Enjoy this Book!
E J Mao

IT'S MURDER IN THE PEAKS

HOW FAR WOULD *YOU* GO TO CHANGE YOUR LUCK?

For DCI Forbes, the discovery of body parts on a moor produces a worrying link to his station. He becomes concerned that his colleagues and their families have become targets.

When the financially compromised, little butcher's assistant with the unfortunate nickname of *Beetle,* is handed an opportunity to become a 'killer for hire' he hopes it might be just what he needs to change his luck and his fortunes.

His first attempt at murder goes disastrously wrong, leaving him afraid for his own life and with two bodies to dispose of.

Then fate lends a hand and his victims seem to be falling over themselves to die for him. His luck has finally changed for the better and he begins to believe that maybe, just maybe, the one thing he wants above all else is almost within his grasp.

KILL FOR LUCK

DCI FORBES PEAK DISTRICT MURDER MYSTERY No 4

Sylvia Marsden

This novel is entirely a work of fiction.

All names, characters, and events in this publication, other than those clearly in the public domain, are fictitious and the work of the author's imagination. Any resemblance to actual persons, living or dead is entirely coincidental.

Copyright Sylvia Marsden 2019

Sylvia Marsden asserts the moral right to be identified as the author of this work.

All rights reserved. No part of this publication may be reproduced, stored or introduced into a retrieval system, or transmitted in any form or by any means, electronic, mechanical, photocopying, recording or otherwise, without the prior permission in writing of the copyright owner and publisher, or be otherwise circulated in any form.

Sylvia Marsden was born in Mansfield, Nottinghamshire, but grew up in the centre of the Peak District of Derbyshire – an area she still thinks of as home. She now spends much of the summer in a campervan, touring Derbyshire with her husband and her rescued greyhound – and of course her laptop.

***

Books in the same series by the same author

ORPHAN KILL

SERENE VALLEY KILL

MINE TO KILL

***

All are on Amazon kindle, kindle unlimited and in paperback.
Visit and like my Facebook page for up to date news…
fb.me/sylviamarsdenbooks
Or catch up with me on twitter @MarsdenSylvia
Or email me on sylviajanemarsden@outlook.com

***

This novel is dedicated to all the small businesses and individuals out there who help us to keep our lives real, with a special thanks to the lovely High Peak Bookstore and Café near Buxton for the faith they have shown in me.

***

Chapter 1

With a nickname like Beetle, how could he fail... crawling along wooded lanes in search of prey ought to be second nature to someone such as him. He shrugged the tension from his shoulders. Windscreen wipers swooshed away wet snow... again... and again. Up ahead was the gap in the trees... almost there... time to dip the headlights. He was nervous, but more than that, he was determined.

Seatbelt released, gears shifted, he reversed into the forest entrance, reassured by the feel of the handgun digging into him as he moved in his seat.

The waiting car was exactly as expected, its two occupants sitting in darkness. He'd been told not to expect choirboys, warned they might be tooled up, so he'd come well prepared. Sharpened, polished knives lay on the passenger seat beside him, each blade positioned, as always when he left home, in its own allotted slot in the handcrafted, brown, calfskin, leather sleeve. A handgun could misfire, but a blade was always trustworthy.

He was ten minutes late, but only because, true to form, fate had thrown an obstacle in his path. A canopy of branches shielded the dark forest floor but already the tarmac was virgin white. Swirling flakes of snow that had until now only messed with the beams from his headlights were sticking to the car's windows.

He shut off the engine and waited for the youths to approach, their hands full of folding money and their heads full of anticipation. "Dumb and dumber," he muttered.

Larger and larger flakes swirled between the two vehicles and condensation began obscuring what little view he had of his targets. "Come on, I haven't got all frigging night."

He squinted across the five-metre gap but saw only fragmented silhouettes – heads thrown back, body language suggesting the youths were happy and relaxed. He guessed they were laughing.

He had been nervous, now he was irritated. He hadn't driven out on a winter's night to be ignored like this.

But then why wouldn't they be laughing? They surely wouldn't have been expecting to see their medications delivered by a middle-aged man in a rusty old Vauxhall Corsa Estate. They were most probably wetting themselves – swearing never to be seen dead in such a thing.

However he'd pictured them being out of their car – off guard.

His irritation ratcheted up a notch. "The lazy little twats!"

He was going to have to be the one to step out into the snow – in shoes that had ceased to be waterproof while still with their previous owner.

Rage was rising up through his chest.

He counted to ten, slid the longest knife into his coat pocket, grabbed his torch and opened the car door into a blast of ice-cold wind and wet snow.

Beetle, a butcher by trade, didn't blink. Only his left hand moved as the beam swept the interior of the car, the metallic odour from inside so familiar it hardly registered. The mess of glistening dark fluid, ripped flesh and splintered bone didn't turn his stomach, as he expected it would with most people.

Why he was even surprised? Repeatedly, fate had dumped the worst scenario onto him that it could possibly conjure up.

He pictured the lettering he intended having carved into his own, nicely polished, granite headstone – his epitaph, assuming of course that he ever had sufficient funds in his account to invest in one:

Here lays the man known as Beetle
Beloved son and brother
He expected nothing from life
And received even less
1980 - ?

This was a new level of screw-up, even for him. Here he was, a virginal, gun-wielding, would-be assassin with eyes bulging from their sockets and a black woollen hat almost at the point of falling from his head.

Parked high in the hills above the Derbyshire market town of Matlock, with damp snowflakes landing on his cheeks and eyelashes and a fully loaded gun in his gloved right hand, he leaned back and checked the car – a fancy, two-seater sports coupe. He was standing beside the correct car – but that was where his plans for the night curled up and died.

Instead of turning from drugs pedlar to executioner, he was looking at two, shot-up corpses, and whoever had beaten him to it hadn't held back on ammunition.

He was surprised rather than shocked. So now what?

This should have been his hit, his contract, his change of luck and change of lifestyle. This single night's work hadn't just been about the money – it had been a stamp on his entry card into one of the most powerful gang of criminals in the Midlands.

Some hope!

He reached past the first corpse and opened the glove box – no weapons, but no cash either.

Just his luck!

But why him?

All his life he'd worked hard. As a teenager, he had helped look after his mother and sister, and he'd been a loyal employee, all with little or no thanks or recognition.

He'd lived his life as an ordinary, boring, law-abiding citizen, apart from the occasional joint of cannabis, that is.

As for killing someone... he'd had to steel himself for the task of killing in cold blood. Cutting flesh and bone was what he did for a living, but the carcasses arrived at the shop ready cleaned, he didn't have to look them in the eyes.

He was one of life's 'also-rans', he knew that. He was a dreamer who'd had to dig deep to find the courage needed for this night's work.

He let his forehead drop onto the car's roof and melt-water trickle down his cheeks.

How was he supposed to kill two men whose feet were already in pools of blood, whose brains were splattered across two headrests, and whose life-fluids were making the snow appear red whenever his torch beam penetrated the windows? What was he to do... shoot them again... walk away... what? Of all of the scenarios running through his head in the early hours, none had come even close to this.

He raised his head, looked towards the road and blinked melting flakes from his lashes.

He'd thought the offer was too good to be true – too good for the likes of him. He should have sensed something about it hadn't been right. After a lifetime of relentlessly rotten luck he was probably being set up and looking at spending his remaining years behind bars. And the worst of it was that he only had himself to blame.

He shivered, but still couldn't get his legs to move.

He'd recently taken out a funeral plan, so buying a gravestone would be the next logical step. Before he could do even that small thing, his finances needed a serious injection of capital.

Something among the trees rustled. His skin prickled and he shivered again. He looked around but saw only regimented trunks, and beyond them impenetrable blackness.

The reality of his predicament hit him like a sledgehammer.

Minutes earlier, snow had already been deep enough to creak beneath his shoes but, in typical Beetle fashion, he hadn't thought to look down. He hadn't thought to check for other tyre tracks, or other footprints.

The killer could be out there – index finger looped into a trigger – waiting and watching.

His lungs froze. His senses were on high alert. Clumps of damp snow, from overhead branches, were hitting both cars. A vehicle rumbled up the hill on the distant main road. Over those sounds, his heartbeats thundered in his ears.

He flashed the beam of his torch along the ground. There were no fresh tyre tracks and the only fresh, clear footprints matched those of his leaking shoes.

Maybe the real killer was long gone. Maybe being late had been the best thing to happen to him tonight. Maybe it had saved his life.

Road conditions on the high ground were deteriorating. Realistically, he wasn't likely to be disturbed, although with his luck he ought not to rely on the assistance of the weather.

He leaned back into the car, looked at the angled heads, at the similar build and hair colouring of the two young men and at what remained of their features. He'd expected his main target to be sitting in the driver's seat, but the features of both youths were distorted beyond recognition.

The identity of the passenger was irrelevant; he'd been instructed to leave no witnesses.

Satisfied he was alone, and out of ideas, he blanked out the scene. His brain raced off on a track of its own, trying to picture what he could have done differently. This afternoon, at three p.m. precisely, he'd lit his last remaining joint and sometime later and with his eyelids drooping and his fingers still loosened by the drug, he'd fumbled with the alarm feature of his mobile phone and attempted to set it to seven p.m.

At seven-thirty, he'd forced open his eyelids and cursed.

He'd only gone and set the damned alarm for seven a.m. the next day!

No matter… he'd slept fully clothed, apart from his boots that he'd left under his bed ready to pull on. He'd emptied his bladder, splashed ice-cold water onto his face and picked up the only things of his still left in the flat – a loaded handgun, his knives, car keys, phone, warmest and oldest coat, and finally his woollen hat and gloves.

Then he'd gently closed the door of the one-bedroomed flat for the final time.

No one had been around to notice his quiet progress to the external door, but that was where his short interlude of good luck had ended.

At seven-forty-five, after passing through the communal doorway onto the street and almost falling on the ice-covered yard, he'd cursed himself again.

In the dead of winter, why the hell hadn't he checked the weather forecast before arranging to meet his target in such a remote parking spot?

The layer of frost stuck fast to his windscreen had defied his gloved hand and he'd never seen the point in buying de-icer. With a small plastic scraper from his glove box, he had scraped a large enough hole in the crystals to see the road immediately in front, and then turned his ignition key.

Even that had defied him for a few seconds. The old banger needed a new battery, or a new starter motor, or something else equally expensive. In addition, its MOT test was due in two weeks' time.

It wasn't as if calling for a taxi had been an option, even if he'd been able to afford one.

Finally, the car's engine had sprung into life. He'd steadied his heartbeats into an even rhythm, slid the gear stick into first and gently eased the car out onto the ice. Fifty metres further on he'd looked down at the clock on the dashboard and begun fishtailing up the street.

As soon as this job was over, he'd get the car fixed – or even treat himself to a newer one…

…this job… he was back in the moment. What was wrong with him? It had to be the cold that was affecting him, and surely shock was setting in by now. Why else would his mind be wandering like this?

He stamped his feet. His limbs all felt numb.

His heart was pounding again – he ought to be doing something… anything rather than just standing here… potential target practice… but what?

Big Stevie Hall wanted the driver to vanish without trace until further notice, and that part of the contract he could accomplish.

He looked around again.

By now, he should have been shoving the bodies into the plastic-lined boot of his car.

His plan had been to take them the five or so miles back to his late mother's empty house, midway between Matlock and Chesterfield, on the even bleaker hilltop of Beeley Moor.

Therefore, that was exactly what he would do.

He stuffed the gun and the torch into his coat pocket, took a deep breath and reached into the car.

No one was on the road to notice Beetles' whitened knuckles, or his sweating hands clamped to the steering wheel as he corrected one skid after another. No one was around to see how fear and shock was causing him to bite into his lower lip until blood trickled down his chin. Even if anyone had been at the entrance to the snow-covered lane he'd been aiming for, they couldn't possibly have realised the intensity of relief washing over the white-faced little man as he turned the car off the unclassified road.

He was home and he was safe. The property he was moving into, the property where he'd spent much of his childhood and all of his adolescence, was in sight.

His mother's voice prattled on inside his head. *"We're all born with a certain number of spots,"* she was telling him, as she so often had. He knew what she meant. He'd always known what she'd meant. That was why she would never have understood why tonight had been so important to him.

She hadn't been able to change the way that she was, weak and gullible, but his problems were different from hers. At an early age he'd realised he had to be one of the unluckiest people on the planet, and that the hand he'd been dealt with at birth had been a mean one. In his mother's language, he'd been dealt an odd number of spots.

He'd tried many things to change that luck, from risking the ridicule of his school friends by picking up pennies from the street, to avoiding cracks in the pavement, to wishing on every shooting star he saw, to moving from one flat to another but nothing had made the slightest difference.

He could still lose a pound and find a penny.

Becoming a contract killer seemed a touch extreme, even to him, but desperate times had called for desperate measures, as the saying went. Taking a human life was something he'd never tried, something he'd never even considered, but after much debate between himself and his conscience, his conscience had lost. He'd told himself that if he could pull off such an act then his fortunes, and maybe his luck, might finally change forever.

He relaxed his grip on the steering wheel and rolled the tension out of his shoulders once more.

Creepy, crawly Beetle, they'd nicknamed him at school, and the handle had stuck. The schoolyard bullies might have thought twice, though, if they could have looked into the future – if they could have seen into his late mother's garage – seen the almost empty chest freezers, the array of razor-sharp knives, the chain saw and band saw and the strong plastic food bags waiting to be filled.

The car crunched the final few metres of snow down into two ruts and he pictured Stevie Hall, a tall, powerful man who no one with any sense would cross. With the bodies safely stashed away, he'd lose no time in explaining everything to him. He'd assure Stevie that he'd done his best. Then hopefully he'd receive some payment, even if not the full amount, and salvage something from his cold evening's work.

Fear was still tightening his stomach muscles. However hard he tried, he couldn't gloss over the fact that there was a real killer out there, that he'd failed in his first contract, and that Stevie Hall was not reputed to be a forgiving kind of man.

Only one thing was certain about this night, and that was that inside the dark property his mother's dog was waiting for its supper and a short walk.

Chapter 2

Beetle snapped open his eyes and out of habit took in the clear sky and full moon. For as long as he could remember he'd slept with his bedroom curtains open, not wanting to miss the one shooting star which might turn his fortunes around. Satisfied none were there he turned his head and looked upwards at the grey outlines of his knives. As always overnight, they hung in an orderly line from the steel rail above his bed. They were, without doubt, his most treasured possessions, his pride and joy, his adult equivalent of a security blanket. Memories from the previous evening flooded back and he counted the blades down the length of the rail and then counted them back up again. He scanned their sharpened edges and felt soothed. Whatever his problems, however badly things twisted and turned in his life, his knives could calm him just by their presence. He released a deep sigh, pulled the duvet up around his chin and drew up his legs until he was curled into a tight ball.

The knot remained in his stomach. There was a real killer out there, and he was the imposter.

Last night, after seeing to Angus he'd levered the two bodies from the boot of his car and dragged them through the snow into the garage. Every step had been hard work. On a positive note, the weather would allow him ample time to dissect the bodies and bag them up neatly, with no need for a fly swatter or can of insecticide. Every cloud...

He was reasonably sure he hadn't been followed to Hill Top Cottage, but he'd still slept fully dressed and with the loaded gun beneath his pillow and his wet shoes beside his bed.

His hand slid under the pillow and found cold steel.

Next, he clicked on the bedside lamp and saw his knives winking down at him. He was in a familiar house, but not yet as familiar as his old flat. He'd spent his last night in that expensive dump and was looking forward to some solitude.

He and his sister, Sophie, had inherited the property from their mother but Sophie's lucrative employment took her well away from Derbyshire. She was happy for him to live here and hadn't been back since the day of the funeral.

He threw back the covers and staggered to the bathroom. Angus, the black lab he'd driven up to the cottage twice a day to feed and exercise for the past few weeks, padded after him and began whining at the bathroom door. He opened the door, allowed it in, and the noise stopped. What was it with dogs that made them think you needed accompanying to the toilet?

He'd promised his mother that after her death, he'd look for a new home for the thing, but last night he'd been thankful for failing her. The presence of another heartbeat in the house had allowed him to snatch a few hours of much-needed sleep. Not that he felt any better for it.

Angus followed him down the stairs and around the house as he checked his previous night's attempts at securing the property. They were all good. The ground floor curtains could remain closed, the makeshift barricades and locked doors could stay as they were, and no way was he allowing the whining animal outside.

Angus even sat beside him as he picked up the phone. "Boss," for once he didn't have to force the quiver into his voice, "I'm really sorry but I feel like death this morning. I feel sick and I'm just off the toilet for the third time in the last hour. I'll try and get in to the shop tomorrow." It wasn't an excuse he used too often, but it was a reliable one and difficult to disprove. Any rumour of sickness and loose bowels in anyone working in a butcher's shop could result in an environmental health officer shutting them down. This morning it was no excuse.

Predictably, there was nothing wrong with the dog's bowels. Before twelve noon, he'd cleaned up two steaming piles from beside the barricaded kitchen door and, not daring to open the door even a crack, wrapped the offerings in layer after layer of plastic. That hadn't helped his stomach. At lunchtime, he switched on the television, but with the volume on low.

There was no news of the car.

He'd been in and out of the shower in less than one minute, afraid of missing any sounds from outside. If he was to get through this, he had to stay on the ball.

A quick peek through the curtains, early afternoon, told him it was a crisp, clear day – far too clear to risk venturing out. Hill Top Cottage's nearest neighbour was a quarter of a mile away with both properties surrounded by open moorland and rough pasture. He could easily be in the sights of someone's rifle or shotgun and never know.

The bite of a cheese sandwich was sticking to the roof of his mouth.

He offered the crust to the dog.

Like being in an underground bunker, without an internet connection, and with the signal to his mobile so feeble, the television was his only window on the world.

He poured out a small measure of whisky and waited for the minutes to tick away. Finally, the early evening local news began.

Alcohol splashed his trousers and his empty hand knocked the plate and the remainder of his sandwich to the floor. The car, as he'd left it, was the main news of the evening.

Angus looked up at him with a puzzled expression and then seized on his unexpected treat.

Two faces stared back at him from the top of the screen. They could have belonged to brothers. The young female reporter, who looked as though she'd rather be anywhere other than up in the hills, in the freezing cold, at the scene of a double murder, was saying that they were friends…

"… and police have just confirmed that from the material found inside the car, which is registered to one of the missing youths, at least two murders appear to have taken place here, in this gravelled, woodland entrance, sometime late yesterday evening or early this morning. Paul Biers and Gary Jones, both twenty-five, were last seen at approximately seven o'clock last night driving up Sydnope Hill, just over a mile from where the car was found at eleven o'clock this morning. A statement released a few minutes ago confirms that the blood types found in the vehicle match those of the Gary and Paul. Relatives have been informed and are awaiting the results of DNA tests. If anyone has any information about the crime they are asked to contact the Matlock Police Station or phone the Crimestoppers number on screen now."

Chapter 3

Eleven months later.

The working week was over and detective constable Martin Jones was on his way home to his wife and five year old son. A minute ago, he'd been relieved to be finishing his late shift at the Leaburn Police Station, in the heart of the Peak District of Derbyshire. He checked his rear-view mirror for the tenth time in sixty seconds and the chill in his stomach turned to ice-crystals. This was the third time in as many weeks that he'd felt he was being followed, each time by a different car but with a lone male of similar build in the driving seat. Martin had a more powerful reason than most to be cautious, or paranoid, as his wife sometimes accused him of being. It was almost a year since his younger brother, Gary, was murdered in the hills above Matlock, about fifteen miles away, and neither his body nor his killer had ever been found. The thought that this might have been how the night of Gary's murder had begun was making his heart pound against his ribs. Had Gary been followed before being targeted for a reason that had so far escaped everyone involved in the long investigation?

On the previous two occasions he hadn't been certain enough to do anything other than drive on home and park up, whereby the vehicle had driven on, out of sight, each time with a number plate too dirty to read.

Tonight though, Martin intended putting his fear, or paranoia, to the test.

He turned sharp left without indicating. The car, almost out of sight behind him, did the same.

His family was waiting at home and he did not intend to lead a killer back to them.

In the thirty mile an hour zone, he accelerated to fifty for about five hundred metres. Then he slowed to twenty. Lights faded and then reappeared. He wasn't a trained pursuit driver, confident driving at speed on narrow roads in built-up areas, but he knew this maze of back-roads as well as anyone. He knew they were normally quiet after ten at night.

He pulled another left turn but this time observed the speed limit. He wasn't trying to lose the car; he was drawing it ever closer to the rear of the police station, and a dead end.

He took the final left turn needed for his idea to work. The car behind turned right.

He was sure now that someone local, someone as familiar with the road system as he was, and someone who knew where he lived and knew his car had followed him. Tomorrow he'd get in-car cameras fitted, front and rear, and he'd ask to drive home in a pool car whenever one was available, if only for the comfort of having a police radio instead of just a mobile phone, which was all he had right now.

He pulled up and stared at his reflection in the rear view mirror. The eyes looking back at him could have been those of a terrified child.

Gary was dead, they'd all had to accept that, but the list of suspects for his murder, mainly drug dealers and gang members, had dwindled to nothing over the eleven months since. The absence of a reason for Gary's death was one of the hardest things he'd had to deal with. He'd survived that nightmare, and with the help of his colleagues and his family was getting his life back on track, but every now and then, something happened to drag him back into those dark days. Something had happened again tonight; he'd seen it and he'd felt it.

He picked up his phone and jabbed in his home number, not concerned that he might be waking his wife and sending her into a state of panic. He needed to hear her voice reassuring him that she'd checked all the doors and windows, and that their son was safe.

Only then, could he drive to the front of the station, park up, and run to the safety of the building.

"Hey, Martin, I thought you'd gone home," divorcee DC Ryan Wheeler had no one waiting for him at his home. With his jet-black hair and steely blue eyes, he hadn't been short of female company since moving into the area from Preston five months earlier but none of his relationships had lasted. He was highly skilled with computers and regularly worked more hours than he was paid. "What's up, is that lovely wife of yours making unreasonable demands in the bedroom again? I've told you before – you can always send her to me if you need help in that department."

Martin flopped into a chair. He was a seasoned police officer. How did he begin a conversation that would make him sound a complete wimp?

"Mate... she really is wearing you out, isn't..."

"Give it a rest, Ryan," he snapped. His colleagues might laugh but he had a wife and son to consider, and, as tough, as his father was he wouldn't survive losing another son. "I'm scared, all right? No one at this station's been through anything even close to the experiences I've had over this past year, and right now, I need either help or protection, and I'm not sure which..."

"Whoa... steady on there, old chap. You know me, I was only joking. It's serious... right? Back up a bit... I'm all yours. Let me get you a drink, and then you can tell me what I can do to help."

He had to be honest with himself, and with Ryan. Between sips of coffee, he described the events of the previous twenty minutes. "I sound like a drama queen, don't I?"

"Hardly... look, I'm clocking off now, so I'll follow you home, and on Monday we'll put in a request for a panic button to be installed in your house." He was saying it as if it was the most natural thing in the world. "What are you and your family planning on doing this weekend?"

"Hiding...," he laughed nervously.

"Come and stay with me... tonight if you like. I have plenty of room and a bedroom with two double beds that I keep ready for visiting family. I also have beer and wine in the fridge and an old pool table to keep your boy occupied. How old is he?"

"He's five, but I don't know if Sarah will want to move out at this time of night. She'll have my super waiting..."

"Phone her. She can bring the food. We'll share it if there's enough. Ask her to throw a few things in a bag and we can return tomorrow for whatever else you need. We'll have a great weekend. To tell you the truth, I'd welcome the company. What do you say?"

The obviously heart-felt offer produced a lump in Martin's throat. His hands and legs were shaking and he felt sick. If Sarah was in agreement he'd gladly accept, and next week, if his bosses still wanted to send him for counselling, then fine, he'd gladly accept that as well.

*

Winter was Beetle's favourite time of the year – it always had been, even as a child, especially that one year when his father had been in a better mood and had built a sledge from old broken pallets and then spent hours with him and his sister on the snow-covered fields around his grandparent's house on Beeley Moor.

Thirty years on, Beetle still favoured the wintery weather, but for different reasons.

It made it easier to park up and watch people, or to follow them, without attracting attention. It was almost too easy sometimes, while driving the top-of-the-range, cloned cars Stevie Hall kept entrusting him to deliver. They were an absolute pleasure to drive.

However, that particular pleasure was over for the day and now he was back in his own old banger. Not that he minded. Fewer people were active after midnight on the unclassified moorland roads and those who were weren't likely to take notice of a battered old Vauxhall Corsa parked at the roadside, or a lone figure climbing out of it, carrying a rucksack, out for a solitary walk.

The fresh, cold air felt good on his face. It proved to him that he was alive.

He stepped off the tarmac onto the rocky entrance to the ancient burial site of Stanton Moor and looked up at the scattered clouds and the new moon resting on its back.

The Bronze Age stone circles, the King Stone, the Cork Stone, and the Nine Ladies Standing Stones, who someone had once told him came to life to dance at midnight on the nights when a full moon lit the sky, created an inconvenience as far as he was concerned. They drew too many people, locals and tourists alike, on to the high plateau and restricted his work to the hours of darkness. Even then, he had to choose his times and weather conditions carefully.

What he was about to do needed no living witnesses.

He stumbled on the uneven ground of the first fifty metres or so of well-worn, but rocky footpath, cursing the straps of his rucksack as they dug into his shoulders and altered his normally upright posture.

As the path became sandier and easier to navigate, he lengthened his stride. Fifteen minutes later, he was at one of the highest points of the moor. He paused to make sure of his bearings before turning right and leaving the path to cross the more difficult, overgrown ground.

The stalks of heather, black, sinewy, and invisible against the spongy black peat and sheep droppings that together coated most of the moor, grappled with his boots. He stumbled repeatedly. The thin, low branches could have been ancient fingers, reaching up, attempting to stop his determined, measured strides. He batted that thought away.

Apart from the sheep and occasional hare, rabbit, fox, badger or deer, he sensed that he was the only entity breathing in the cold, sweet-smelling air.

The narrow moon might be his friend but he cursed at the racing clouds that seemed hell-bent on darkening the moor and hampering his progress. With what he was carrying, he couldn't afford to injure an ankle.

His eyesight was first-rate. It always had been. It adjusted rapidly to the fluctuating light levels. He remained focused on the ground. He wasn't on the open moor for either the wildlife or the limited views.

Finally, he slowed his pace, mainly to appease his sore leg muscles, and felt sure enough of his footing to look up. The dark shadows were there, as expected, swooping and flickering across the open ground. They didn't scare him. He knew they were only fragments and shadows of the low clouds skittering across the night sky, and not, as some of the locals believed, some of the many souls of the long dead haunting this moor.

Cold air was seeping through his winter coat and his two thick jumpers. He tugged his woollen hat hard down over his ears and returned his concentration to the ground.

As if in reverence to the moorland graveyard well-trodden paths criss-crossed much of the area but he was avoiding them. Even in poor light, he knew the topography well enough. One outcrop of rocks after another, some silhouetted against the sky and others blending into the dark landscape, served as his navigational tools. He stopped just ahead of his final marker, bent down, and fumbled with gloved hands for the spade and crow bar he'd left hidden in the undergrowth.

He shrugged the rucksack from his shoulders and placed it gently on the ground, then straightened up and stretched his spine. He looked around at the silhouettes of leafless silver birch trees and weathered rock formations that together were creating the ragged edge to the black horizon closest to him.

The longer branches were rocking back and forth against the wind, but other than those, and the few dead stalks of coarse moorland grass that had so far escaped the attentions of the sheep and the wildlife, the moor was still.

The neighbouring Beeley Moor loomed black against the more distant horizon, beyond the ribbon of twinkling lights in the valley below.

Suspended in time, the ground he was on was special to him and sacred to those souls lost in the mists of time. He felt a warm glow at the thought of sharing it with his lodger.

For half an hour, he gasped the sweet-smelling, cold air in and out of his lungs, a limitless tide of energy surging through him as he dug at the hard ground and levered loose rocks from where they'd been stuck fast for hundreds, maybe even thousands of years.

He stopped, dropped his tools and pressed his hands against his back. His neck angled forwards and he peered down into a black hole just large enough to hold the contents of his rucksack and a few inches of soil, plant debris and stones. His muscles burned. It would have to be good enough.

He looked around again.

All clear – it was safe to open the rucksack.

The narrow moon broke from its cover as neatly sawn slices of grey flesh, bone, and gristle slid from the plastic bag. The mixture nestled into the tiny grave and reflected back the luminescent glow of the moon for just a few seconds before the hole fell back into darkness. A metallic tang of blood, strengthened by the plastic and the warmth from his car, drifted upwards, mingled with the sweeter smell of peat and damaged foliage, and then faded into the night air. He walked around the site, aware of the beads of sweat dripping from his forehead onto the cold ground. As long as they didn't fall into the grave, it was of no concern. They'd soon break down, and anyway, his DNA was not on any files anywhere.

Ten minutes later, he straightened his complaining back once more and admired the small mound of earth at his feet.

To mark a burial spot and protect it from scavengers, he covered it with a dozen larger stones. Finally, he could add his personal touch, something floral to mark the spot. He always chose blue flowers. He liked blue. Blue had been his mother's favourite colour. Six crocus bulbs nestled in his coat pocket, but because they wouldn't bloom for several months, he'd brought a spray of blue silk flowers. If anyone did notice his work – well it wasn't uncommon today for people to scatter the ashes of a relative or a family pet on a favourite site and then to place flowers there occasionally.

With the blue tributes in place, the moor looked less grey and less threatening.

The shadows were keeping their respective distances and it was time to leave.

Walking back, he could have sworn he felt each molecule of sweat as it evaporated off his face into the night air. He was so invigorated, so alive. Things were going his way – life was going his way. This was his time.

With the homemade magnetic registration plates and empty rucksack safely covered on the back seat he changed into his driving shoes and slid into the front. He decided to sit for a while, too exhilarated to drive and wanting to savour the moment, and this was the perfect location for taking stock of his new life.

The days of looking over his shoulder and jumping at every sound and every shadow had merged into weeks and then into months. If the real killer had intended making his identity known, then he'd have done so by now, Beetle reasoned.

His new part-time employer, Big Stevie Hall, together with his minders, had assumed that he'd killed two people that night eleven months ago. They'd called at Hill Top Cottage to offer their congratulations and he'd been too much of a nervous wreck to put them straight. He'd nodded his head like a plastic toy in the rear window of a seventies motorcar and they'd mistaken his lack of speech for modesty. They'd slapped his back in honour of his achievements before putting more mundane, but highly profitable and illegal, jobs his way.

Then one month ago, unexpectedly, Stevie had given him permission to do as he pleased with the frozen remains, just as long as they didn't lead police back to him or any of his many employees. He'd assured him he had plans, and even made Big Stevie's muscular frame shake with mirth when he'd joked about how working in a butcher's shop meant he was ideally placed for the disposal of unwanted flesh.

The one dark cloud swirling in the back of his brain could still bring stinging tears to his face, but he'd grown used to swallowing them down and getting on with his life.

By day he remained the mild-mannered, jovial butcher working on the shop counter, making the female customers either laugh or blush, and by night he was out and about distributing drugs to minor suppliers and collecting outstanding debts, all the while growing in confidence, certain of not being challenged because of his growing reputation. He never went anywhere without his knives. He was moving in a world where extreme violence was currency, and he loved it. The thrill no longer centred on the money, though he wasn't about to turn any of it down, it was about being somebody.

The speed at which he'd been welcomed into a world he'd known next to nothing about still filled him with amazement. A larger-than-life gang leader seemed to be under the impression that his new hit man was 'the dog's bollocks', and that the unassuming little man from the butcher's shop was a character not to be messed with, an up-and-coming power in the criminal world, even.

He'd never appreciated the allure of power until the night he'd been taken on a tour of the night clubs of Manchester, where the bar staff had plied him with drinks but refused his money, and where the women had actually come up to *him* to talk. He was growing quite used to witnessing respect in the eyes of the men he associated with and drunk real ale and malt whisky with. He was the right side of forty, just, he wore designer clothes, sported an expensive haircut, and he had envelopes bulging with used twenty pound notes hidden all over his house.

The old car's interior light flickered and he leaned across to stare at his reflection in the rear view mirror. A few lines were appearing around his eyes, but they gave his face character. Youth and opportunity didn't always go hand in hand, as he'd once believed. He had two bodies under his belt and was eager to try his hand at contract killing again. He had a reputation to uphold.

He shivered. It was time to make a move.

Still feeling thankful for the turn his life had taken, he carefully avoided the parked cars on the narrow, steep village street that led away from the moor. He was vaguely familiar with Stanton-in-the-Peak, the village most closely associate with Stanton Moor, the village he'd visited as a child with the man he and his sister had briefly looked upon as their future stepfather. Back then, if he'd had even a glimpse of his immediate future, things could have been very different for him, his sister, and his mother.

However, looking that far back in time served no purpose. The solitude of the moorland suited him and Angus was all the company he needed. Sophie's work meant that when she wasn't working she was with one of her boyfriends in some city or other – he didn't really care which or where as long as she stayed well clear of the cottage. In her absence, he could keep odd hours. He could load up his rucksack and travel the ten or so miles between the ancient graveyard and the welcoming open fire of the living room without having to answer awkward questions. In addition, there was no one to ask why he no longer worried about paying the heating bills, or how or why he had a wardrobe full of new clothes, or why there was a constant stream of stolen or cloned vehicles on the property.

He rolled his shoulders. It was becoming a habit. His muscles ached from digging and his bed was calling. He needed sleep. Christmas was only a month away and already the shop was taking orders. From now on, it would get busier.

He felt a rush of cheer at the prospect of celebrating the festive season with his new colleagues in a way he'd never even thought possible this time last year.

One day he might to have to pay a price for his change in fortune, but for now, he was going to enjoy it.

Tomorrow the shop would close at twelve noon, and in the afternoon, he would drive to Chesterfield for his arranged meeting with Big Stevie. He'd rather have been clothes shopping, but no one ever said *no* to Stevie.

Maybe there was another important job coming up, in which case, after tonight, he might just have to shelve his own pet project for a while.

Chapter 4

DCI Michael Forbes was at his desk in Leaburn Police Station and looking over the weekly reports of incidents. He'd been the area's head of Homicide and Major Crimes for thirteen years without ever wishing to climb higher on the political ladder. He enjoyed the vast majority of the work. Apart from a brief spell at University, he'd spent his home life in a six-bedroomed family property on the outskirts of Leaburn where his father had still been in bed when he'd left at six this morning and where his sister, Louise, had already been up and dressed for a couple of hours. Her daughter, Gemma, who was almost three, had been grizzling for most of the previous afternoon and nothing had changed overnight. The poor child seemed to be sickening for something, as his father would no doubt say when he eventually surfaced.

Whether they were quiet or not he liked to come in early for a few hours on a Saturday morning. The station had experienced an unusually peaceful few days although Martin Jones's semi-breakdown late last night had been an unfortunate ending to the week. Installing a panic button in his house would be a priority, for everyone's peace of mind. He was also going to recommend counselling, despite Martin refusing it earlier in the year.

Martin, however, was a reliable and experienced officer and Forbes wasn't about to dismiss his fears out of hand.

Martin's father, Godfrey Jones, had been a superintendent at Leaburn for ten years before his retirement eight years ago. At the time of Gary's murder, one theory floated was that one of Godfrey's old cases had caused someone to seek revenge. Nothing had been proved one way or the other, despite exhaustive enquiries. If Martin's panic attack turned out to be anything other than paranoia then that theory would have to be revisited. As he prayed that it wouldn't, he picked up his jacket ready to leave his office for the day.

*

For once, Beetle was out after nine p.m. on a Saturday night without being suited and booted. His wish from the previous evening had come true and he was a little apprehensive, but at the same time thrilled. That afternoon he'd met with Big Stevie and been issued with instructions, two clean handguns, and just over four hours in which to prepare for a reputation-enhancing opportunity. His state of mind these days was calm, determined, and organised, so the rush-job didn't bother him. With less time to worry about what could go wrong his fear of failure was becoming a thing of the past.

He was wearing the old clothes that he'd kept for just these occasions, standing in a dark alleyway, tugging his woollen hat down over his ears and blowing on his gloved hands. The cold breeze wasn't bothering him; he was simply using the actions to occupy his impatient fingers.

A sudden gust brought the stench of tomcat urine down the alley and he wrinkled his nose. On the opposite side of the street, an empty crisp packet barrelled along the pavement. His gaze left the doorway of the Community Hall for less than a second.

In his right-hand coat pocket was one of the two guns Stevie had personally handed to him, and in his left was his boning knife.

Life changing events came no bigger than this. This weekend he was on for a double payday, and he was mentally prepared, and even looking forward to it.

The first of his targets was alive and well and in the next few minutes expected to leave Matlock's Saturday evening youth club gathering to walk the short distance to his home.

The youngsters had already gone their separate, noisy ways and he was watching as one by one the lights were being turned off on the other side of the Community Hall door.

He'd been given very scant personal details on his victims and he hadn't enquired further. The biggest flaw in his character, as far as he could see, was his conscience. It was a hell of a thing for a contract killer to suffer from but, just like his strange and rotten luck, it seemed it was something he was stuck with. But then – no one was perfect, and his new lifestyle more than compensated for the odd twinges of guilt he occasionally felt after downing more than a couple of pints of real ale and a couple of whisky chasers.

His fingers curled and uncurled inside his coat pockets and he imagined his mother's high-pitched laughter. Her voice was never far from his thoughts. *"A contract killer with a conscience... and how is that supposed to work? You've got ideas above your station in life again, my lad. Why can't you be more like me and just accept the way you've been made?"*

However, he wasn't the one making the life or death decisions – and if it wasn't him pulling the trigger tonight, then it would be someone else... someone else... his heart lurched and he reached out to the wall to steady himself. The other thing never too far from his mind was the fact that another killer was out there, a killer who, eleven months ago, had remained in the shadows, just as he was doing now.

He fought back the urge to step out into the glare of the streetlights to check his watch. His phone would have been handy, but it was back at home on his bedside table. When left on standby, a mobile phone checked in with its network provider every twenty minutes or so. Should he ever become a murder suspect, and his phone checked, had he brought it, it would have put him right on the spot.

The door opened and closed and keys rattled.

His heart pounded against his ribcage and his fingers curled around the two handles inside his coat pockets.

His target turned the door handle once more, presumably checking it was secure, and then turned and with long strides began walking in the direction of his home and his wife and children. Beetle waited until the family man was almost out of sight and then he stepped from the alley.

His legs were trembling slightly, from excitement as much as nerves, but his hands were rock-steady. Stevie's instructions had been clear. *"One clean shot to the back of the head, execution style, as close to his home as you can and where he'll be easily found."*

Family man turned right, onto a more exclusive-looking residential street and Beetle lengthened his strides. They were the only two people on the street and he was wearing rubber-soled shoes.

Adrenaline pumped through him – blood roared in his ears, his body preparing for 'fight or flight', only in this case it would be 'execution followed by flight'.

Semi-detached properties whizzed by, and in front of them, where once there had been areas of well-tended lawns and flowerbeds, there now sat car after car on stretches of gravel and tarmac. It was the same everywhere, too many cars owned by too many people, and more importantly for him right now, too many places from which those people might be watching. He couldn't look everywhere, and he couldn't afford to look suspicious, not before the moment he pulled out the gun. Curtains and blinds were all tightly closed, and apart from him and family man, and the few leaves left over from the autumn which were tumbling along as if looking for somewhere to hide, nothing was moving on the quiet, residential street. His target had a hat pulled down over his ears and a head bent into the wind. Good. He wasn't likely to turn and look, even if he did hear footsteps growing ever closer.

A clean kill, as instructed, was the best he could offer this man and his family now. The knowledge that he hadn't suffered would eventually offer them some comfort, and wouldn't offend his own conscience too much either.

He shortened his stride and checked the closest properties, looking for twitching curtains.

The gun slid from his pocket, nestled into his hand and took aim almost as if it had a life of its own and had been waiting for this moment. He tightened the muscles in his arms and shoulders and a loud, sharp crack echoed along the respectable street.

A dog barked.

Family man staggered and then stumbled sideways towards the road.

Beetle muttered a string of curses.

So much for a quick, painless kill!

He raised his arm to take aim again.

The road became brighter – not from house lights as he'd first thought, but from an approaching vehicle.

"Shit... shit... shit..." He dropped to his knees on sharp gravel at the rear of the nearest parked car and screwed up his face. His ears were still ringing from the shot but there was no mistaking the sound of screeching tyres and a body colliding with several tons of oncoming metal.

The joints of his knees cracked as he slowly stood and looked around. Curtains and doors opened and voices seemed to be coming from every direction.

The dog was still barking.

Residents were beginning to rush down garden paths and Beetle calmly walked away.

At the end of a sleepless night, Beetle almost didn't accept the call on his second mobile. He'd botched the previous night's killing. He took a deep breath and pressed the accept icon, as ready as he would ever be to be vilified by Stevie Hall before being relegated to the role of small-town butcher once again.

"Beetle, my main man," he almost dropped the phone there and then but Stevie drawled on, "I wanted to personally congratulate you on your timing last night. It was an act of pure theatre to try to make the assassination appear as a road traffic accident. From what I've heard this morning, you fooled everyone just long enough to make your getaway. I like your style – I really do."

"He's dead...?"

"What sort of a question is that? I'm taking valuable minutes out of my busy morning to congratulate you, aren't I?" An edge had crept into the voice, but it disappeared as quickly as it had come. "My little colleague, are you all set for tonight?"

"I think so."

"Think so...? You're teasing me, Beetle. You crack me up, you really do. I look forward to tomorrow morning and hearing how efficiently you've eliminated another one of my little problems."

"I'll do my best."

"Sure you will, Beetle, sure you will."

Beetle heard genuine laughter before the call cut from the other end. He sank back into his pillow and sobbed with relief. Angus's wet nose slid into his hand. "It's all right boy. I'm happy really. Look at all this money around the place. Think how many doggy biscuits we can buy with it. What's not to be happy about?"

The dog's tail wagged.

"I've got to leave you again for a while tonight, but you're getting used to that, aren't you my lad?"

He was in too deeply now. In the world he was operating in it was kill or be killed, and right now he was situated somewhere in between those two outcomes. The police would hopefully be chasing their tails in Matlock, looking for clues to the identity of the previous night's shooter and leaving him free to complete the second half of his weekend's work in the nearby market town of Bakewell.

A fine, cold drizzle made him regret not bringing his umbrella. It would have been something extra to juggle in his gloved fingers but it would also have provided him with an extra layer of camouflage.

He'd been assured that, whatever the weather, target number two walked his dog along the banks of the River Derwent at ten p.m. every night. He only had to follow until a suitable location for a kill presented itself, and the rain should help with that.

His fingers curled around the handle of the gun. He was still riding high from Stevie's words of praise earlier in the day and he wanted more of the same. He was determined not to mess up again.

His target and a small white dog walked past, less than a metre from where he stood. Neither of them turned to look at him, not even when he fell into step behind. A smile twitched on his lips but he suppressed it.

Under his watchful eye, the man would take his last few steps in blissful ignorance.

As expected given the weather, the grassy path bordering the meandering river was deserted. There were no twitching curtains to worry about here. "Relax," he murmured, "take your time." He pulled the gun from his pocket, slowly took aim and began to squeeze.

"Hey, what are you doing?" A woman's voice sounded from the opposite bank of the river.

His fingers flexed, as if on an automatic system of their own. He heard the ear-ringing, loud crack, but this time followed by a woman's screams, and then by two splashes.

He shook his head in disbelief, and then hurried away. What else was there to do?

After a few paces, he risked turning round and saw the small white dog scrambling to safety up the opposite bank, out of the fast-flowing water. He squinted to see beyond the animal. There was something floating in the centre of the river.

The woman had gone and her screams had stopped.

All was good with the world.

Chapter 5

Beetle had slept soundly until six a.m. and was now enjoying breakfast in front of the television. It was past seven and the anticipated phone call hadn't yet come through, though as Stevie had pointed out the previous morning, he was a busy man. The local news was reporting on a body recovered overnight from the River Derwent in Bakewell. He threw a square of toast to Angus and smiled. This was almost becoming too easy. Now, if Big Stevie would just call to congratulate him and tell him when to expect his payment, his morning would be complete and he could set off to work in the knowledge that he'd moved another rung up the ladder in Stevie's world.

*

The towns of Matlock and Bakewell were both situated outside DCI Forbes's immediate area of responsibility, but as he'd been the general area's officer on duty for the weekend, for Homicide and Major Crimes, and as both police stations closest to the shootings were manned on a part-time basis, he'd been called out on Saturday and again on Sunday evening.

Leaburn and its surrounding villages had enjoyed a quiet weekend; due in part to the cold, wet weather, so as he sat in his office on Monday morning the two shootings had his full attention. His detective sergeant, Adam Ross, was approaching. "Have you read these reports...?" As he spoke, an e-mail pinged into his inbox.

"The shootings...?"

"Yes... and we're being asked to attend the two post mortems this morning. Grab your coat, Adam. Let's go."

"Sir, before we go, DC Martin Jones has just told me he believes someone may be following him. I think he's trying to hide the fact that he's quite shaken up, and concerned for his family... and in the light of his brother's disappearance..."

"I am aware of the situation, Adam, but we can't deal with it now. Ask DI Lang to handle the problem until we return from the mortuary, and tell Martin, under no circumstances is he to be allowed out of the station unaccompanied. I'll meet you at the front."

*

The phone call Beetle had been anticipating came as he was climbing into his old Corsa to go to work.

"Beetle, my man, you did it again." Stevie's voice drawled. "You sent people on a body-fishing expedition while you made your retreat. I congratulate you. Some crazy woman raised the alarm, I believe?"

"She didn't see..."

"But it still took them a couple of hours in the dark to find the body. Brilliant, I couldn't have planned it better myself."

"It was nothing..." He could get used to this sort of adulation. He'd been practicing sounding modest.

"Nothing, he says... nothing," there was a voice in the background but Beetle couldn't determine whether it was male or female.

"It's just a job... all in a day's work."

"Speaking of which – I've another job for you this coming weekend – if you're up for it?"

"No problem, Stevie, anything for you." He was being used, he knew that, but he wanted to prove himself further. The work was coming in thick and fast and who knew where it would take him next?

"Good man, that's what I like to hear. Now I want you to take my young nephew, Liam, along with you for this next one. See if you can't instil some of your flair for the dramatic into him. He's been pestering for months for a chance to take someone down and I think you're just the man to show him how it should be done. Have you met my Liam?"

"Twice, I think," twice exactly, and they were two occasions too many. Beetle pictured the sharp-faced young youth, a couple of inches smaller than he was, who'd somehow managed to appear to be sneering downwards at him. He'd neither liked nor trusted him then, and from rumours he'd heard since, his instincts had been spot on.

"Next weekend... I'll be in touch. As usual, I will leave the final arrangements in your capable hands. Good man." The phone went dead.

*

"Right, listen up," DCI Michael Forbes stood at the front of the only incident room in the Leaburn Police Station. As stations went it was well behind modern times, but unlike Matlock and Bakewell, was permanently staffed. It was also open to the public every day, and had its own team of detectives. "Adam and I have just returned from the mortuary."

"I thought there was a funny smell," DC Harry Green, the station comedian with the scouse accent, muttered.

Forbes ignored him. "At ten-fifteen on Saturday evening a shooting took place on the edge of a housing estate in Matlock. The right shoulder of the victim was hit, and from an eyewitness account, we know that he then stumbled into the road and into the path of an oncoming taxi. Skid marks on the tarmac indicate that the vehicle was travelling at well above the speed limit for the area and consequently the victim was killed on impact."

"If the gunman doesn't get you, the traffic will..." Harry chimed in again. "I guess his time was up."

"Thank you Harry. The single bullet didn't cause serious injury, and passed through the body. It has since been retrieved from the pavement and sent to the lab. All information gathered to date from Matlock should soon be in our system. Now, was the gunman intending to maim, or to kill? Matlock officers are conducting door-to-door enquiries but as usual, we need to gather as much background information as we can on the victim. Who would want to frighten him, warn him off something, or someone, or dispose of him permanently?"

"The files are through from Matlock, sir," DC Emily Jackson added.

"Good. There should also be a batch of files coming from Bakewell. The second victim of the weekend was also incredibly unlucky. He was out walking his dog when a bullet grazed the side of his head, toppling him, unconscious it's assumed, into the swollen river. If it hadn't been for a woman, also out walking her dog but on the opposite side of the river, the death might have gone down as accidental. There was alcohol in his system, and if he hadn't been found until the next day, the damage from the river might possibly have masked the scrape on the man's skull. So, do we have a gunman who's an extremely good shot, or an extremely poor one?"

"Has that bullet been found?"

"Yes, an hour ago, courtesy of a local man's metal detector."

"Are we to assume there's one gunman or two?"

"For the moment we'll assume one, and I don't believe these were random attacks, so what I don't want to do is alarm the public. The Matlock and Bakewell stations are issuing their own press statements. Now let's get to work."

*

Beetle showered and dressed for his evening meal. He had a steak cooking in the pan, a bag of ready-prepared salad waiting to be opened and a jacket potato in the microwave. Now he could afford, it amused him to try out his new clothes in the comfort of his own home. His mother would have thought it hilarious – him – dressing for dinner – all posh like. She'd have laughed her old head off.

His phone had been by his side all day. He could hardly wait to find out about his new contract. It had to involve murder for Stevie to be so mysterious.

The suspense was killing him!

He sniggered at his own joke, and then frowned. If only he'd had someone other than Angus to share it with...

Chapter 6

It was Tuesday afternoon and Beetle had been offered overtime, something that didn't happen too often. Although he no longer needed the extra money, he did need to keep up the pretence of living an ordinary life, and to be able to pass for legitimate. And since his money worries had become a thing of the past he'd found he enjoyed working in the shop more than he ever had before. He enjoyed the gossip and the banter with customers. In all the years he'd worked there, the worst thing to happen had occurred five weeks earlier when his boss had hired the weasel-faced university graduate with the ponytail and manicured fingernails, supposedly to improve the business.

After so many years of loyal service, he should have been the one offered the responsibility.

The newcomer, Adrian, who seemed taken with expensive suits and designer shoes, and who looked as though he hadn't eaten a decent meal in months, had miraculously found five days of outside work with an events and catering firm. A family farmhouse, on the outskirts of Leaburn, was to host a wedding, followed by a reception, in one of its huge barns.

On Thursday and Friday Beetle was expected to help with the setting up of the barn, on Saturday he was to be in charge of the cooked meats as well as being a waiter and a general 'dogs-body', and on Sunday and Monday he was to assist in the clean-up of whatever mess the drunken yuppies left behind.

But before then, with so much newfound confidence coursing through him, he intended having some fun of his own, while getting the measure of young Liam.

The air temperature had stayed below freezing all day and already a half-moon and full array of stars lit the late afternoon sky. Beetle walked to his car and his eyes automatically swivelled upwards, but only for a few seconds at a time, and only until he saw the skinny youth with the smug grin, leaning against his car.

At that moment, Beetle liked Stevie's nineteen-year-old nephew even less than when he'd first met him a month ago at one of the drug pick-ups.

"Uncle Stevie said you wanted to see me as soon as you'd finished work." Liam whined. "I'm not used to waiting around in car parks, especially in this weather. Couldn't whatever it is have waited?"

He pushed out his chest and glowered at the impertinent youth. "Lean against my car again and I'll hammer you until you don't care what hour of the day or night it is, or what the weather's doing." This was an occasion when it was best to start on the right footing.

The youth responded by stepping forward quickly, in a way that Beetle would never have expected anyone to respond to him a year earlier. It was heady stuff. "You're Liam, right?" He smiled diffidently. As far as he knew, this lad was scum.

"To my mother, I am."

"What does everyone else call you?"

"Ripper..."

"Ripper, what sort of a name's that?"

"It's on account of my first two visits to the snooker hall. Both times, on my first games of the night, I ripped the cloth of the table while taking a tricky shot. Uncle Stevie had to step in to stop me getting barred."

He tried not to laugh. Maybe this youth wasn't so different from him after all. "You don't look old enough to be in those places?"

"I'm nineteen. I know I don't look it, but I am."

"Got a driving license…?"

"Of course… Uncle doesn't like any of us breaking the law unnecessarily. That's my car, over there… the silver Audi." He pointed unnecessarily towards the only other car on the park.

An hour later, they were sitting together in the warmth of Ripper's silver Audi, just ahead of a left turn into a quiet residential street in Leaburn. The sky had clouded over, the ice was softening, and snow had been forecasted for the early hours of the following morning. No one walking past was going to look twice through the steamed-up windows. They ran through Beetle's plans one more time.

"You intend kidnapping a policeman – man, you are one crazy dude," Ripper spoke in awe. "I see why Uncle Stevie likes you."

"Not crazy, no, just lucky these days… lucky in everything that I set my mind to doing. You could learn a thing or two from me if you pay attention. Did you see the shooting stars last night, before the sky clouded over?"

"Err… no, what rubbish are you spouting now?"

"Shooting stars – if you make the same wish often enough, whenever you see them, the wish eventually comes true."

"You're bullshitting me?"

Beetle couldn't help glaring at the youth. The jury was still out on whether he liked him or not. "You'll see."

"Whatever… Uncle Stevie said you were a bit out there… now I know what he means."

"If you intend making a living from crime you're going to need a slice of luck every now and then. Anyway, back to tonight. Have you got the plan fixed in that head of yours?"

"I have, but I still say you're crazy."

Not for the first time, Beetle wondered if ought to abort his mission but, as young as he was, Ripper seemed intelligent and able to suss out a situation rapidly, even if he wasn't on the same page yet. Changing plans rarely worked out – best to stick with it. "There's one loaded handgun in the glove box and I've got one on me. Just being caught owning a gun means a mandatory prison sentence these days. Do not flash it about unless you absolutely have to. Wait here until you see me, either on foot or driving the copper's car. OK?"

"OK, but I still say you're crazy," Ripper giggled as he spoke; ignoring the scowl shot back from Beetle.

He opened the car door and spoke slowly in reply. It amused him to feel the air temperature plummeting inside the car. "I'm a quiet, overlooked, blend-into-the-background little shop worker, and there are far worse things to be in this life. When you're old enough and hard enough to begin insulting me, come back and try it again. Until then, keep your thoughts to yourself."

Ripper stared ahead and rubbed his hands together.

He'd made his point. It was time to exit the car and quietly close the door.

Beetle dodged behind a hedge. He was taking a risk – a calculated risk, but a risk non-the-less. It was a time when most people were home, but unlikely to be opening their curtains or their blinds again to look out onto a wintery road.

Martin Jones and his family must have been away for the weekend, they'd been missing every time he'd driven past, but the wife and son were in the house now. A television and several lights were on. Last night a marked police car had followed Martin home, but it hadn't stopped. He was relying on the same thing happening tonight.

He'd checked the layout of the property, looking the best places to stand and making sure there were no alarms where he intended to be. In fact, there were no alarms anywhere on the property. For an officer of the law, security was very lax – but then wasn't that the case in many professions? Mechanics seldom maintained their own cars until they had to, and builders neglected their own properties – luckily for him.

A car passed by. Seconds later, he'd drilled out the lock of one of the two garage doors, slowly and quietly raised the metal door just far enough, and slipped into the dark interior.

This was new ground, a more intimate glimpse into the police officer's life, and it smelt of turpentine and oil. Two small windows faced away from the glare of the streetlights and a modest car occupied half the floor space. His eyes adjusted. He located the door to the adjoining house, returned the drill to the poacher's pocket of his oversized coat and pulled out the stocking he'd taken from his late mother's bedroom. It would work as a crude but effective disguise. His face wasn't as well known in Leaburn as in Matlock, and Martin didn't have a dash-cam fitted inside his car, but he didn't see the point in taking unnecessary risks. Finally, he checked the roll of duct tape and the rope, pulled the gun from another pocket, and sidled along the wall until he found a clutter-free place to lean and wait.

*

Five minutes after taking the ten-second call, DCI Michael Forbes was driving at speed back to the station and praying someone had overreacted.

He burst through the entrance doors and took the stairs to the first floor incident room two at a time. He halted when he saw DC Emily Jackson's flushed face. She was one of his more laid-back officers, the eldest from a brood of eight, and it normally took more than an average crisis to fluster her. DS Adam Ross and DC Harry Green were the only others in the room. "What the hell happened... how much do we know?"

"Sir," Emily answered. "I was the only officer left upstairs when Sarah phoned in. I've alerted all traffic units to look for Martin's car as a matter of urgency and everyone else I've been able to contact is on their way back to the station now."

"We know he arrived home safely...?"

"Yes sir, Ryan followed Martin's car as far as his driveway and Sarah heard his car pulling up. She switched on the kettle in the kitchen, which unfortunately prevented her hearing much else for a couple of minutes. I've just been speaking with her again and she's understandably distraught."

"A family liaison officer...?"

"PC Wilson's on her way over there now. When Martin hadn't entered the house by the time the kettle boiled, Sarah looked outside and saw the garage door wide open but no sign of Martin or his car. That was just over half an hour ago." She paused as if she thought her boss might need time to digest the unlikely statement. "It's looking as though he wasn't mistaken in thinking someone was following him."

"I never thought that he was..." Forbes waited for her to continue.

"Sarah's been phoning him, and so have we. His mobile goes straight to voicemail."

"One of you – see if you can get a fix on his mobile from the phone companies."

"Adam was just starting on that, sir."

"You've done well in less than an hour, Emily. Let's hope your hard work pays off." The first hour after any abduction was the most vital. "And I want the CSI at Martin's house ASAP."

"I'll get on to that, sir."

Ryan was the next to burst through the door. His face was grey. "I'm so sorry, sir. I can't believe it. I watched him pull into his drive. I should have waited and watched him into his house."

"It's not your fault, Ryan, now think, did you see anyone at all on the street, or any vehicles parked close to Martin's home? Unless the perpetrator arrived on foot we could be looking for more than one person."

"I've got dash-cam footage, sir, and I've been trying to picture the side-streets, but I honestly don't remember seeing anything that might help."

"Get the footage uploaded." How he handled this investigation in the next few hours might determine whether Martin was ever found. "Is anything coming in yet from any of the ANPR cameras...?" Automatic number plate recognition cameras were rare away from the A515 and A53.

"Nothing yet, sir," DC Harry Green shouted back.

There was a strong chance that the abduction of Martin Jones, if that was what it was, would turn out to be linked to Gary Jones's murder, and it was pointless trying to pretend otherwise. It didn't bode well. "I want a uniformed officer to stay with Godfrey Jones tonight, whether he likes it or not. Someone could be targeting the whole family."

"I'll see to that, sir," Harry responded.

It was hard to admit, but the answers they desperately needed now might lie in files created over the previous eleven months. Had they wrongly dismissed a name, or overlooked some vital clue? But there were so many documents and his team had so little time. He was in no mental state right now to go trawling through the backlog of information. His place was in the incident room, co-ordinating the search and working towards a better outcome for Martin than for his brother.

By thirty minutes to midnight the two confirmed sightings they'd had of Martin's car, on the Buxton to Ashbourne road, were old news. All available cars had been dispatched to the area but for two hours, nothing new had come in.

At fifteen minutes to midnight, a phone rang in the reception area downstairs.

PC Katie Brown had volunteered to work through the night on the switchboard and she transferred the call upstairs.

"To quote the male caller," Forbes addressed the stunned room, "we'll find Martin, trussed up like a Christmas turkey, on an unclassified road behind a hermit's cave."

"That's it... that's all he said? What hermit's cave?" Emily broke the silence. "Is he alive?"

"He didn't say. Katie's requesting a trace, but the call came from an unregistered mobile so the caller could be anywhere by now or may even have disposed of their phone or their sim card."

Adam switched his attention back to his screen. "I'll search for possible hermit's caves."

"It's bloody cold out there," Emily added, "and it's beginning to snow."

Adam raised his hand. "The most famous 'hermit's cave' is at Dale Abbey, Ilkeston, but I've found another, much closer. It comes up as Cratcliffe Hermitage, on the side of Cratcliffe Rocks, between the villages of Elton and Birchover."

"Get a grid reference. How far is it from here?"

"About ten miles, sir, and Martin's car was clocked heading in that direction."

"Alert the Ilkeston force and ask them to check Dale Abbey. We'll check the nearest one with that name. Do we have any vehicles in that area now?"

"We should have, sir. Danny Grant is on the radio. He'll direct all cars in the area to the site."

His voice dropped into a lower register. "Tell him to also arrange for an ambulance to be at the scene. At the very least, in these conditions, Martin may be suffering from hypothermia. Let's get moving, folks."

Forbes resisted breaking the speed limit. The roads were slick and other cars were already closer to where Martin was hopefully awaiting rescue. It was bitterly cold and sleet was hammering the windscreen as he drove, with Adam beside him, in convoy with four other vehicles. He wondered if the weather was coming out in sympathy with them. He'd thought Martin wasn't in any immediate danger, but he'd been wrong. The panic button and alarm system booked for installation in his home at the end of the week now seemed a pointless gesture. He should have pushed for immediate installation as a matter of urgency. If Martin wasn't found alive it was something he'd never forgive himself for.

Adam knew when to sit in silence. They'd worked together closely enough and for long enough to recognise in each other the occasional need for quiet. Ten minutes into the journey, the darkness of the A515 seemed endless. The left turn had to be coming up soon.

The car radio crackled into life and PC Katie Brown's voice sounded alien. She was shouting. "Martin's alive… he's been found. He's alive and conscious," her voice screeched.

Forbes tried to hold his tone neutral while Adam laughed with relief. "Where is he?"

"Are you sure?" Adam suddenly sounded sceptical.

The two men looked at each other. No other words were necessary.

"At the Cratcliffe Rocks location that you're headed for," she continued. "A traffic officer from Matlock was first on the scene. He found Martin in the boot of the car, trussed up with tape. He's taken a blow to the head and is possibly suffering from hypothermia and shock, but otherwise he's all right. A second car and an ambulance have just arrived on scene. That's all the information I have."

"Call his wife and father," Forbes eased his foot off the accelerator. For the first time since leaving the station, he acknowledged the vast expanse of farmland and woodland in this dark, snow-covered, unfamiliar part of Derbyshire. Without the phone call, Martin might not have been found until it was too late. "And remind the traffic officers to preserve as much of the scene as they can. Our ETA is approximately ten minutes. I want to see for myself that Martin's all right."

"Yes sir."

He glanced at Adam again before refocusing on the road.

Chapter 7

DC Jade Sharpe poked her head around the door of Forbes's office. "Martin's father has arrived, sir. He's come straight from the hospital. I must say he gave me quite a shock. He's aged since I last saw him a couple of months ago. As he used to be one of us, DC Bell's bringing him up to date with the enquiry. I hope that's all right?"

Retired detective superintendent Godfrey Jones had never fully recovered from the murder of his youngest son. That and the death of his wife two years earlier had left him with one son, who last night had been attacked, abducted and then dumped for no apparent reason, and one daughter he rarely saw and who lived and worked in London. Forbes called in to see him whenever he could. "That's fine, Jade. I'll speak with him as soon as Robert's finished."

Gary's murder had touched everyone at the station. Eleven months earlier, outside officers had been brought in to the station and Godfrey and Martin had been interrogated, and their houses and gardens searched. It had been considered routine by the chief constables but had been a bad episode for everyone involved.

"It's strange, sir, don't you think, that no more traces of either Gary Jones or Paul Biers have ever been found."

Gary's car remained in the pound, along with obscene quantities of dried blood. Forbes shrugged. "Whoever killed those young men and then lifted out their remains could be capable of anything. Unfortunately, until we have a motive we have to assume he may kill again. Eventually, we'll get a break in the case. We have to keep on believing that, or else what are we all doing here?"

"I do believe." She smiled and blushed, "That came out as if I was at a Gospel meeting, didn't it? I never had the opportunity of working with the superintendent but I know of his reputation of being a hard-line, no-nonsense officer while at Leaburn and throughout his long career. He must have made more than a few enemies, but to be targeting his entire family..."

"We have to keep an open mind, Jade. CSI are still searching the fields and roadside around where Martin was found. If there is anything there to link the incidents, they'll find it." Crime Scene Investigators was the latest name for the mainly private group of individuals previously referred to as the Scenes of Crimes Officers.

"What about the anonymous call...?"

"That was from a pay-as-you-go phone. Identifying the general location of the call hasn't helped us. We need to find the phone itself. Unlike on most television shows modern technology doesn't always work in our favour. Where's Godfrey Jones now?"

"Robert was taking him to the canteen."

"Bring them both to my office. We can't rule out the idea that last night's abduction and Gary's murder could be connected, or that they could be related to an old police investigation." It wasn't unheard of for criminals to harbour grudges against arresting officers, but he'd never come across one being held against an entire family – not in Derbyshire anyway.

However, that did not make it impossible.

Godfrey's appearance was worse than he remembered noting just two weeks earlier, and not just because of last night's trauma. His hair was unwashed and hadn't been near a barber for months. Looking at him now, no one would ever correctly guess at his past career, or at his current handsome pension. "Come in Godfrey; I understand Martin will be in hospital for a day or two for observation. Concussion needs careful monitoring." He watched the retired officer collapse into a chair.

Forbes saw a broken man, but at the same time a tough man. He understood Godfrey needed to be in the building, and that his police-brain was methodically searching for reasons and answers.

"I'll be happier when he's home with his family," when Godfrey finally spoke the words tumbled out. "Martin said the man was waiting… in the garage. He said he went to open the door, saw that the lock had been tampered with but before he could react, the door was shoved open in his face. A masked man with a gun told him he wouldn't hurt him if he co-operated. He made him drive for miles and then whacked him on the head. When he woke, he was in the boot of his car and trussed up. After what happened with Gary, he thought he was going to die. My Martin has never hurt anyone in his life. Why would anyone do that?"

"We don't know, Godfrey. I've requested that an armed response unit be on standby in case of further developments. Crime scene investigators are still working in Martin's garage and I understand that hair, fibres, and possible DNA samples have been found in the car. There are also footprints and tyre tracks in the area where he was found indicating another vehicle was involved."

"What about those two shootings at the weekend… could they be connected to what happened to Martin? He remembers the man saying something about sending a message – but not what that message was about, or who it was for."

"He told us that. Godfrey, are you absolutely sure that you've no idea who might be behind this latest attack on your family?"

"Don't you think I'd tell you if I had? There will be ructions from this… mark my words. I'd give a small fortune to know who was responsible…"

"It's too early to consider offering a reward."

"If I find him before you do…" His hand went to his chest and his eyes rolled.

"Are you all right, Godfrey, you look done in."

"I'm just tired, that's all, tired of all of it, tired of wondering what's coming next." He paused to catch his breath. "I don't understand any of it. And what about my Gary's murder — what are you doing about that these days?"

"You know how these things work, Godfrey. The case is still very much open but we've had nothing new to work with since we last spoke. In the light of what's happened with Martin, is there anyone, anyone at all, who you can think of who might still be bearing malice towards you and your family from your years on the force?"

Godfrey looked genuinely surprised. "Do you really think there might be a connection between the attacks on my sons? I provided a comprehensive list of names when Gary first disappeared."

"Those were checked out and eliminated at the time, along with everyone released from prison whose case you'd been involved with. But can you think of any others, either connected to your work or to your personal life?"

"One or two... maybe, but you know how it is in this line of work; people threaten and bluster, and then think better of it and continue on with their lives. This morning Martin told me of a hit-and-run fatality he'd been working on involving a minor drug dealer called Stephen Monks. Could his death be relevant?"

"That investigation's been running for two weeks now and Martin was only one of several officers working on it," Robert replied.

"I doubt there's a connection," Forbes added, "but we'll certainly take a closer look."

"Three families on the Ashgate Estate in Leaburn have been users and dealers for at least two generations." Godfrey's eyes searched his, as if hoping to see the answers he craved.

"We know those..."

"I was involved in the arrests of most of them at one time or another and on one of those occasions things went badly wrong. You must both know the case. James Daley was as high as a kite when we brought him in for his own safety, but while waiting for an ambulance he suffered a cardiac arrest and died. His family complained that we should have taken him straight to the nearest hospital instead of back to this station, and in hindsight, they were probably right. I ordered him to be brought here first, and his family knows that, but that happened ten years ago and I gave you their names when Gary disappeared. Was Stephen Monks related to that family in any way? Could everything that's happened to my sons be related to my mistake all those years ago?"

"You mustn't think like that. What happened to Gary might not be even linked to Martin's ordeal. Last night, whoever was responsible could easily have killed him, but instead he called us. I've never heard of anything remotely similar before, not involving a police officer, and to me it suggests a kidnapper with an overblown ego, or someone's sick idea of a joke. He may make contact again and give us a better idea of what his game is."

"I know there were rumours at the time of Gary being involved in the drug dealing scene but I never believed them. I'm sometimes glad his mother didn't have to live through these traumas. That's an awful way to think, isn't it?"

"It's understandable, Godfrey. She was a good woman who loved her boys, and her daughter, with a passion. We found no evidence of Gary's dealing, only that he sometimes bought small quantities for his own use, but we'll take another look at the names you've just suggested."

"What about the friends and family of Paul Biers? I know some of them blamed Gary for his death at the time, claiming my Gary had involved him in some kind of gang warfare."

"We can take another look at them, but I'm sure they all now see Gary as just as much of a victim as Paul."

"I expect you're right. I wish I could be more help. All this on top of…"

He watched the man press his lips together and sink further down into the chair. He was visibly shrinking. "Robert, go and find someone from downstairs to escort Godfrey back to his home." He wanted a private chat with the man who used to be his superior, and whose quick brain he was still in awe of.

Ten minutes and one mug of coffee later, PC Tracy Wilson, the family liaison officer, poked her head around the door. She'd worked thirty out of the last thirty-six hours but was still smiling. The high that everyone involved in the search for Martin had experienced, at midnight last night, was keeping every officer unnaturally cheerful and alert. "I've got a car out front for whenever Mr Jones is ready to go home," she beamed at them.

He felt he was in a parallel universe – in a happiness home for demented and overworked police officers. "Tracy will see that you get home safely, Godfrey. Look after yourself and we'll be in touch."

The smiling PC held open the door to the corridor but Godfrey hesitated, reluctant to leave what at one time had been his office.

"This latest case needs a firm hand, Michael, and although you haven't found my Gary's remains, or his killer, I'm placing my trust in you again. Don't let me down. Go with your own gut instincts, as I used to. I've always maintained that if you have two or more people around a table then nothing meaningful will ever be achieved because of time spent bickering instead of focusing on the job in hand. Remember that, and I'll expect to hear from you soon."

Forbes felt reprimanded. He was uncomfortable turning away the shell of a fellow officer who so clearly wanted involvement in the investigations, but he had no choice in the matter. Godfrey had retired eight years earlier, and even then, many of his methods belonged to a system of policing which no longer existed. The best thing for him to do was to go home and eat a good meal. The second of those things wasn't likely to happen and Forbes made a mental note to call on his old colleague in the next day or two, with or without any news concerning his sons.

As Godfrey was leading Tracy down the stairs, DS Adam Ross strode through the open doorway. Adam and Godfrey's paths had to have crossed on the stairs. Forbes briefly wondered if words had been exchanged.

"What's next, sir?"

"Adam, you and I are off to the outskirts of Leaburn, to pay another visit to the family of Stephen Monks."

Forbes had met Gillian Monks once before, shortly after her brother's death, and as far as he'd been able to ascertain at the time she was the opposite of her late brother in every way imaginable. While he'd been stick-thin, his body ravaged by years of drug abuse and with a reputation of being able to start a fight in an empty room, she was a healthy-looking, well fleshed, friendly twenty year old – *a comely girl*, Forbes's father would have said. She had no need of make-up, and although she'd obviously been crying shortly before opening the front door to them, a genuine smile reached her eyes as she beckoned them into the heart of her parent's home.

The semi-detached, three-bedroomed, stone-built property probably dated back to the turn of the twentieth century but had been tastefully and sympathetically modernised and furnished. From what he'd read in the reports, only the antics of their son had blotted this family's upper-working-class lifestyle. Forbes knew how that felt.

"Mum and dad are in the living room. Go through, I'm making them a cup of tea. Would you like one?"

"No, thank you, but you carry on," he nodded to Adam to follow Gillian into the kitchen.

"Stephen's death wasn't an accident, was it?" Mr Monks began before further condolences could be offered. "Have you found out yet what was he doing on that road that night?"

"We're still not sure, I'm afraid. Our best guess is that he was expecting a lift that never materialised. No one has come forward." A wailing sound came from Mrs Monks and he saw her reach towards the box of tissues on the coffee table beside her chair. "What we'd like from you both today, if possible, are any names and addresses of Stephen's friends that we might have missed, and your permission to access any electronic devices he either owned or used."

"His phone was with him," Mr Monks sounded surprised.

"We've identified all the contacts on that, but we didn't want to overlook anyone whose details weren't stored in his mobile."

"You'll need to go into his bedroom," Mrs Monks turned her tear-streaked face towards her husband. "You'll have to show them. I can't go in there – not yet." She ended the statement with an accusing look at the intruders to her home. "When can we have our Stephen back?"

"Soon, Mrs Monks, soon," he didn't want to commit the forensic pathologist, his long-term girlfriend, Alison Ransom, to a timeline. The post mortem had been completed within hours of Stephen's death but once the body was released, if it was cremated, there would be no opportunity of going back to it to confirm or rule out the relevance of any new evidence. He moved the conversation on to the main reason for the visit. "We've come to keep you updated, Mr and Mrs Monks. Last night, the detective you've mainly been dealing with, DC Martin Jones, was attacked and injured. Until he's back at work, Detective Inspector Robert Lang will be in charge of the case. He'll be along to introduce himself later today."

"I saw something on the local news about that. I didn't realise it was our detective. You believe his being attacked is something to do with Stephen's death, don't you?" Mr Monks was already ahead of him. "Why else would two such senior officers be coming round here today looking for more information?"

"It's a line of enquiry we're following, and nothing more." He quickly moved the conversation on. "This may be a coincidence, but Martin told us today he'd recently discovered your Stephen had been friendly with the missing youth, Gary Jones."

"That's right, and Stephen was terribly upset when Gary's car was found in such a state, but he hadn't seen Gary for several days before that. He had absolutely nothing to do with it."

"I wasn't suggesting that he had, Mr Monks. Did Stephen know the other victim, Paul Biers, do you know?"

"I remember him saying that he'd never met or even heard of the other youth in Gary's car that night."

"But he knew Gary quite well...?"

"They went to school together and were the best of friends for years."

"Stephen's name never came up during the original enquiry."

"From what we saw in the papers, and on social media, your investigations focused on drug dealers, and there's no shortage of those. No one was interested in two-bit users like my Stephen, though I'm sure that if he'd had any information at the time he'd have come forward."

"I'm sure. I have to tell you that Stephen had moderately high levels of heroin in his bloodstream at the time of his death. I'm sorry if that comes as a shock to you."

"It doesn't," Mrs Monks sighed as she spoke.

"We'll let you know as soon as we have any more information. Now if you'd be kind enough to show us into Stephen's room, Mr Monks, we'll be as quick as we can and then we'll leave you all in peace."

Adam settled back into the passenger seat, "That could have been any family home in this country," he commented.

Forbes turned the ignition key and pictured his younger sister, Louise, whose demons had come from bottles of vodka rather than drugs, and who now, fortunately, had come through her private hell with a determination to make something of her life. "Bringing up a family isn't easy today. Did you learn anything from Gillian?"

"She loved her brother, but she acknowledged he was his own worst enemy and that his lifestyle was slowly destroying her parents' mental and physical health. She's a straight-talking girl, in her first year at university and happy enough to talk." He reached into his jacket pocket. "She also knows considerably more about his life than their parents do. She gave me a list of Stephen's suppliers and customers."

"Excellent – so now we know for certain he was dealing, which of those suppliers on the list will his customers turn to now, I wonder? All of a sudden we have two possible motives for Martin's abduction, and two lines of enquiry."

Adam looked confused.

"No one has offered us any explanation of what Stephen Monks was doing on foot on that country road, miles from town, and Martin claims that his memory of what his abductor said to him is sketchy. If we assume that Stephen's death wasn't the result of an accident where the driver panicked and fled the scene, but was deliberate and premeditated, we have to ask whether it was possibly a drugs related confrontation and that someone is trying to warn off the investigating officer. The alternative is that it's part of an elaborate vendetta against ex-superintendent Jones and his family."

"Someone's begun killing off Gary's friends...? That's a bit of a leap, isn't it?"

"I'd agree with you if the man who abducted Martin hadn't told him that he wasn't going to hurt him, and that he was sending a message. I'm also wondering if maybe Stephen Monks wasn't meant to die that night."

"Sending a message to whom – to Godfrey Jones?"

"I'm not sure... possibly. We need to look again at Stephen's movements during the days before his death. It's time to get a team together. It's possible all three cases could be parts of one major incident. I'll call for a team briefing as soon as we get back."

Adam took a deep breath. At the risk of feeling foolish, he spoke out. "What about the weekend's shootings? We don't have too many firearms incidents in this area, fortunately. Is it too much of a co-incidence to think that they might be linked to last night's incident with Martin, and if so, that they're also related to the other three?"

"Now who's making a leap of judgement, but I follow your line of reasoning. For now, the Bakewell and Matlock stations are treating the shootings as isolated incidents, mainly because the two bullets were fired from two different guns.

But I do agree that, in our station, we should be ready to assume that all the recent cases, plus the two murders from last winter, could be linked, and could have something to do with Godfrey Jones or his sons."

"Bloody hell… we could have one hell of a crazy fucker on our patch," Adam seldom swore but Forbes understood his friend's outburst and said nothing.

Chapter 8

Stevie Hall rarely went anywhere alone. Beetle stared back at the minder – the man-mountain overflowing the front passenger seat of the silver Mercedes who'd turned his shaven, tattooed head just far enough to watch the rear door being opened and closed.

He slid onto the cream-coloured leather seat. "What's this about, Stevie?" There was something going down and he was excited about being involved.

"All in good time, my impatient little friend. Buckle up and enjoy the ride."

Beetle did as he was told. He was too shrewd these days to do otherwise. He was thrilled with the prospects this man had opened up for him and didn't want to risk irritating him with more questions.

Stevie had a dark, gypsy look to his features, and a permanent air of menace, but with a cool and calm way of talking to the people who hadn't offended or dared to criticise him. He was someone who was, 'once seen – never forgotten', as Beetle's mother would have said. Women seemed drawn to his looks – Beetle had witnessed the phenomenon for himself in the clubs, and while he was very occasionally seen with a young female on his arm, he didn't think Stevie was the type of man any woman ought to consider as a long-term prospect.

There were rumours of one female in particular, somewhere in Stevie's background, although, assuming she actually existed, Beetle had no desire to meet her. The big man himself was quite enough for Beetle to be dealing with and he felt that any woman who'd allied herself to a man who thought nothing of putting out contracts on the lives of other people was a woman to be steered well clear of.

But he respected Stevie. He'd found him to be a man of his word and, more importantly, a generous and prompt payer. If anything, Beetle was conscious of being paid almost too handsomely, and consequently living the good life a little too freely. Some of his new clothes had become tight of late and in the bathroom mirror, he'd noticed a developing paunch. He was going to have to chase another new experience, that of joining a gym. He could afford it, after all, and in his new line of work it wouldn't do to become complacent about fitness levels.

"Whether you take this job or not, you don't tell a soul about it. Have you got that, Beetle?" the tattooed man drawled.

"You can trust me." Beetle breathed deeply and settled into the soft leather. His nickname had first come about because of his late mother's passion for owning and driving around in the ridiculous-looking vehicles, although in his mind the Volkswagen car company had to accept some of the blame for producing such objects of ridicule in the first place. They were desirable cars nowadays, but back when he'd been a youngster they'd been at the opposite end of his classmates' scale of cool. His mother had delivered him and his sister to school in one of the damn things every morning for years, and to make matters worse had stencilled multi-coloured flowers and insects all over them. Not that his school days had been made any easier by his own appearance – with one leg a good inch longer than the other, ears Dumbo the elephant would have been proud of, and a childhood stammer, he sometimes considered he'd done well to make it to adulthood at all. His appearance hadn't changed much, he'd just become bigger and clumsier. Sophie, on the other hand, had blossomed from a short, freckled, skinny youngster into a blonde haired stunner with model figure and looks to die for, but that was just typical of his luck.

The car he was in now could not have been any more different from those of his mother's. It screamed class. It exuded an aroma of expensive aftershave and expensive leather, rather than the cigarette smoke and fried onions that had accompanied him into the first class of every school day.

His own car, these days, was something he felt comfortable in, and now that he had the funds to maintain it properly he'd found he was perfectly happy driving around in an easily forgettable, grey Vauxhall Corsa Estate, in the occasional fug of cannabis smoke and with his trusty walking boots and rucksack on the covered rear seat. On his drug runs, he used stolen and cloned vehicles, and he marvelled at the fact that now he could afford a better car for himself, he no longer desired one. These days he was all about business.

With a few miles and the busiest of the traffic islands behind them, he felt comfortable enough to speak. "Where are we headed for, Stevie?"

"We're going to the spa town of Buxton, my friend. I need you to take a look at one particular woman, in the flesh, so to speak, so you'll recognise her when you see her again on Saturday."

"This Saturday...? I'm working that day. That lairy little ponce my boss has just set on seems to think I'd make a half-decent waiter at some posh wedding out in the sticks."

Stevie startled him by letting out a genuine belly laugh. "Beetle, you surprise me – Adrian too is in my part-time employ. I thought you might have sussed that out by now. I take it you're not a fan." He laughed again. "You're right though, he is a lairy little ponce, but he's sending you there under my instructions. I have a job out there for Liam and your good self. It's a bit out of the ordinary, but I need it doing quickly and with the minimum amount of fuss, so there'll be no opportunity for your fancy trick-shooting this time, understood?"

"Anything for you, Stevie, you know that." He settled into the sumptuous leather again and studied the rear of the expensive seat and expensive haircut in front of him, both of which his hard-earned money had once contributed towards. He smiled. It sounded as though he was once again about to recoup considerably more money back than he'd ever invested in Stevie Hall's empire.

*

Naomi Proctor's body was on high alert. Through the splatters of dirt on the car's rear window, she'd seen she was being followed.

A month had passed since she'd last visited Stevie Hall's apartment, and since she'd uncovered some of the sources of his limitless income. Pretending to be clueless hadn't been an option and so she'd challenged him, and then taken a beating for her trouble. Being on the same street as him now was enough to spark prickles of fear.

There was a supermarket up ahead. Maybe there'd be someone in there she knew. She pressed down on the accelerator, for once willing a police car to appear from nowhere. Why was it they were never around when you needed them?

She had hoped never to have to see Stevie ever again, or be reminded of how he'd humiliated her. Role-play was one thing, but she now knew that bondage, pain, and safe words within sex were the markers of a dangerous individual.

She'd withheld details of Stevie's life from her friends, but with what little she'd told them they'd all encouraged her to distance herself from him as swiftly as possible. She'd finally done that, but his threats to herself and her sister had worked. Going to the police at the time had been out of the question.

The larger bruises from that day had faded to a pale yellow, not that they'd concerned her. She'd considered them the price paid for her steep learning curve.

Her sister, Emma, who was the only family she had left, was going off to America to work in a few days' time, and until then she couldn't risk placing her in harm's way. Even contacting a solicitor for advice, as some of her friends had suggested, was out of the question. She was under no illusion about the spread of the Hall family's influence, and she'd been left not knowing whom to trust.

She turned her car into the park and found a floodlit space.

Through her rear view mirror, she saw the Mercedes parking in the shadows, close to the entrance.

After a deep breath, she launched herself into the drizzle, hoping to appear calmer than she felt, and hurried across the supermarket car park.

The coloured lights around the massive windows of the Morrison's supermarket were mirrored on the wet tarmac. And as if that wasn't enough to remind shoppers of the time of year a perennial Christmas song with a modern beat grew louder with each step she took.

Metal trollies in the floodlit, covered bay looked reassuringly substantial, but to get her hands on one meant spending longer outside. She marched past them, and past the unnaturally cheerful couple in the foyer who were dressed in red and white floor-length coats and who were shaking their red plastic buckets at anyone and everyone. She'd normally have dug out a few coins, but she mouthed the word '*sorry*', and hurried past.

Inside the doorway, she tested the weight a wire basket from one of the stacks.

As a defensive weapon, it would be useless.

She headed towards the aisles of tinned goods.

"Are you all right, Miss?" The purple-haired, youngish woman sitting behind the till was staring at her.

She blinked. The two items she needed, along with two tins of vegetable soup and two large tins of potatoes that would probably sit in her cupboard until they were well out of date and destined for the bin had all moved along the conveyer belt as far as they could while she was still standing at the opposite end. Her next few steps would place her in full view of the car park. "Sorry... I just... I don't wish to be a nuisance, but do you think someone could walk with me as far as my car. I don't feel too well."

"Are you sure that you should be driving?" The young woman glanced downwards.

Maybe she had a panic button in easy reach.

"Quite sure, thank you." Once in her car, she could phone around her friends until she found someone willing to drive out to the shop. She could invite them for a drink. Miss purple-hair couldn't be aware of the outdoor threat – she was probably assuming the woman standing in front of her was either unstable and unpredictable or about to collapse into a heap in front of her without first paying for the goods on the conveyer belt.

"I just need some air." That part was true. A wave of heat had rolled up her chest and her neck, and then accelerated up her face to her cheeks.

"I'll get a member of the floor staff for you."

"There's no need for that." A man's voice cut through the beginnings of yet another butchered Christmas song. The dark haired, dark eyed man standing beside her had already unloaded his wire basket of its six tins of cat meat, one packet of apples and two litre container of milk without her noticing him. "I'm a policeman," he was reaching into his jacket pocket.

"I'm sorry... I don't know..." She struggled for the right words as he produced a small black wallet, flipped open what appeared to be an identity card and held it up in front of her face. She'd never seen one before. How did anyone tell a real ID card from a fake? She scrutinized it for a couple of seconds anyway.

"And I'm trained in first aid," he was smiling at her – a sympathetic but at the same time warm and friendly smile. He most probably was a real police officer – they were good at things like that. Putting people at ease was a part of the job, or so she believed.

"I don't want to be any trouble…"

"I've just come off duty so please allow me to help you. It will be my final good deed of the day."

She looked again at Miss purple-hair.

"It's all right, Miss. He really is a copper. He lives on my street. I went to school with him. You'll be safe enough."

The seasonally dressed couple in the entrance foyer optimistically shook their plastic buckets at her again, but this time she blanked them. Through the icy drizzle, she was watching the red taillights of a car with darkened windows speeding out of the car park.

"I'm feeling better, thank you, I'll be fine from here." Was that something you normally said to someone you didn't know – to someone offering to do a good deed and who you didn't really want to walk out of your life too quickly? As they reached the doorway she shortened her steps and looked up at him. "I'm sorry; I'm being an ungracious bitch, aren't I? We weren't introduced properly. I'm Naomi Proctor." Her vow to herself to steer well clear of men for the near future was in danger of being broken – at least, she hoped that it was. This was showing all the signs of being the opposite of her last close encounter with the opposite sex. A good-looking, cat-loving police officer could be just what she needed now.

"And I'm Ryan Wheeler – DC Wheeler actually, originally from Preston and now stationed at Leaburn." He held out his free hand and she awkwardly accepted his handshake.

A formal introduction – whoever did things like that these days? "That's my car over there, thanks for the escort, but I promise you I'm feeling better now." She smiled at him, desperately hoping he wasn't thinking she was a somewhat neurotic, attention-seeking bimbo. A couple with a pushchair and a screaming toddler glared at them as they edged past. "I think we're standing in the way."

Together they stepped to the side of the door, and out of necessity, closer to each other.

"I hope you don't think I'm being forward, and if you have a boyfriend, or a partner, or other plans, please say no, but would you care to go somewhere with me for a bite to eat?"

"Now, do you mean…?"

"Well… yes… I thought that maybe a lack of food or drink might be the cause of you not feeling well back there in the shop. I'm sorry if that sounded presumptuous of me."

"I'm just tired, that's all, and I've had rather a stressful day, but… I'm attending the wedding of a close friend tomorrow and my sister should have accompanied me. She's been unexpectedly called away on business… so…" She hesitated. "I'm rambling on a bit, aren't I? I'll pass on tonight… thank you anyway… but if you're not doing anything tomorrow… would you care to put on a suit and tie and accompany me to a rather swanky wedding out in the country? You don't need to buy a gift; I've done that. And I've got a taxi ordered so I can pick you up if you'll let me have your address."

Chapter 9

As was his custom on a Saturday morning, Forbes sat in his office going through the week's crime sheets while most of his officers were still in their beds. The deaths of Paul and Gary last year, and last weekend's shootings of James Goodall in Matlock and Darren Reed in Bakewell, bore the hallmarks of professional killings. They'd taken place outdoors, where evidence would be easily destroyed and where so many people walked that DNA samples would be almost impossible to isolate, even if they survived the wet weather.

The forensics team had taken casts of indistinct footprints and tyre tracks from the scene of the first two murders, and that was it for tangible evidence. From the second two his officers had found private CCTV footage in Matlock of a person walking away from the scene of the shooting, but that too was blurred, and they had a distraught woman's vague description of the gunman in Bakewell. The hit and run fatality case was no nearer to being solved than the day it had been reported and Detective Superintendent Christine Price had been chewing his ear off about that. Overall, they could do with a break in at least one of the cases.

The abduction of Martin Jones was the odd one out, and the only incident to provide some real evidence – quite a lot, in fact, including clear footprints, size ten – male shoe, clear tyre tracks, four short brown human hairs and ten black canine ones. The DNA from the human hair follicles didn't throw up a name from police records, but the forensics team was still working on Martin's car, and none of Martin's family could remember being in recent contact with a black dog.

Forbes straightened up in his seat and closed his eyes. The weak links between the cases were gnawing at him, along with the lack of motives in any of them. If nothing new came in before dinnertime, he'd take the rest of Saturday and all of Sunday off to rest his brain.

*

Beetle snaked between the small groups of wedding guests while awkwardly balancing a tray of filled, lead cut, crystal wine glasses. He smiled at those who condescended to make eye contact with him. He was finding the experience really quite enjoyable, though with his rolling gait he was hardly cut out to be a swanky waiter.

He was working for cash-in-hand, he'd been issued with a false name, and he intended rehoming a few of the glasses before the weekend was over... so far so good... but the best was yet to come.

Since leaving school he'd only ever worn a tie, under his mother's instructions, to attend either a wedding or a funeral, and without exception, they'd taken place in cold and draughty churches. The organisers of this particular shindig had gone overboard with the heating. It was unrelenting, and he really was out of condition. He deposited the tray of empty glasses on the edge of the nearest table, mopped his brow with a clean handkerchief and fingered the irritating knot at his throat.

Feeling slightly more comfortable, he picked up the tray again and scanned the room. The fabric and flower strewn barn was heaving with overdressed people and for the last five minutes not of them had looked beyond the drinks he'd been offering. None of the guests were likely to be taking any notice of him now – now that they were all glass-in-hand and focused on finding their allotted place at one of the over-dressed tables.

Naomi and her date were together, over in the far corner.

He watched the couple but his mind was wandering. His knives weren't within reach, and not being able to see them or lay his hands on any of them, in such a crowded space, left him feeling cornered. He was sweating again.

He'd been in butchery since leaving school and for the most part enjoyed it. His first paychecks had gone on the set of Sheffield steel blades and he'd never regretted it. Now though, guns and knives lay side-by-side in his car, in position and ready and waiting for the phone call from him instructing Ripper to set off.

The reception couldn't end soon enough.

The couple were taking their seats at a table close to the edge of the room. Naomi obviously wasn't in one of the bride's or the groom's inner circle of relatives – she was busy focusing her green eyes on her smartly dressed boyfriend's face. They were locked in conversation, leaning towards each other.

Enjoy the meal you two. It will be your last for a while.

His head was buzzing as he carried endless numbers of plates and dishes to and from the tables. Just for fun, in his imagination, he replaced the faces of some of the guests with the faces of the handful of customers who regularly looked down their noses at him. He pictured them looking up at him while he dropped a carefully worded question into his usual chatter of which type of sausage was the best tasting, or the most superior quality:

'Ladies, would any of you care to peruse the latest updates to my CV? Kidnapper... butcher... murderer... as you're all such good customers to the shop I could work out some special rates for you.'

He imagined them laughing politely... the stuck up fools.

His thoughts were working quite independently of the rest of his body now. It passed the time and was a skill he'd perfected over many years.

Plates and glasses were filled, emptied, and then removed without upsetting the other beetle crawling around inside him.

He was quite looking forward to kidnapping two people instead of carrying out a killing. The Browning 9mm automatic pistol, the one that he'd still never actually fired was his favoured weapon. Ripper could have one of the used ones. Between them, they should have no trouble persuading Naomi and her off-duty police officer friend to co-operate.

He'd had time to prepare for this new venture, but it hadn't fazed him, as he'd feared it might. Before leaving home, he'd cleaned the residual grease from his gun, oiled it carefully, and pulled at the top slide. The weapon had cocked without making a sound. He'd squeezed the trigger and listened to the click of the hammer hitting the firing pin. Feeling a thrill ripple through him, he'd loaded one of the two magazines, each holding thirteen 9mm high-velocity bullets, into the pistol and placed the other magazine into the glove box of his car. Then he'd polished his knives and added them to the cache. Experience had taught him it was always better to be over prepared.

Sometimes, late at night, he lay awake worrying about just how long his run of good luck was likely to last – how long the name of Beetle was going to command respect. He hadn't heard his real name used in years, not even by his mother or his sister. Only his employer and those who'd known him at school were even aware of it. That was the way he liked it.

The nickname his classmates had given him was apt.

He remembered writing in a class essay: *Have you ever felt that you must have been born during the most incredible electrical storm ever, and that somehow the life that should have been yours had been whisked through the ether and come to rest in the body of some other lucky sod, because I have?*

He'd been proud of it, until reprimanded for the three-letter swear word, and for refusing to apologise to the over-sensitive English teacher. Now though, he was on the up, and he was one of those other lucky sods.

As far as he knew, only one person out there knew that he was no killer, and for some reason that person had held his secret. He'd reasoned that it had to be someone who knew him – maybe even someone who came into the shop to buy his sausages or meat pies. For months, those types of thoughts had reduced him to little more than a quivering wreck, but although they still occasionally interrupted an otherwise good day, he'd learned to live with them.

His inner beetle swept him through the boredom of the speeches, and then through the cleaning up operation. Finally, the winding down of the party in the main barn was the signal for the new, emboldened Beetle to make his move. He dried his hands, donned his new jacket, and set off on the hunt.

"It's Naomi, isn't it?" This was going to be easy. On the edge of a roomful of inebriated people, she appeared lost.

"Yes, do I know you," she hiccupped. "Sorry, I think I've overdone it a bit. I'm meant to be meeting someone at the front door, but I can't seem to find it," she hiccupped again and then giggled. "He's gone to the bathroom. Perhaps he can't find the door," another hiccup.

"Your boyfriend...?"

"Yes, kind of... yes, really... his name's Ryan. What's yours?"

"I'm anything you'd like to call me. Look, I'm leaving shortly, and someone's coming to pick me up, so can I offer you both a lift home?" He steered her to the side door and out into the fresh air. "Wait here a minute. I'll find Ryan for you, phone for my lift, and then we can all leave together."

"You don't know where I live…"

"I've seen you in Leaburn and in also the hospital when I was there with my mother. I know neither of you live far away, or else I wouldn't have offered," he smiled reassuringly. "Stop worrying. Just lean against that wall and relax. I'll find your boyfriend and be back again before you know it. Trust me." He sneaked another glance at her full figure before he walked away. "Shame," he murmured.

He'd told them to walk on ahead, and that he'd meet them at the end of the drive in a few minutes. They were doing just that. There was a touch of frost in the air, a clear sky and a full moon – not that either of them were likely to notice. A single shooting star sent his pulse rate soaring. All he had to do now was keep them in sight while not letting the other guests who were leaving think he was anything to do with the couple. Surreptitiously, he checked his phone.

Timing was everything.

The phone vibrated in his hand.

ETA 1minute, the text read.

Naomi and Ryan had come to a halt at the roadside and he was closing in on them.

Chapter 10

Forbes reached into his desk drawer for a cough sweet, rather than the square of chocolate he normally treated himself to straight after his morning's mug of canteen coffee. The streets of Leaburn and its surrounding areas had been quiet over the weekend, compared to the previous one when two men had been shot at and then bizarrely lost their lives.

He opened up his files. No new evidence had surfaced over the weekend.

The two upcoming court cases were straightforward enough. The first involved a knife attack which took place at the end of a work's party where the accused was claiming he'd been provoked, and that he hadn't realised he'd been holding a knife until he'd seen blood. The second was a domestic assault where the wife was pleading not guilty to murder but guilty to the manslaughter of her husband of thirty years. The paperwork for those cases was up-to-date and the courts would decide the outcomes.

The tickle in the back of his throat was a new worry. Some of his officers had minor colds – it was that time of the year, but his two and a half year old niece, Gemma, had yesterday been diagnosed as having the chickenpox.

His father, Gemma's grandfather, had been no help when asked about the family history. "Your mother, bless her, dealt with everything like that," he'd said. "I contracted them back in the sixties, when I was a teenager, but I really have no idea whether you ever caught the virus, and I don't remember your sister ever having it either. Your mum believed in natural remedies and only ever called in the doctor as a last resort."

Great! At the age of forty-six, chickenpox could develop into any number of serious conditions, the first symptoms of which were often similar to those of the common cold.

Michael had been eighteen when his sister, Louise, had been born and because he'd helped to raise her after their mother's death when Louise had been only two months old, he could have told his father that she'd never caught the virus. Unless he'd had it as a very young child, he could be 'at risk'. He threw the sweet wrapper into the waste paper bin and with a shrug of his shoulders pushed the thought to the back of his mind. Then his phone rang and the virus was forgotten.

At eight a.m. DCI Michael Forbes suppressed his anxiety and entered the busy incident room. "Attention everyone, it seems that one of our own is unaccounted for." The room fell silent. "DC Ryan Wheeler's whereabouts is unknown, and in light of what happened to Martin last week, and until we know otherwise, we're going to treat his absence as a serious incident. The last contact he had with this station was at five p.m. on Friday when he radioed in to report following a known drug dealer who was in a car with two other men. Half an hour later he radioed in again to report that he'd lost sight of them and that he was going off duty. It was his weekend off and he definitely attended a wedding in Leaburn on Saturday with a young woman believed to be Naomi Proctor. The couple then went on to the reception at the bride's home, at Home Farm on the outskirts of the town." He wrote the relevant names on the only remaining blank whiteboard. "We know this much because his flat-mate was concerned enough to phone this station a few minutes ago to enquire whether Ryan had turned up for work. Since yesterday evening the flat-mate has been phoning and e-mailing their mutual acquaintances, and some of the wedding guests, but so far hasn't been able to find anyone who saw Ryan or Naomi after about eleven p.m. on the night of the wedding. He is now one hour late for the start of his shift."

"Do you know if the flatmate's checked the hospitals, sir?" DC Emily Jackson spoke and several heads nodded. "People do daft things at weddings, if they've drunk too much."

"His date might still have him tied to a bed in a hotel room somewhere – the lucky sod." DC Robert Bell looked around the room for smiles, but none came.

"His flat-mate called the local hospitals yesterday evening and officers downstairs are checking again now. He didn't take a change of clothes with him on Saturday morning, but he did take his wallet and his phone. He left in a taxi, organised by Naomi, leaving his own car parked on the street. I've only just been informed of this so that's all I can tell you at the moment."

Ryan Wheeler, stationed at Leaburn for five months now, was a promising, well-liked young detective. Forbes considered him promotion material, with a flair for computers and technology, and in those five months had never been late for work.

"Our first priority is the home address of Naomi. Begin by contacting Mr and Mrs Buchan, the bride's parents. Presumably, Naomi was an invited guest. We'll also want the names and addresses of everyone who attended, and we'll need to see as many of the guests' videos and photographs as possible, from both the inside and the outside of the property. And we need them uploaded on to our systems as quickly as possible. Don't forget to include the names and addresses of the wedding organisers and caterers, and taxi drivers."

"Do we know the name of the drug dealer Ryan was following on Friday?" Robert Bell had struck up a friendship with Ryan the day he'd realised that the new DC was a distant cousin on his father's side of the family, incredibly, one he'd known nothing about. "Only he hadn't said anything to me about any drug dealers. That would have been more of a job for the uniformed officers downstairs."

"No name, only that he recognised a face from the past and that it concerned him."

"I'll check his bank and credit card details for any activity since Saturday," DC Jade Sharpe offered, "and can we get a fix on his mobile?"

"Robert, you organise the phone check. I want to know where he called from on Friday when he first reported having someone under surveillance, and where he was when he reported losing him or her. Wherever that was may have CCTV footage. Adam, I want you to take a uniformed officer with you to Ryan's' flat to pick up his laptop, and anything else you think might provide a clue as to where he is. There's still a chance he's gone off somewhere with that woman. Tracy, you can make the initial contact with Ryan's parents; I believe they still live in Preston, and Harry, I want you to contact the Preston station and put them in the picture. Ask whether they know of any enemies Ryan made while stationed with them and whether he's made contact with anyone at the station lately. And ask if they can think of anyone who might be upset enough with Ryan to follow him down to Derbyshire, especially anyone involved in the drugs scene."

"Yes sir," DC Harry Green nodded and clicked on his computer. Every other officer had been stunned into silence.

During the twelve years he'd been a DCI, he hadn't lost any officers in the line of duty. There had been injuries, some serious, but none uncomfortably close to life threatening. The risks associated with this job were generally accepted but rarely spoken about, and he was proud of his record of accomplishment. Ryan hadn't been on duty when last seen, but the fact that he'd called in an interest in an old face without naming him was making Forbes apprehensive.

He knew of the Buchan family, though he didn't move in their social circle. They'd farmed in the area for generations and the wedding would have been a high point in the county's social calendar. If a major incident had happened there on Saturday night, and coming less than a year after two of Leaburn's young citizens were murdered, the residents of the area would begin to feel justified in looking differently at their friends and neighbours, and at people they'd known all their lives.

With any luck, Ryan would appear in the next hour or two, full of apologies for doing something unbelievably stupid... but for some reason, he doubted it.

What sprang to his mind next was as alarming as it was unexpected.

*

Naomi Proctor woke from a dreamless sleep. Her head was pounding, the front of her dress was covered in dried vomit and her body was shaking. Enough natural light was filtering through the small, cobwebbed window for her to see that nothing in her prison had changed overnight. She remembered slipping in and out of consciousness through what must have been Sunday, so now it had to be Monday. Every muscle ached, and she was so cold. It didn't require her training as a nurse to recognise that although her body had pretty-much recovered from the hangover, her problems were just beginning. She was hungry, thirsty, and above all terrified beyond anything she'd previously thought possible. Her wrists were tightly bound with a rough rope that was in turn secured around the two vertical lengths of copper piping running from floor to the ceiling in the garage, or outhouse, or whatever the hell that it was she was in. She could either remain seated or, with difficulty, stand on the concrete floor, but that was as much as she'd been able move since the early hours of Sunday morning.

She screamed in frustration.

The pipes were the older type, similar in appearance to the ones down in the boiler room of the hospital where she worked, far more rigid than those used nowadays, and anchored into the concrete block wall.

For the first time ever she'd gone out on a date with a police officer. She'd felt safe. He'd promised to look after her.

Some joke that had turned out to be!

He hadn't been able to protect her against two gunmen and for all she knew now, DC Ryan Wheeler, defender of the town of Leaburn, was lying dead in a ditch somewhere. Anger took over and she screamed again.

The room window was about half a metre square and one metre below the ceiling. The only things in the dimly lit space, apart from the bucket that the man had placed beside her, were two large, old, dirty chest freezers, both humming away on the opposite side of the room. The older styles produced heat, but supposing they caught fire and no one noticed? She stifled another scream, this time from sheer terror.

She had to try to remain calm. There might come a time when she could escape. She had to keep her wits about her.

The man who'd abducted her, the one who'd been at the reception, had brought her nothing except one mug of water and the plastic bucket that she'd been forced to use yesterday. From being too terrified and hung over to think about food, she now had hunger pains to deal with and a thirst that was almost driving her crazy. She'd licked the condensation from the copper pipes. Her eyes stung from lack of sleep but, as tempting as it was to escape again from her waking nightmare, she was determined to stay awake.

If the winter sun had shone yesterday she didn't remember it ever reaching the window, and there were no signs of it yet this morning. She had to move a little, had to generate some body heat, or risk passing out from hypothermia.

'Stay positive, Naomi, stay positive,' she whispered repeatedly as she flexed her arms and legs. Her muscles felt like jelly. *'You are going to get out of here alive."*

The motor on one of the freezers juddered into life and fear spiked through her again. She hadn't seen or heard anyone since some time yesterday, although at one point the sound of an engine, or possibly a mechanical saw of some sort, sounded close by. Someone had to have been working, but at what? Why had no one been to her? But, when they did come, maybe things would be considerably worse.

It had to be her ex-boyfriend, Stevie Hall, behind her kidnapping. It just had to be. It was too much of a co-incidence, after seeing him following her a few nights ago. Not that knowing that was going to help her. Degrading her in this way would be typical of his idea of fun. Had going out with a police officer been a huge mistake? Had Stevie assumed she'd gone running to the police to report him for assaulting her, or to tell tales about his drug dealings, or money laundering schemes, or human trafficking?

Shouting for help yesterday had only resulted in a sore throat. No one had answered and no one had come to her aid, neither her police officer nor her captor. Perhaps she was going to be left here – her remains found in a crumbling garage by some property developer years from now. She feared that almost as much the alternatives. Whatever Stevie had planned for her was bound to be degrading and painful. He was a sadist, who wouldn't lose a single wink sleep over her suffering but, after being seen in public with her a few times, would he want her to die?

No one was likely to miss her for some considerable time. She rented a basement flat where she lived alone, and all her bills were paid by direct debit with her account holding enough to cover everything for the next six months. Her colleagues knew she was thinking of moving to another town, and another hospital, and her only family, her sister, would be in America for the next twelve months. When her body turned up years from now, would they all be wracked with guilt? Suddenly she felt even more isolated and afraid. She didn't want to die, but if that was to be the outcome of her only date with a police officer, she realised she wanted a few people to at least miss her and be sad for her for a while.

*

Since being discharged from hospital DC Martin Jones had been feeling disembodied. He blamed the bang on the head and his wife's fussing. He couldn't seem to move past the feeling that an important chunk of something was missing from his memory – something to do with a message – something from seconds before he'd been unceremoniously dumped in the boot of his car. By mid-morning, as he walked into the office of DCI Forbes, he was almost operating on autopilot. "I'm sorry sir, I know you wanted me to stay at home for a few days, but I just couldn't settle. It didn't feel right not being here on a Monday morning."

"You only left hospital yesterday afternoon. You look like shit."

"Thanks for that, sir. The in-laws were on the doorstep before we were dressed."

"Ah... I see."

"And I heard about Ryan. Robert phoned to ask if I had any ideas of where he might be. Ryan and I have become good friends. I wanted to help in the investigation. Please don't send me home, sir."

"All right, Martin, but you know I'll have to keep you at your desk. You can check video and CCTV footage as it comes in, but if you start to feel unwell, even slightly, for heaven's sake tell the person closest to you."

"Thank you, sir."

"Before you start... I had a quiet word with your father the other day and he told me a curious thing. He said that a fortnight ago, his house was broken into but nothing taken. I'm surprised you didn't report the incident at the time."

"He told me not to. He knows how busy we are."

"And when your father says jump, you ask how high. Am I right?"

"You know how he is, sir. Since Gary's disappearance especially, my sister and I find it easier to go along with whatever he says."

"Mmmm... quite... if ever there was a man born to take charge of every situation he finds himself in, it's your father."

"It has its advantages, sir, and growing up we all just accepted his ways, but I know his personality isn't to everyone's liking and that he's made more than his fair share of enemies over the years."

"That's what concerns us now – that and what the intruder to his house left behind..." He paused and held eye contact with Martin. It was a loaded comment – a wild guess inspired by a gut reaction after Godfrey Jones had stuttered and stammered through his account of the break-in.

"The note... did my father tell you about the note after all? He swore that he wouldn't."

His gut instinct had been spot on. "What was your impression of it?"

"It wasn't threatening as such... just made us feel uneasy. Why would anyone break into a house only to leave a note promising to make contact in the near future? It didn't make sense."

"Has he still got it?"

"No, it went on the back of the fire. But he did have all the house locks changed and he altered his bank account numbers and passwords. He insisted he wasn't worried so what could I do? My sister knows nothing about it."

"Your brother's murder happened almost a year ago and we treated it as an isolated incident. However, last week you were attacked and now I'm learning someone broke into your father's house and left a veiled threat. We have to consider that the same person could be involved in all the incidents. Is your sister still down in London?"

"Yes sir."

"Put her in the picture. Tell her to be on her guard and ask her to report directly to this station if anything unusual or worrying occurs."

"Yes sir."

"And despite us being busy I'd still prefer it if you took a few days leave, to keep an eye on your father as well as to allow yourself time to recover fully."

"I suppose... Sharon could go and stay with her parents in Ashbourne for a few days while I moved back in with dad – just until we know what we're up against."

"That might be for the best. Your father won't admit it but I think he'll be glad of your company, if Sharon doesn't mind."

"I'm sure she won't, but I'd really like to help in the search for Ryan, if only for a few hours, now that I'm here."

"Put in a couple of hours on the computer and then see how you feel." He hadn't wanted to voice the thought he'd had just minutes before Martin entered his office – the thought that maybe his station, or his officers were actually the intended targets of someone with a grudge, or someone with an unbalanced mind. He needed to talk his concerns through with someone, but Martin wasn't the right person.

Chapter 11

Naomi took a deep gulp from one of the two mugs of cold water brought to her earlier in the day. Their delivery hadn't made her feel any better. She was still breathing for a reason.

She was being kept alive for a purpose, yet no other attempts had been made to ease her discomfort. Every inch of the concrete was as hard and cold as an iron slab, her wrists were sore and her backside was hurting.

To Big Stevie Hall, sex not involving some sort of bondage was almost unthinkable. She wiped tears away. He had to be the one behind her imprisonment – any other scenario would probably be far worse than anything she'd so far endured with him. She was going to have to enter Stevie's twisted world at least once more, but as long as he believed that her friends knew his name, and that they'd recently been an item, surely he wouldn't risk killing her. She had to keep hanging on to that thought.

Her stomach churned and she swallowed back a mouthful of diluted bile. How long could she survive on water alone? She was a nurse. She ought to know a thing like that. It had to be several weeks, maybe even months for a healthy young woman. And what had happened to her police officer – was he in fact dead, or had the whole thing been a set-up from the beginning? Had Ryan Wheeler been in Stevie's employ all along, and was she the butt of some elaborate joke aimed at keeping Stevie's associates entertained for a while? Was she destined for the sex-trade industry, permanently drugged out of her mind and forced to work until contracting some disease or other? From some the things she'd discovered about Stevie's world in the short time they'd been together, she wouldn't put any of those things past him.

*

Eight o'clock on Monday night found Martin Jones driving alone on the familiar route to his father's house. He felt he had no choice in the matter. Having another family member snatched away from him forever would be more than he could handle.

Sharon's parents had collected their grandson from school while Martin and his wife had hastily thrown clothes into dusty suitcases and then spent a pleasant hour in bed together. So pleasant in fact that he hadn't wanted to let her go. Unable to shake the feeling that his family was under threat from an unknown source, he'd wanted to retain the memory of the feel and the taste of his wife's damp skin for as long as he could.

He'd more or less adjusted to the idea of never seeing his brother again, of never knowing the truth of what had happened to him. What he'd never quite been able to dispel, was the lingering idea that maybe... just maybe, his father had had a hand in Gary's death. He wished things were different, but he was under no illusions that his father wasn't anything other than a hard man and a bully, and quite prepared to stand up to anyone who challenged him in any way. Was that what Gary had done, had he stood up to their father once too often?

He'd never stop loving his younger brother and, however many years rolled by, never stop hoping to one day uncover the truth, however painful it may turn out to be.

With his windscreen wipers switched to intermittent and a flicker of snow in the light rain, he felt the old feelings of helplessness and dread. He wasn't helped by the thought that, for the first time since his marriage, he would be living apart from his wife.

He recalled the look of joy on her face when, at the end of a tranquil walk through the picturesque valley of Dovedale, he'd dropped to his knees on the famous stepping stones in the very centre of the River Dove and proposed to her. He was missing her and his son already.

With each mile covered, the knot in his stomach tightened.

*

Naomi's shrunken world had been in darkness for hours. The sound of a chain saw being used somewhere close by had ceased long ago. As terrifying as that noise had been it had offered her a few minutes of escape by transporting her back to her childhood, to the happy times spent in her grandparent's kitchen hearing her grandfather sawing logs before helping him load them into his shed ready for winter. She closed her eyes and felt herself transported back to a roaring open fire and hot buttered crumpets, and a black and white collie dog looking adoringly up at her.

She woke and was amazed to find she was smiling. She was actually going crazy. It hadn't taken long; she'd thought she was tougher than this. Maybe comforting dreams were how lack of food first affected people – maybe they were the brain's way of dealing with horror.

The thick pain throbbing across her temples had almost gone but she'd lost all sense if time. It felt like Monday evening, at the earliest.

The freezers fell silent and only the hoots from a family of owls broke the silence. For at least two days now, no one had answered her screams for help. She was in the countryside – somewhere remote enough no body to stumble past and for the property owner to need those two chest freezers to be full of provisions – ice creams, strawberry gateaux, meat pies... God she was hungry, so hungry she felt sick. Her mind was drifting in and out of reality. She had to keep a grip if she was to come through this.

Her ex was far more likely to be associated with a remote cannabis-growing farm than with a cosy country cottage with open fires and home-cooked meals and roses growing around the door. The freezers were probably full of weed.

Her eyes closed and she allowed her mind to drift back into her grandmother's kitchen again. She drew in the aroma from the pot of beef stew simmering away on the stove. A masked man was entering the humid room, pointing at the bubbling pan with one hand and pulling off his mask with the other.

Behind the mask was half a face, sneering, one eye staring and bloodshot and the other a bloody mess… a dog was barking… an aggressive-sounding dog… Kim the collie had passed away years earlier… and anyway she'd never sounded aggressive… had her grandparents got another dog without telling her?

Her eyes snapped open.

A vehicle was close by.

A dog really was barking.

Voices became louder… at least two men, maybe three… and a police dog…? Her heart pounded with relief. She'd been found… saved… rescued… she wasn't going to die alone here after all. She opened her mouth, ready to shout, but nothing came. Her heart and lungs hammered and the room spun.

No… not now Naomi… you can't pass out now… stay with it…

She pulled herself back. One minute passed by, and then another. She was desperate to see the smiling face of DC Ryan Wheeler, to see his jet-black hair and his steely blue eyes. If he'd escaped he wouldn't have stopped searching for her.

What could be holding up her rescue?

The police would be going after her captor first — she'd seen it on the television. They always secured properties to minimise the risk for those entering it. Yes, that had to be it. She only had to wait a few minutes more.

The dog had stopped barking.

More minutes passed. It didn't have to be Ryan coming through that door first. Any friendly face would do. To know that he was safe would be enough. Anyway, she couldn't have him seeing her like this — she was such a mess. He'd never be able to think of her or look at her in the same way again.

Footsteps were growing louder.

Instinctively she smoothed down her blonde hair.

She recognised a voice and her questions were answered, all bound together in a jolt of terror. She'd been wrong about being rescued, but right about who was behind her imprisonment. Ryan was undoubtedly dead and she would have to dig out every ounce of bravery that she possessed just to stay alive. Stevie Hall would be planning on hurting her, of that she was in no doubt. He'd enter the room threatening her with death or mutilation if she reported him for assault, and then, with any luck, he'd release her. That was his style. He'd done it to her before, not like this, but he had left her tied to his bed for half a day and then raped her before cutting her loose.

The dog yelped and a door slammed. She could hear nothing except the humming of the freezers.

Her body shook and her breaths were ragged. Safe words weren't going to help her here. She'd touched the edges of Stevie's twisted world but had no idea of where his boundaries lay.

She closed her eyes and began to hum the tune to the only hymn she could remember, *'all things bright and beautiful'*, – anything to blot out the unfolding nightmare. Two verses were enough. Her voice cracked and she began counting her pounding heartbeats instead.

On the count of eight hundred, and above the thrumming of the motors in the chest freezers, she heard the footsteps.

She wasn't ready… she was never going to be ready… but the door opened anyway. Two bare light bulbs coming on felt like a physical shock. The man she'd met at the wedding, and who'd brought her and Ryan to this place at gunpoint stepped into the light. His short, dark hair stood in spikes from the top of his head, she noticed just before he stepped to the side of the open doorway. Her ex filled the doorway, his chest puffed out and his face smiling, but not in his usual charming, seductive manner.

Stevie stepped into the room, and past the first man. "Hello Naomi, it's good to see you again." He spoke calmly, as if everything about their meeting were normal. "You're looking a bit rough girl, but I suppose that's only to be expected."

She looked past him and saw the outline of a third male in the shadows behind them.

Stevie turned to the spiky-haired man. "Strip her off and hose her down, Beetle. Our guest wants to have some fun here tonight. I'm content just to stand here and watch."

Chapter 12

DCI Forbes had been at his desk since six a.m. It was a cold, dark, Tuesday morning and he couldn't recall ever feeling less in control of an investigation. One officer was recovering from an assault and DC Ryan Wheeler and his girlfriend were still missing. Was someone targeting his colleagues and his station, or were they simply experiencing a run of bad luck? He'd voiced his fears to his superior, Detective Superintendent Christine Price, and with her agreement asked everyone in the station to be extra cautious with their own safety and with the safety of their families. His main stumbling block had been that he'd issued the warnings without any real idea of whether there was an actual threat, or even where that threat might be coming from. His words had felt empty and he'd drawn some enquiring looks from his team.

The eleven-month long investigation into the disappearance of Gary Jones had only ever produced a trickle of useable information, and even that had now dried up. Morale in the station would be at rock bottom if, God forbid, the search for Ryan followed the same pattern.

He reached for the second cough sweet of the morning. Maybe he should alert everyone in the station to the possibility of him carrying the chickenpox virus, just in case anyone else was as unsure of his medical history as he was.

He decided to announce it at the first briefing of the day.

The sweet wrapper landed in the waste paper basket as his office door opened. Martin was standing there. "I thought I'd told you not to come in today."

"I was driving past, on my way home to collect a few clothes, and I wondered whether there'd been any progress in the search for Ryan."

"We've nothing positive yet. Come on in and give me some good news, I could use some – has your wife settled in with her parents and is your father all right this morning?"

"Yes thank you, sir."

"And how are you?" Dark shadows below Martin's eyes suggested a sleepless night. His mouth was set in a grim line.

"The break-in and the business of last week's assault affected Dad almost as much as it shook me. I hadn't realised that until last night. He'd hardly any food in the house and he hasn't been eating properly, so I'd like to thank you for your suggestion."

"I'd rather not have had to suggest it in the first place, and I hope it won't be for too long, but until we get deeper into these latest investigations I think it best you both remain vigilant and look out for each other. As much as I could use you here, I'll extend your leave on the grounds of family problems and work-related stress – not that I'd expect you to take an indefinite leave of absence."

"I understand, sir. However I'd like to work for an hour or two, now that I'm here. And if it's all right with you I'll gladly take the remainder of the week off... if that's all right?"

"I'm sure this station will run perfectly well without you after this morning."

Martin entered the incident room and sat at his desk. Four others had also come in to work early but the room didn't possess its usual relaxed early morning feel or strong smell of coffee. The officers simply nodded acknowledgement of his presence and then returned their attentions to the screens in front of them. The atmosphere in the station had been tense since the late afternoon of the previous day when Ryan and Naomi were officially listed as missing. Naomi's car registration had passed through the Police National Computer and confirmed her identity as Naomi Proctor, from Bakewell

Road in Leaburn. She hadn't turned up for her work on Monday morning and her mobile continued to go straight to voicemail.

His colleagues were searching for any sightings of her as desperately as they were searching for any of Ryan.

He fired up his computer. Two trips to the printer later he had the information he'd come for tucked inside his jacket pocket and he began studying more CCTV footage.

When DCI Forbes stood at the front of the incident room again, his whole team was present. Martin noticed he looked red-eyed – not that he was alone in that – the cold virus had affected almost everyone in the station while Martin had so far escaped it.

"This is the Tuesday morning, eight a.m. briefing of Operation Anchor," Forbes began. "Naomi Proctor's basement flat was searched last night and found to be unoccupied and her car remains parked on the street in front of her flat. She has still neither shown up for her work at the London Road Hospital in Buxton nor phoned in sick. Also the taxi firm she used to pick up Ryan and then take them both on to the wedding venue has confirmed that it was expecting her to call them back late on Saturday night, but that the call never came in. I think it's safe to assume that whatever has happened to Ryan may also have happened to Naomi. So, who took them and why, and where are they now? Or... did one of them, either deliberately or accidentally, do something insanely stupid to the other and then panic and take off?" A rumble of negative comments spread through the room.

"As unlikely as that is, we can't rule it out completely. From the guests' statements, we know they'd both been drinking. In the heat of the moment, did they borrow or steal a car and subsequently crash it somewhere they haven't yet been found? Are we looking for one body or two? We'll release a press statement later this afternoon, and I don't expect to hear any public rumours of a possible vendetta against this station."

Martin realised Forbes was looking at him.

"Martin, if you're feeling all right I'd like you to continue looking through the CCTV footage that's come in so far."

He nodded. His DCI was making sure he stayed at his computer again. It was only what he'd expected.

"The rest of you already have your actions for the day so let's make some progress."

"Yes sir," voices murmured in unison.

PC Danny Grant, a traffic officer, entered the incident room. "We've finished checking other taxi firms in the area, sir. None reported picking up Ryan or Naomi from the wedding reception, and no vehicles were reported as being taken without permission within a ten mile radius on Saturday evening or on Sunday."

"So that's one possibility pretty much ruled out – we're probably not looking for a crashed car containing two bodies. Robert, alert the local mountain rescue teams. It's time we began searching mine shafts, rivers and woodlands, spreading out from the point of the wedding venue. Emily ..."

"Yes sir?"

"Has there been recent activity on either of the couple's bank accounts?"

"Nothing so far, sir."

"There's one other thing I feel I ought to share with you all. I happen to have been in close contact with someone who's contracted the chickenpox virus. If any of you think you might not have had the disease during your childhood, I'd suggest you go online and familiarise yourself with the symptoms and if at all worried to report to your own doctor. That's all for now."

Martin smiled at a memory. He and his brother and sister had scratched the spots off each other while their father had been away on some conference or other. They'd driven their poor mother to distraction with bottle after bottle of calamine lotion. He was ready to leave the station now but didn't want the others to see that. There was something he wanted to do. The legwork for the hit-and-run incident had been handed to uniformed officers downstairs and, if it wasn't for a tenuous link to the current abductions, his ordeal from the previous week would already be old news.

It was understandable that DC Ryan Wheeler's case took priority. He was one of their own and there was a chance that he and Naomi had been abducted and trussed up, just as he had. There was a very slim chance they were still alive and captive somewhere, for some obscure reason.

DCI Forbes was of the opinion that his team were being targeted, but he wasn't so sure.

He turned his attention back to his computer screen.

At ten-thirty Martin couldn't believe his luck. He burst into his DCI's office without knocking, "Sir, thanks to the phone companies I've found Ryan on a video from Friday evening, filmed minutes before his final call to the station. He's in the car park of the Morrison's supermarket in Buxton, talking to Naomi. They can both clearly be seen arriving, entering the shop, and then driving away in their own cars."

"Was anyone else with her?"

"No sir, but get this, Naomi's car entered the park at five-thirty, followed twenty seconds later by a silver Mercedes which parked close to the car park's entrance, just beyond the reach of the cameras. Ryan's car was the next to enter the park."

"So was he following the silver car or accompanying Naomi to the shops?"

"The former, sir, definitely; you need to see the tape."

Forbes watched the tape and felt a momentary pang of genuine sorrow, as though sensing this would be the last anyone would see of Ryan alive. He straightened up and addressed those still in the room. "Someone get this footage enhanced… and the rest of you… we're now looking for a silver coloured Mercedes with darkened side windows which Ryan possibly followed on Friday evening. There can't be too many of those around. Where was it before five-thirty and where did it go after that? Someone contact the DVLA for a list of registered owners of similar vehicles. I want names and addresses, and I want them as quickly as possible."

"I've just had a call back from the Preston station." DI Rob Lang added. "They said Ryan was a respected and well-liked officer, never in any trouble, and particularly keen on investigating the drugs scene. They're e-mailing over a list of all the drug-related cases he worked on."

DC Robert Bell looked up from his computer. "Naomi Proctor has no police record at all, and her employers say they never had any problems with her."

He saw Rob Lang scratch his arm and he made a sudden decision. Just in case he hadn't had the childhood virus, and in the hope that he'd so far managed to avoid it, he would move into Alison's flat on the outskirts of town until it was safe to return home. Alison had already told him of her own childhood days of sitting in a wicker-backed chair, plastered in calamine lotion and ordered by her mother not to scratch the spots against the wonderfully uneven surface.

Her flat was on the small side, ideal for a single person, and because of that it was always Alison who came over to stay with him, rather than the other way around. She had her own, constantly full, wardrobe space in his bedroom and her own bathroom cabinet next to his. He couldn't remember the last time he'd even visited her in her flat, but he was sure she wouldn't object to his company for a week or two.

Chapter 13

Martin strolled into his father's house, trying to act as though he chose to be there, rather than being there from a sense of duty. A faltering voice beckoned him towards the kitchen. It sounded feeble and reedy. He took a deep breath, did as he was asked, and then stopped in the kitchen doorway, face to face with the white faced man.

"It came in this morning's post," his father nodded towards the kitchen table. "I left it there."

In the centre of the wooden table was a single sheet of paper and scattered around it were dried flower petals. Spilt coffee soaked some of the petals, and one corner of the paper. On the edge of the table, a half-empty mug sat in a brown puddle.

Martin stepped past his father and saw yet more petals and an A4 sized brown envelope, addressed to Mr Godfrey Jones, lying on the floor. "You should have called me as soon as you'd opened it, Dad. Better still, you shouldn't have opened it at all. You knew I was coming back." He felt irritated with his father, and wary of touching anything from the parcel. "You should have waited. It could be contaminated with any number of dangerous chemicals."

He couldn't see any writing on the paper – just five brown, equally-spaced smudges. He looked up and held his father's gaze for several seconds. Both of them had been around crime scenes often enough and for long enough to recognise dried blood when they saw it.

"This needs to go for forensic testing, straight away. You of all people should know that."

"This is my house and that letter is addressed to me." His father glowered at him. "It goes when I say it goes."

Martin's chest felt tight. He fought the impulse to stride over to his father, grab him by the shoulders and give him a good shake. This wasn't the time, and wouldn't serve any purpose. Impulse suppressed, he stood and watched as the man he felt he'd never completely bonded with staggered into the living room and slumped into a reclining chair. He should have felt some sympathy as he watched normally proud shoulders dropping and bony hands rising to cover a lined face, but he didn't.

His father wasn't thinking clearly, he could accept that. The elderly man's cognitive senses had diminished over the eleven months Gary had been missing. He'd aged twenty years, both physically and mentally. Despite that, at that moment Martin felt only irritation. He swallowed down his inclination to ignore his father and walk away, and instead followed him into the living room. He placed one hand on the old man's warm back, but only because it was a gesture he felt he ought to make. A difficult few days loomed with just him and his father in the otherwise empty house – days of unspoken accusations and an unspecified threat. "The letter may mean nothing, Dad, but we can't take that risk. I have a wife and child to consider."

"Don't patronise me, Son," Godfrey raised his head slightly.

Martin heard a hint of the all too familiar anger in the order.

"Someone sent that message directly to me; surely you aren't too dense to realise that?"

Martin lifted his hand from his father's back. "A message about what…?"

"That this person knows where my Gary is, and what happened to him, and that I won't ever be at peace until I also know those things."

"You can't be sure of that."

"Can't I… well maybe not, but I intend to find out. And if that means withholding information or evidence from the force, then that's what I'm prepared to do. I want this person to contact me directly."

Martin shrugged. There was little point in arguing. "Well if you're happy for the person responsible for terrorising us all not to get caught…"

"Don't…"

"Dad, you do realise that there appears to be a full set of fingerprints on the paper?"

"I'm not blind, Son."

"If it turns out to be human blood then a crime has most probably already been committed. They're not Gary's prints – they're far too small. Gary had large hands... do you remember?"

Silence.

"Dad... you have to let me hand in that letter."

"All right then; get the damn stuff gathered up and off to forensics – but don't expect me to help you."

His father had given in far too easily. That in itself was a bad sign, a sign that something else was going on, and that Martin wasn't getting the whole picture. "I'll fetch some evidence bags. Stay there." Every detective in the country carried a box or a bag in their car of what was considered essential for their work – protective over suits and shoes, evidence bags, latex gloves, a first aid kit, a powerful torch, collapsible traffic cones, a paperwork box and many other odds-and-ends. One item of equipment no longer carried was the infamous bulletproof clipboard, after it had been pointed out to management that, when faced with a gunman, an A4 sized clipboard was about the last thing that anyone would want to protect themselves with. "As soon as I've got everything safely secured I'll call it in, and then I'll make us some food we'll sit down together and try to figure out what the letter could mean."

The term *safely secured* was a relative one. The envelope had been through the hands of the postal service for at least one full day, half of the crumbling petals were strewn across the kitchen floor, and the remainder, along with the paper, were resting half-in and half-out of the remains of a mug of coffee. The petals all appeared to be shades of blue. Maybe that meant something.

Martin placed the damp paper onto a sheet of kitchen roll, to absorb the moisture and the reddish-brown substance.

With everything, including the soaked kitchen paper, into clear plastic bags, Martin moved to where he could see into the living room. His father had a firm grip on the television remote and appeared to be pressing the buttons randomly. "You know I have to do this, don't you?" He still wasn't sure his father understood why he was moving back in with him, let alone the potential importance of the letter. "There's a real chance that someone could be targeting us. That's why I'm here, and why I have to give my colleagues a chance to do what they're trained to do."

Steely eyes shot a familiar, cold look across the room, and with that look came a clear message – *I'm not senile yet, Son, so don't you dare treat me as such.*

He realised that as long as he was staying here, unless he intercepted the morning post, there was very little chance of him seeing any future anonymous packages.

*

A cold-looking moon was high in the sky when the police motorcyclist delivered the package, which might, or might not, be linked to the disappearance of four people or to a threat to the officers at Leaburn station. The crime lab was closing for the day and the package was logged in and placed in a fridge, ready for the following morning.

Forbes and his entire team were working late. No one felt any pull to leave the investigation, at least not before they were in danger of falling asleep at their post. It was almost three full days since Ryan and Naomi were last seen, and it would soon be twelve months since the same could be said of Gary Jones and Paul Biers. Paul and Gary had been murdered, and so far, they'd found nothing to link the two cases. However, the feeling in the station was that the longer Ryan and Naomi were missing, the greater the probability was that they'd met a similar fate.

Buxton mountain rescue team, together with uniformed officers and a small army of volunteers, had found no traces of the couple anywhere in the hills and fields around the wedding venue and the search had been called off and would be resumed at first light.

The bank accounts of Ryan and Naomi remained untouched and the families had heard nothing from either of them.

Neither had they used their mobile phones since Saturday morning, and wherever the devices were now they had to be either switched off, or were broken.

Forbes picked up another cough sweet and muttered to no one in particular. "So how the hell have two more people simply disappeared?"

No evidence to confirm the rumours of Gary Jones being a drug dealer had ever been found. It was the same story for Paul Biers. They were reportedly occasional users, and the assumption was that they went to a parking area on an out-of-the-way road to buy what they needed, but there remained no feasible motive for their deaths.

The hit-and-run victim had been confirmed as a small-time drug dealer, as well as a user, but the questions remained, had he been run down deliberately or had his death been an accident, or was it linked, through a friendship with Gary, to the Jones family?

Godfrey Jones, when he'd been in charge of the station, had done his level best to rid the Leaburn area of drugs, but he'd been retired for years, so why target him now and what did the message left in his home, and now on the letter, actually mean?

As for Ryan and Naomi — Ryan's last contact with the station had mentioned a drug dealer. If only he'd named him…? The team was looking into Naomi's history. She was a nurse and so had access to drugs of all types, though so far no one had had a bad word to say about her — rather that she was sometimes too friendly and forgiving for her own good, and that she'd had a brief affair with a violent man she'd refused to name. Her internet history hadn't named him, and if it hadn't been for the Mercedes in the supermarket car park the evening before her disappearance, Forbes would have been starting to wonder whether the man actually existed. Now though, naming him was a priority.

Did drugs form the links between these cases? It was a slightly more palatable theory than the idea of people involved with this station being targeted for some unknown reason.

If no link existed, had Ryan and Naomi been victims of her mystery, jealous, drug-dealing ex-boyfriend?

There were no named suspects in any of the cases, his team was becoming disheartened and his immediate superiors were wondering what the hell he was playing at.

Forbes stepped over to the window of his office and warmed his hands on the radiator. He looked out over the floodlit area of the Tesco car park. Any one of the men or women scurrying across the tarmac could be the killer; the odds were that they were looking for someone who lived locally. Despite the rising waves of heat, he shivered. There was talk of a cold weather front moving across the Peak District over the next few days and the air temperature outside was already well below freezing.

*

Beetle could hardly believe that Big Stevie was standing on the doorstep of his cottage again so soon, with his hand outstretched and a small packet in his open palm. His minder stood behind him, both of them backlit by the half moon. "Well done Beetle. I knew I could trust you to do a good job. I enjoyed myself immensely last night and I wanted to deliver this small bonus personally, as a thank you. It's the very best of stuff."

Beetle stepped aside and accepted the packet in the palm of his hand as Stevie strode towards the kitchen. "Thanks… umm…"

"Young Ripper's told me how much he enjoys working with you. Just don't go spoiling him. I don't want him growing too cocky, too quickly. He's my sister's only child and I think the world of him. He's the son that I never had and I'd like him to take over my businesses one day. He tells me you're a good teacher, and thanks to your mentoring I feel he's ready to go to Romania to sort out a little problem I've been having over there."

This was unexpected praise. "Um... I like him..."

"Is the girl still alive?"

He nodded, praying that he'd be left alone sooner rather than later. Stevie Hall was known for barking out orders and expected them to be followed – receiving praise from him was something akin to getting blood from a lump of polished granite, while wondering how and why the phenomenon could be happening and feeling more uncomfortable with each drop.

"I'm not stopping," Stevie sounded apologetic, as if he'd been invited, "comfortable and inviting though your little country cottage is, and I've no further interest in the bitch in your garage so you can do with her as you please. You know my rules, and I don't expect her ever to be found." His eyes scanned the clean worktops before settling on the man-mountain who'd accompanied him in. Then he looked back at Beetle and flashed his expensive smile again. "My friend and I both thought you'd welcome some of our best gear. Don't use it all at once, I'd hate for a handy person like you to end up as a gibbering wreck. I might have more work to put your way in the near future."

"Ta..."

A low rumble came from the corner of the kitchen. Angus rarely barked, and even more rarely growled. The dog was remembering the hard, well-aimed boot from the previous evening.

"Quiet Angus..."

Stevie ignored the dog, instead holding his stare on Beetle. "They say there's a storm coming..."

Beetle's insides quivered at the way this conversation was going. "I'm sorry, but I've no alcohol in the house to offer you." That was a lie but he wasn't about to encourage Stevie to change his mind about not stopping. The last thing he needed was the two men getting comfortable at his expense, or worse still, snowed in with him overnight. He glanced at the minder/boyfriend who winked back at him. Beetle felt his stomach lurch. Stevie was known for taking what he wanted, when he wanted, be it money, possessions or sex. An image of the two men forcing themselves onto him flashed into his mind. He felt the colour drain from his face and had to force his lungs to begin working again. He looked back at Stevie.

"The policeman – do what you want with his body, just as long as it doesn't lead back to me, in which case you'll be nothing more than a dead beetle, ground into powder on the soles of my shoes." Stevie's eyes flashed with a mixture of humour and menace.

"I won't let you down," he shook his head to emphasise his answer.

"I'll bid you good night now, Beetle. I'm off to see my old mum – she worries about me. If you need more ammunition, for target practice or anything else," he winked, "just shout."

"Ta...," Beetle followed them from his kitchen, struggling to keep a lid on his sense of relief. His eyes followed the spots of dried blood in his hallway – his mind drawn to the far greater mess in the garage.

He held open the front door and shivered. The sky had clouded over and soft snow had covered the garden path while they'd been in the cottage.

Angus sat at his feet and dog and master together watched the Mercedes drive away. He sighed with relief and could have sworn that the animal was doing the same.

The weekend would be soon enough to clean up and thoroughly bleach the place. No one was likely to come looking for the couple here, in fact, with his sister in Newcastle, or some other equally big city, no one else was likely to be coming onto his property at any time in the near future, as high up as it was on Beeley Moor, and with a storm closing in.

He locked the door and through the small glass panel, set into it, watched the red lights of the luxury car until they disappeared from view.

Stevie was heading to Chesterfield – that was no surprise. He lived in Preston, and had done for years, but his mother had returned to her roots after finally walking out on his father for good. He'd heard about Stevie cultivating regular clients in the town, to fund his trips and his gifts to his old mum. It was even rumoured he'd recently purchased the four-bedroomed property she was now living in.

Anticipation was replacing his sense of relief. An exciting new world was opening up to him. Some of his more recent drugs drops had been to different venues in the surrounding towns and it was rumoured Stevie was expanding his influence. He was on the up, and he intended making the most of it.

He opened his palm, looked at the sealed packet and decided to save it as insurance for the day he needed to stay awake longer than was natural. He'd never enjoyed the stuff, not really, not in the way some people seemed to, and right now he was high enough on life not to need stimulants. The drugs could go to the top of his wardrobe, well out of the reach of Angus.

All three guns were back in his bedroom, along with his knives and enough spare ammunition to eliminate everyone who'd ever upset him. Never in his wildest dreams had he ever thought he'd be in possession of such an armoury. He was now one dangerous, but deliriously happy man.

His least favourite of the three guns had been used on the police officer by Ripper. It had been the boy's first kill, *but not the last*, the lad had boasted afterwards.

A woman had been beaten and raped on Beetle's property, and that was the only recent happening that he didn't feel comfortable with, but that night he'd been given a straight choice – take care of the copper or help restrain the female. He'd chosen the latter, but very quickly regretted it. Her flesh had reflected white and firm from the bare electric light bulbs until the beatings began. Raised red welts covered her back and her behind before he'd been required to truss her into an unnaturally submissive position. Her blue, tear-filled eyes had fixed him with an unblinking glare of hatred. When he closed his eyes he could still see them. Minutes after Stevie and his men left his home, and as he'd been washing her blood from his hands, he'd been physically sick.

Some killer he was going to make!

Stevie hadn't taken part, in fact he hadn't touched anything in the room, he'd simply watched. He enjoyed novel experiences and was unlikely to return for a second helping. He lived in a state-of-the-art property in Preston, and was no more comfortable in a remote cottage than a polar bear would be on the equator.

It was only the second time he'd visited Beetle's home, and that was two occasions too often.

He was happiest left alone. For decades before his mother had inherited it, the house had enjoyed a local reputation of being haunted. His grandparents and great-grandparents had named the ghost, George, and as long as the stories continued to keep the neighbours away, he was happy about that too. His sister believed in the ghost, and that suited him. He told himself he didn't care one way or the other if she never came to the farmhouse again. They met occasionally for a coffee, and he loved her, but he didn't need her poking her nose into his business.

The television didn't hold his attention for very long these days. It paled in comparison to the entertainment he'd found in the cottage – from his mother's letters and diaries which made interesting, and enlightening reading.

He'd been reading one of the letters before his unwelcome visitors arrived.

He was surprised she'd hung onto them, but pleased. They'd cleared up some of his suspicions and answered some of the questions he'd puzzled over for years.

He poured himself a smaller measure of whisky than normal. A clear head was necessary to compose the second letter to retired superintendent Godfrey Jones and his propitious son. If the moorland roads were passable in the morning then he'd be able to post it on his way in to work.

*

Michael Forbes was warm and comfortable, and watching the late news, on Alison's white sofa. He stopped himself reaching for the television remote. This was her flat and he didn't want her thinking he was taking her hospitality for granted. He'd landed on her, suitcase in hand, before asking whether or not it would be all right for him to move in for a week or so. Their relationship spanned twenty-three years but over that time they'd always maintained certain ring-fenced boundaries, and her precious flat was firmly planted inside one of those. At the time of the Royal wedding, back in the summer, he'd jokingly broached the subject of marriage but she'd laughed it off. To be fair, he couldn't realistically have expected any other kind of a response, he hadn't made an actually proposal, but it had dampened his ideas of proposing to her properly, at least for a while.

*

Beetle suppressed the idea of going to check on the woman. "I'll look in on her in the morning," he'd told the uninterested dog. If she was dead by then – well – he could just about find enough room for her in the end freezer, and if she was still alive, then tomorrow would be soon enough to decide what to do with her.

Chapter 14

Martin Jones reached over to his bedside table and wrapped his fingers around his mobile. It was five a.m. and he was thinking of Sarah. He missed her warm body. If she too was lying awake, then maybe she was feeling the same. The only thing stopping him from calling her was that yesterday's letter to his father was playing on his mind. Should he tell Sarah about it? She knew all about the break-in and hadn't seemed unduly worried by it, but since his abduction, she'd been understandably jumpy.

Secrets weren't good for a relationship, but then neither was stress. They'd promised to always be open and honest with each other, and if she'd been beside him right now he'd be spilling out his feelings and his fears, but she wasn't. She been packed off to her parent's home and he'd heaped enough worry onto her lately. He decided to keep news of the letter from her for as long as possible.

He risked clicking the call button.

Sarah answered after the second ring. "Err…hi…" Her voice was soft and slurred by sleep. His body responded as surely as if she'd been beside him.

"Morning sweetheart, did I wake you?"

"What… is something wrong?"

"No, nothing, I was just missing you, at least, nothing's wrong that couldn't be fixed in a matter of minutes by having you in bed with me."

"Minutes… how many minutes?"

He didn't need to see her face to know she was smiling. "I don't know. These things can be unpredictable. Time isn't really the issue here. I wondered if you might like to experiment with something I heard about a while ago…?"

"And what is that… as if I didn't know?"

"Well… I've heard it referred to… by certain nameless parties… as phone sex…"

Three hours later Martin was pushing his supermarket trolley from one isle to another and feeling as though he'd been transported into a parallel universe. This was Sarah's domain, not his, and he hadn't a clue where to find any of the items on the list he'd compiled with his father. To make matters worse, a sprinkling of snow had decorated the outside world overnight, twinkling lights and festive music had greeted him at the shop's entrance and everywhere inside were reminders of the time of year. His childhood Christmases hadn't been memorable occasions and he'd promised himself that for his son things would be different. At the age of five there wouldn't be many more Christmases for him to believe in the magic of Santa Clause, and for the build-up to the big day to be such a huge deal. Whatever stages the investigations had reached, by this time next week he intended being back with his wife and child. They were the ones who most needed his protection and he intended putting them above all else.

After feeling like a suspect for so long in the case of his brother's disappearance, he needed to feel his wife's unwavering trust washing over him again. He only wished that same kind of bond existed between himself and his father. Until yesterday, he'd almost forgotten what living in a toxic atmosphere of mistrust felt like. Gary's death hadn't brought him and his father closer – it had done the opposite, and he feared their already fragile relationship was beyond repair. His father had made it clear that he neither wanted nor needed a minder.

In case another letter arrived, on the pretext of allowing the traffic to clear the worst of the snow from the roads, he'd waited for the morning post before leaving for the shops.

His colleagues were no further on in their investigations into Gary's murder than they had been after the first few days, and so far, there'd been nothing to suggest that the current investigation into two disappearances wouldn't go the same way. Due to police policy, he'd been excluded from the hunt for Gary's murderer and he wanted to feel part of the current one. He needed to get his life back to normal. Over Christmas, his father could either come to him and Sarah, go down to London to be with his daughter and her boyfriend, or stay home alone. It would be his choice.

*

Beetle had suffered another night of broken sleep. At least half a dozen times he'd considered getting up to check whether Naomi was still alive, but the pull of his warm bed and the sight of snow sticking to his bedroom window had persuaded him otherwise. When his alarm woke him from his deepest sleep of the night he found he had a headache.

He switched on his bedside lamp and flinched. He looked to the sky first, but this morning saw only snow on the outside of the glass and ice on the inside. He was due in at work at eight, and who knew how long it would take him to get there?

His head pounded and his stomach was churning round like a cement mixer running on aviation fuel. He stumbled to the bathroom and threw up in the toilet. Feeling slightly better, he staggered down the stairs to the kitchen and switched on the kettle. After finishing the letter last night, he must have had more tumblers of whisky than he'd realised. Again, he considered looking in on the woman, but decided to delay the task until after work. He'd thrown her a bottle of water and a duvet the previous morning, and he'd checked her ropes. She'd been securely tied. She might even be dead by now, and that would be a blessing. It would save him from having to carry out a job that he knew he wasn't cut out for and certainly wasn't relishing.

Two slices of toast and two mugs of coffee had steadied him. Driving along his lane was a bit dicey, but once off the moor two parallel strips of tarmac opened up on each side of the road, thanks to the wheels of the morning traffic. He was going along fine until he stupidly pulled over onto a patch of ice to post the letter and then had to wait for good-natured passers-by to give his car a shove.

Despite that, he was only five minutes late entering the shop.

Outside, pavements had been gritted, and when he turned the closed sign around and recognised the first of the day's customers heading in his direction the display cabinets were brimming with the day's raw and cooked meats. He shouted into the street, "Good morning, Mrs Weaver. How's the decorating coming along?" She beamed back at him. It was the first of her two daily trips to the shop, for a chat as much as anything.

"Slowly, Beetle, slowly, but it'll be grand when it's done." She waddled into the shop and looked longingly into the full cabinets.

"And what do you and Sidney fancy for your breakfasts this morning?"

"I'll take two oatcakes and just two sausages, I think. The doctor has told us we ought to cut down a bit, on the fatty stuff, you know. We'll try it for a day or two and see if we feel any better, but I don't hold out much hope. Sidney and I are set in our ways, as you know, and those medical people don't know everything do they?"

He nodded and smiled. "They certainly don't, Mrs Weaver." If this customer had been a serial killer, she'd have tied her victims to her kitchen chairs and force-fed them fatty foods until fatal heart attacks ended their sufferings. He assumed poor Sidney either enjoyed her cooking or didn't dared to complain. "Your Sidney will miss his morning bacon, won't he?"

"Aye, well, I can always pop back later for a few rashers for our dinner. I see on the news this morning that the police have called off their search around Leaburn for that missing couple."

"What…?" Across the scales where the weight and price of the sausages should have been was a shimmering image of search dogs and armed police officers, running across his yard and swarming through his home. He blinked and the numbers reappeared, but so blurred he couldn't decipher them.

"They're saying that the weather's too bad this morning," she continued. "And Mrs Lucas, from number six, has heard that from tomorrow the police are bringing in cadaver dogs because they're assuming that if the young man and woman are still in that area, that they must be dead."

He blinked again, his vision cleared and he stifled a giggle. Mrs Weaver was too busy rummaging in the bottom of her hessian shopping bag for her purse to notice his slip-up. He chided himself. He couldn't risk giving himself away like that. That would be too cruel after so much recent good luck.

He sealed the wrapping on her breakfast parcel and handed it over the counter as his smiling boss strolled in, followed by the young whizz-kid with the manicured fingernails – the 'Trojan Horse', otherwise known as Adrian. Beetle watched his first customer of the day exchanging pleasantries with the boss but ignoring the newcomer.

Did she know something about Adrian and his involvement with Stevie Hall? But how could she... unless she knew Stevie... unless she was another one of Stevie's many pairs of eyes and ears? Was that why she came into the shop at least twice a day... could she have been the one who'd volunteered his services as a hit man?

He shook his head – his imagination was galloping off again – it was a good thing he'd given up on the drugs.

He stepped over to his precisely placed row of knives and the single steel he used for sharpening them, picked up the largest blade and the steel and began stroking the two over each other. His knives were maintained at maximum sharpness, he'd always obsessed about that. They were his babies – more than that even, they were his comfort blankets, his go-to objects whenever he felt he needed reassurance.

He was feeling reassured now. With the hint of a smile pulling at his lips, he stared at Adrian. The interloper was looking uncomfortable. This was fun.

Over the years, his knives had proved themselves to be multi-purpose, not only in the shop, but also in the cottage. After seeing them in his bedroom, Sophie had sworn never to sleep under the same roof as him ever again. For some reason she'd taken against the metal rail over his bed. He giggled at the memory as he repeatedly slid the steel across the blade.

Hill Top Cottage was jointly owned with his sister, and had to be worth an eye-watering amount of money, but she didn't need the proceeds from the sale of the house whereas his current lifestyle demanded a secluded environment.

Sophie had the face and figure for a well-paid career in the cosmetics and beauty industry and a wealthy partner somewhere down in London, or up in Newcastle – he was never sure which.

He no longer needed the money either, but she didn't need to know that.

Occasionally he missed her, and her wicked sense of humour.

"What's wrong with you, man, are you in a trance or something," ponytail-man's face was white. He'd gone from looking slightly unnerved to positively frightened, "more eggs need putting out, and where are the sandwiches, have they yet to be made?"

The little shit wouldn't dare address him like that outside of the work area. "I'm on it," he growled back, slowly placing the knife back down, parallel to the others and in the order he hung them every night.

After thirty years of loyal service, he'd expected to be the one following the boss around and barking out orders to the counter staff. A change in the order of things was coming, and he had the wherewithal now to make sure that it did. Until then, he'd make-do with his dreams. He dumped a cooked ham onto the meat slicer. As the slices peeled away onto the tray he pictured slices of manicured fingernails, followed by wafer-thin slivers of flesh and spurts of blood.

The gift of a powerful imagination had to have come from somewhere, though he'd no idea where – certainly not from his mother, whose career had consisted of her lying on her back, or whatever other positions her customers required.

The vibrant scenes in his head helped him pass the hours until he could slope off into the rear storeroom to access the internet on his mobile.

Technology truly was wonderful. It allowed him to check the latest local news without anyone wondering why he was so interested. Had his first letter arrived, and if so, had its significance been realised yet, or had it been thrown into the rubbish as a piece of junk mail? Unless the police were keeping it under wraps, there ought to have been something on the news about it by now. Never mind – the second letter was safely on its way – and that one really ought to put a fire under one person in particular.

For the next few hours, he'd have to make do with local gossip while trying not to let Adrian get under his skin.

*

Michael Forbes opened his policy book before looking up at his team. It didn't make positive reading. "This is the Wednesday morning, fifth briefing of Operation Anchor, the investigation into the disappearance of Ryan Wheeler and Naomi Proctor, both now missing for three and a half days. As Ryan is one of our own, however unlikely some of you think this might be, we have to consider that the abduction of Martin Jones last week, the recent break-in at the home of Godfrey Jones, and now the letter, could be linked to this case."

"Is anything back yet from forensics about the letter?" DC Harry Green piped up in his familiar scouse accent.

"I was coming to that. The letter sent to Mr Jones yesterday was blank except for one full set of fingerprints, which a few minutes ago were confirmed as being made using human blood. We're awaiting DNA analysis but the prints match those of Paul Biers."

A gasp rippled across the room. Even he'd been shocked when he'd taken the call. "We know Paul was murdered in a car belonging to Gary Jones, who is also presumed dead. The dried petals contained in the envelope were all blue and have provisionally been identified as a mixture of cultivated, garden plants. Has anyone any ideas?"

The silence in the room confirmed what they all knew — that police officers didn't usually have time for gardening until they retired.

"If it is Gary's blood," DC Jade Sharp answered, "then something must have woken up his killer. But how could they have his blood, or his fingerprints, after eleven months? What could they have done — frozen it?"

"It adds weight to the theory that someone is hounding Godfrey Jones and his family." DI Rob Lang offered. "It might even be the person responsible for the hit-and-run. The victim was a good friend of Gary Jones."

"That may well be the case, and for that reason, with assistance from uniformed officers downstairs, we're resuming control of that enquiry," Forbes answered. "We could be looking for someone with, or access to, a garden."

"Or someone who works with flowers," Jade added.

"We're not talking inner city here," Lang commented. "I'm sure ninety per cent of the population around here could easily lay their hands on those types of garden flowers."

Jade shot him a scathing look. "All the petals were from blue flowers. There can't be too many gardens with that particular combination of plants."

"Unless the petals were from imported flowers they had to have been gathered during the summer," DC Robert Bell added his thoughts. "That suggests pre-meditation by the letter sender, unless it's possible to buy single-coloured dried petals these days. I believe paper confetti is banned at some wedding venues. Should I check for suppliers, sir?"

"Good idea, and check all the florists in the area. We'll keep news of the letter out of the press for the moment. For now the only link between the cases involving the Jones family and Operation Anchor is this station. If there are more then we need to find them, and quickly. And just in case this station is the link may I remind you all to be extra vigilant with your own safety and the safety of your loved ones."

"I have a suggestion which might not be too popular," DS Adam Ross had been standing quietly in the corner of the room. His longstanding dislike of ex-superintendent Jones was no secret. "Godfrey was never totally eliminated as a suspect for his son's disappearance..."

"Carry on..." Forbes noted the hesitation in Adam's voice and respected him for it.

"He's been living alone for years, so is it not slightly convenient that the letter should arrive when he has someone with him to witness it? Is it conceivably possible that he sent it to himself?"

Someone in the room whistled.

*

Beetle had had a tough day. There'd been nothing on the news about his letter, and to top it off he almost hadn't made it back onto the moor. Finally, he was turning left onto the narrow road where black ice gave way to hard snow and where his tyres had some degree of grip. He was back where he belonged, above the snow line and with a shimmering grey landscape ahead of him. In the moonlight, the few random fields were indistinguishable from the open, heather and bilberry covered moorland, at the heart of which sat Hill Top Cottage and one very cold, or even dead, young woman.

Seeing the uneven terrain reminded him of the grubby, uncovered duvet he'd thrown to the woman the previous morning.

He accelerated gently onto the track linking the road and the cottage, relieved to see that the only imprints were from his own vehicle's tyres, made much earlier in the day.

He crossed the yard, the air entering his lungs feeling ten degrees colder than that down in the streets of Matlock – he could have been back in the cold store at the rear of the shop. If the girl was still alive she'd most likely be in a bad way, but he couldn't put off the moment any longer – he had to take a look.

The frozen hinges on the wooden door of the garage creaked open and he groped along the wall for the light switch.

Naomi was breathing; he could tell that much without getting too close. Dark smears on the duvet showed she'd been trying to keep warm. He saw the side of her face and a spark of hope flickered inside him. Almost indistinguishable from the dirty cover pulled up around it, where her face wasn't bruised and blood stained it was a deathly shade of grey. She was showing no signs of being aware of his presence, so had to be either unconscious or pretending to be asleep – either way, she was quiet. In an hour or two he'd return with food and water, and, if his conscience was still gnawing away at him, an extra duvet.

Bedding was something he had no shortage of – his mother, God bless her, had hoarded cupboards full of the stuff, along with items from his and his sister's childhood and piles of other clutter.

But first-things-first – the living room fire needed lighting and Angus needed feeding.

Chapter 15

Detective Sergeant Adam Ross picked up a slice of buttered toast and the previous day's paper to pass the ten minutes he knew it would take Jane to shower. The paper was Wednesday's – he checked, but it was the date that he couldn't quite believe. A deep furrow creased his brow. He'd been so wrapped up in the investigations that he hadn't realised more than a month had passed since his last visit to his wife's grave. It was five weeks, to be precise. His heart fluttered and he felt a lump rise in his throat.

He'd always gone alone, but time was marching on and their son had turned six. He'd been thinking the child ought to be taken along to visit his mother's resting place occasionally. He'd ask Jane what she thought.

It was never an easy subject to broach. After his marriage proposal, she'd confided in him her fear of never being able to hold a candle to a dead woman, *a bit like Rebecca in the classic novel*, she'd told him, and despite never reading the book he'd understood. However, a monthly ritual visit to the cemetery wasn't something he felt he should ever have to give up.

Jane's footsteps sounded on the stairs. He put the paper down, still staring at the date, and bit into the cold toast.

"Can you believe that I've had a text this early in the morning?" Jane walked into the living room wrapped only in a towel. "The children aren't even awake yet – typical, thoughtless Kevin. He wants to know whether he can take

Lucy to Disneyland, Paris, during the Easter break. And he wants to know before lunchtime today."

Eight and a half year old Lucy was from Jane's first marriage, to one of the most successful businessmen in the Leaburn area. During the brief marriage, he'd tried to control every moment of Jane's day, refusing to allow her to take on anything other than voluntary work. Being a trained police officer, she'd gone along with his demands and worked as a volunteer special constable at Leaburn station when Adam had been struggling to come to terms with the death of Erin and the prospect of single-handedly dealing with a new-born son.

The rest, as they say, is history.

"It won't be a problem," he shelved the idea of mentioning Erin. "The three of us can visit Alton Towers and a few other places while she's away. How long will they be gone?"

"He wants her with him for a fortnight." Jane sank into an armchair and spread her hands out as if she couldn't quite believe her own words. "He wants to take her touring around France. He'll spoil her rotten, I know he will. She'll be impossible when she gets home."

"We'll keep her well-grounded – don't worry."

"It's ironic, isn't it," she continued, "that now I've *chosen* to take a year or two away from the world of work to be a full-time mother, I feel she's being taken away from me."

"That isn't going to happen and you know it." He sat on the arm of the chair, gave her damp shoulders a firm cuddle and kissed the top of her head. "We're luckier than many families," he reminded her. "We know Kevin has Lucy's best interests at heart, we're financially stable and we're all in good health."

"You're right. It's just that, when I hear from him it flicks a stress-switch in my brain. I need to learn to relax when I have to deal with him."

He felt her shiver and squeezed her cold, bare shoulder. "Go and get dressed, and if I was you I'd wait until the morning was over before giving him an answer. It won't hurt to remind him that you're in control of his access to Lucy."

Whenever Jane mentioned relaxing, he inwardly flinched. The wine bottles in the recycling box were the result of her 'trying to relax', but she had promised him that she was cutting down. The effect her drinking might have on the children was his main concern, but the last thing he wanted was for her to feel pressured. She'd refused counselling and he couldn't risk her hiding her problem. Only if she was open with him could he help her fully recover from her traumas of the last few years and get her drinking back under control.

*

Martin Jones was buttering his morning wedge of toast and listening to the local news when he heard the latch of the wrought-iron gate click back into place. Snow had become slush overnight, but the television weather reporter was talking about another cold front due to be arriving in the Midlands sometime over the next few hours. He dropped the knife and strode to the front door. Even in the dead of winter, the post arrived before most people on the street were out of their houses. The orange glow from the streetlight met the white of the newly installed security light mid-way up the short garden path, and through the frosted glass of the door panel, anyone could be forgiven for thinking a spectacular sunrise awaited.

The body of the postie blocked out the light and the letterbox opened. Martin recoiled for a second, then recovered and held a clear plastic bag just below the letterbox.

The toilet upstairs flushed.

A brown envelope with a handwritten address on it slid into the evidence bag he'd have given all the material things he possessed not to be holding there.

Back in the kitchen, he pulled on the latex gloves he'd left ready, but not really expected to use, and then spread a sheet of clear plastic over the kitchen table. The envelope slid from its protective sleeve and with a trembling hand, he reached for a small, sharp knife.

Almost as if his old sergeant was whispering into his ear, his police training kicked in, reminding him this wasn't the way to open a suspect package, and that there was no guarantee of this envelope containing anything similar to the previous one.

He placed the knife back down and gently ran his gloved fingers over the A4 sized package, feeling for tell-tale wires or small lumps and bumps which might indicate an incendiary device. Reasonably satisfied, he pushed the knife to the edge of the table and reached for the scissors. Then he cut a narrow sliver from the side of the envelope furthest away from where the sender would be expecting him to open it, and gently tilted it onto its edge.

Familiar blue petals tumbled out, this time followed by two sheets of paper. With tweezers from his detective's bag, he opened out the folded papers. His brother's name leapt out at him from the top of the first page. A crudely drawn map jumped out from the other.

"I told you there'd be more." Father had been listening for the post. "What's written there? Let me see." For a doddery old man, supposedly in shock, he was crossing the kitchen with a determined, aggressive stride without waiting for an answer.

Martin's open hand thudded against his father's chest. "Don't touch it. I'll read it to you." He pronounced the written words as steadily as his throat would allow. "So, Godfrey, I expect you want to find your son? If that is the case, take a spade up onto Stanton Moor. Follow the directions on this map until you find blue flowers. Then dig. And good luck."

"This is one sick, bloody joke... surely?" Godfrey's face showed bewilderment, followed a second later by rage. "Some little shit thinks he can terrorise us and then sit back and watch us squirm, does he? When I catch up with the little bastard, I'm telling you now, he'll wish he'd never been born."

"The letter you opened on Tuesday morning was no joke, Dad." He lowered his voice. It was time for his father to hear some painful facts. "I've just taken a call from DCI Forbes. Those fingerprints were made using human blood, and they were those of Paul Biers."

"Paul Biers...?" Godfrey's anger dissipated, leaving confusion in its place. "But... this letter names our Gary."

"Paul was the youth killed the same night – in Gary's car..."

"I know who he is, Son, I'm not senile, but what I don't understand is how or why his prints, or his blood, should be on a letter addressed to me."

Martin shrugged. "The theory at the station is that Paul's blood had been frozen, possibly along with his hand, but that's yet to be confirmed by the lab. As to why it's been sent to you... no one's any idea yet. I'll photograph this letter before I call it in and it gets whisked away."

"That letter's going nowhere until I've followed the directions on that map. Gary's been gone almost a year – how will holding on to it for a few hours make the slightest difference one way or another to the investigations?"

"Dad, no, it could be an elaborate set-up. There's a killer out there whose motive we still have no idea of and you could be walking into his trap. Don't be foolish. Let trained officers go up there and dig."

"Not a chance. I'm going to follow those directions myself, and unless you've suddenly begun to do everything by the book, you'll be coming along with me."

"We could both land in serious trouble for tampering with evidence, assuming there's anything there to be found. You've got a pension and I've a mortgage and a family to consider, besides, it's started snowing again."

Godfrey sighed heavily. "In that case, we'd better get going, hadn't we? I'll get my coat."

Martin weighed up his options as he traipsed into the hallway. Either he defied his father and phoned in the arrival of the second letter, or he went along with him at the risk of losing his job. He felt forced to change his life to fit in with his father wanted. He should have been willing to stand by him, no matter what he thought the old man may have done, but it wasn't easy.

Nothing short of closed roads was going to stop his father and, despite their differences, if he were to lose him in the way that he'd lost his brother he'd never forgive himself for not putting someone else's feelings ahead of his own. "OK

Dad, we'll do as you say and get going before this weather worsens, and before I change my mind about this." He hoped his father could read the concern in his face.

Many people, friends and enemies alike, thought of his father as obsessive. Others, those who knew him slightly better, called him a bully, but never to his face. Martin considered him both of those things. Sitting back in the passenger seat he silently prayed that this morning's course of action wasn't one that they'd both come to regret.

The rush-hour traffic was doing a reasonable job of keeping the main roads clear of snow. Within minutes they were clear of Leaburn, driving through limestone hills and on towards the sandstone plateau made famous by its stone circles, its ancient burial sites, and its quarries. He'd heard of Stanton Moor, but never visited the place. It wasn't going to be a comfortable introduction.

They covered the main roads at reasonable speeds and then drove more slowly along a winding, tree-lined road before taking a sharp right onto a steep incline. Snow was building on the road sign but Martin could just make out the name of Birchover.

"This is where the all-wheel drive comes into its own," Godfrey broke the silence for the first time since they'd left the main A515.

While the territory was unfamiliar to Martin, his father had barely glanced at the road map. The atmosphere in the car told him not to question the route.

The car's engine fell silent on what they hoped was a parking area beside the road. To the right of them was Stanton Moor and, judging by the undisturbed snow, on it they would be alone. Martin felt his skin crawl. Images of what they might find had been running through his mind from the moment he'd read the letter. He'd seen two badly decomposed bodies and had no desire to add to that tally.

There had to be more than one access point onto the moor but he thought it unlikely anyone would be waiting for them, not so soon after the letter's arrival, and not given the weather. It was still barely light and no one had followed them – he'd been watching the wing mirror and his father had varied his speed, telling him he'd been thinking the same.

He got out and walked to the driver's side, to where his father was changing into an old pair of wellingtons.

"Grab the spades – we may as well go prepared now we've made it this far." Godfrey sounded tense.

"Dad..."He could imagine the local newspaper headlines if this got out – *vigilante cops loose on the moors*. And even if they didn't find Gary, supposing what was there turned out to be gruesome enough to catch the attention of the dailies...? Instead of opening the letter, he should have taken it straight to the station, and if his father had raged at him then, at least he could have returned to his wife and son with a clear conscience and a continuing career. He missed them both so much, and hindsight was such a wonderful bloody thing.

Snow had stopped falling but and as far as Martin could see the sky resembled polished lead and clumps of grey cotton wool.

"Well... what are you waiting for?"

There was no going back now. He grabbed the two spades and slammed the boot of the car shut. "I'm ready – let's get this over with."

He cleared enough snow to allow them to pass through the wooden gate, and with their heads bowed against the cold wind, they marched on.

Walking at speed in wellingtons was neither easy nor comfortable for either of them. The paths resembled white ribbons disappearing into the distance while the ground alongside them had dark stalks and scrubby-looking bushes poking through the white blanket. They trudged on, his father using the spade as a walking aid to keep himself upright.

They were easy targets in the open space. His father's weathered face was glowing and his eyes were alert. He'd never been what some might describe as *an oil painting*, but now he looked positively demented. The idea of finally finding Gary's resting place was driving him on.

On leveller ground, they walked side-by-side, past an enormous, upright stone, which to Martin resembled an enormous cup cake topped with a thin layer of vanilla icing. He could imagine the area being popular with walkers in the summer, but on this bitterly cold morning, theirs were the only man-made footprints.

Godfrey stopped suddenly, took out his phone and studied the photograph of the map. "The site has to be over by those rocks… see… towards where the moor drops away. This is where we leave the path." He was breathing hard, but then so was Martin.

Martin thought again of his wife. *'Your father needs you too,'* was one of the last things she'd said to him over the phone the previous night. She obviously didn't know him as well as she thought.

"Dad, in these conditions we're never going to find the exact spot to dig. We've taken a look, so please, let's go home."

"We're not close enough. You wait here if you must, but I'm going on."

"I'm coming with you," he groaned.

Minutes later the rough terrain ahead of them fell away sharply into a long valley, with a ribbon of dwellings and a black road at its base. Beyond the houses were more wooded areas than fields. For a moment, he struggled to get his bearings, but then realised what he was seeing — on the far hillside lay the forest entrance where Gary had died. He pushed the thought away. He had more than enough to deal with in the present.

Looking down again, fields, trees and rooftops all appeared white. He could have been in a toy factory, admiring a Christmas display of finely produced models. The pain of missing his son gripped his insides even more intensely and for a few moments, he struggled to place one foot in front of the other.

His father stopped abruptly again.

"This has to be the right area," Godfrey shouted into the snow-flecked wind, "but where are the flowers? There are no flowers... blue or any other colour...?"

"We've been the victims of a hoax, Dad." He wanted to calm him. His own heart was crying out for his brother – the brother who'd been shot like a rabid dog. He looked around. Gary's killer could have them in his sights at this very moment.

"But nothing is going to bloom in the wild... not at this time of the year... not up here."

"Dad, let's go... There's nothing to be found here."

"You said yourself that the first letter was for real. I have a gut feeling the second will prove vital in finding our Gary."

He couldn't argue because the moment he'd seen it he'd felt the same way. He just hadn't expected his father to become so convinced, so quickly. "Come on Dad." He placed an arm around the old man's shoulders and felt a tremor. Through the thick duffle coat he was wearing, his tension was visible, as was the devastation on his face.

"Let's go now. This isn't a job for us. Let me report that letter."

"All right, Son, I know you're right. Do it as soon as we get home."

*

Beetle's sleep patterns were unpredictable these days. As a result, he'd nodded off while sitting on the toilet in the shop and twice almost driven his car off the road. And he couldn't remember when he'd last seen the ending to a television show. When he did sleep in his bed, as opposed to the lumpy sofa, he was plagued almost every hour by nightmares. Last night, at nine o'clock, he'd taken food and water and an extra duvet to Naomi. Unbelievably, she'd looked slightly better, with a touch of colour in her face, and he'd gone to his bed feeling marginally less guilty. At midnight, he'd woken up in a cold sweat, convinced she'd escaped and gone running to Stevie. At one a.m., he'd sat bolt-upright in his bed, believing she'd escaped and brought the police to his home. And at two a.m. he'd opened his eyes in terror, imagining she'd escaped, found his knives and was sitting on his bedroom floor sharpening them. After that, he'd slept soundly for a couple of hours.

When he next opened his eyes, his bedside clock showed four a.m. Thursday. His pillow was soaked on both sides and there was no point in lying in his bed, trying to stay awake. He got up, showered and dressed, and then fed Angus. In place of his usual morning coffee he poured himself a tumbler of whisky.

He'd never lost sight of the fact that there was a killer out there. It didn't worry him the way it used to, but someone knew who he was and how he lived his life. And living alone, in a remote location, it was sufficient reason to keep loaded guns handy at all times.

The alcohol slipped down his throat and on an empty stomach was soon having the desired effect – taking the edge off his conscience. He returned to his bedroom and picked up his favourite gun. Deliberately slowly, he descended the stairs. It wouldn't do to have an accident. He ordered Angus to stay on the pile of blankets in the corner of the kitchen, and headed out into the freezing air.

Naomi lay still with her eyes closed. She was either feigning sleep or she'd fallen into unconsciousness, either way she was making what he had to do seem a whole lot easier. He raised his arms straight out in front and aimed the gun at the centre of her chest. A shot to the head, as he'd been instructed, would have been a cleaner, kinder end but his hands were shaking and he couldn't trust his aim. He didn't want to have to squeeze the trigger more than once.

He half-closed his eyes and gently squeezed.

A freezer motor juddered into life, his eyes opened wide, and he gasped.

He was staring straight into Naomi's open eyes and they were pleading with him. This was the stuff of a fair few of his nightmares.

That's it, he thought, I'm having another nightmare... if I could wake up...? He bit his lower lip and it hurt. Despite the cold he felt sweat prickle on his forehead.

He relaxed his grip, hoping she could see in his face how sorry he was. He couldn't go on like this. He began to squeeze the trigger again, but it was no good, he couldn't do it. He was a pathetic failure. Angry with himself, but not angry enough to shoot a woman in cold blood, he lowered his arms, turned on his heels and tramped back to the warmth of the house.

She was still alive. More than that – she was awake and wrapped in the two duvets. Her face was a mess but it was healing, and despite the swellings, her eyes had held him as surely as if he'd been hypnotised.

Another tumbler of whisky was called for. If he didn't have the guts to kill her, what the hell was he going to do?

More to the point – what was wrong with him? He was a killer for hire, for heaven's sake. He had a reputation to maintain. A gang leaded with a reputation of wiping out those who let him down or crossed him, actually trusted him. Why... he'd never been quite sure, but the fact was that he did.

Those he'd already pulled a trigger on had been nameless and faceless, but he knew that this woman's name was Naomi and that she was a nurse who would otherwise be out in the world caring for sick and vulnerable people. He'd seen her at her most vulnerable. He'd heard her screams and tasted her blood. He'd held her down, watched her being raped, and scrubbed her from underneath his fingernails.

He took a deep breath, wrapped the gun in a tea towel and placed it in the kitchen drawer. Then he turned to the dog. He could have sworn Angus was smiling up at him, and as he reached down and stroked the soft black fur he heard the echo of his mother's voice, *'I told you so, didn't I, you silly boy, you aren't a killer'*. His hands shook and he reached for the bottle and the tumbler.

He flopped into the nearest kitchen chair, dropped his head into his hands and tried to block out the speech Stevie had delivered to him while sitting at this very table. *'Do what you* want with her, as long as nothing ever leads back to me... I don't expect her ever to be found... Thanks to your mentoring, Ripper will soon be jetting off to Romania to sort out a little problem I've been having there...'

'You can rely on me, Stevie,' he'd replied as if he'd meant every syllable.

So now what?

Just what the hell was he going to do?

He'd come so far in the past year; sometimes he'd pinched himself. But what use to anyone was an assassin who could only kill if he didn't have to look his victims in the eyes?

Despite trying not to, he liked the woman. He really liked her. He'd liked to have had sex with her, but had always considered rapists as the lowest of the low.

He wanted to be sick. He couldn't allow Naomi to go free – she'd go straight to the police and Stevie would have him killed – for sure, and he couldn't leave her to die of thirst, or hunger, because that would be too cruel.

He had a young woman restrained in his garage and he couldn't bring himself to use her. What was wrong with him? Had his rotten luck returned to haunt him, as he'd feared that one day it must? If so, would killing her be the ultimate trigger required to change his luck for ever?

He would have asked Ripper; he should have ordered Ripper, as a part of his mentoring, to shoot the woman in cold blood, but that thought might not have come too late. If the lad wasn't half way across Europe already, maybe he'd care to come up to Hill Top Cottage for a little last minute tutoring.

He picked up his phone and willed Ripper to answer.

He was going to delegate. He was becoming a man of importance, and the art of delegation was something he needed to learn.

Ripper's voice made him feel a whole lot better. The lad was already on his way to the cottage.

There was just time to sober up a bit. He pulled a loaf of bread from the cupboard and shoved two slices into the toaster then picked up the kettle and moved to the sink.

The police had been searching about twenty miles away for Naomi and the copper, but soon they'd be extending their area. He probably had a week at most to get Naomi's and the police officer's bodies cut up and into the freezers.

When Ripper had done the deed for him he'd have a proper breakfast, drink as many mugs of coffee as he could, and then set off for work as normal. He'd be late but he could blame road conditions.

Chapter 16

"I can't stop for long, I've a plane to catch," Ripper breezed into Beetle's kitchen, "and it's a good thing I have a four wheel drive motor, that lane of yours is a right bastard, do you know that? Is the female still in the garage?"

"She is, and as you've never killed a woman, I thought it might be an interesting experience for you to have before you went jetting off around the world, another notch on your belt, so to speak."

"I appreciate the offer, Beetle, and thanks for asking me." Ripper reached out for a handshake. "It's because of your teaching that I'm been given the chance to visit the sources of some of Uncle Stevie's income streams in Europe."

"You're very welcome." If this lad was ever to take over Stevie's empire then maybe he could be his right-hand-man. A little creeping wouldn't go amiss. "You're a good lad, you remind me of myself when I was your age."

"We make a good team, don't you think – a team to command respect – Ripper and Beetle?"

He laughed. "You mean Beetle and Ripper."

"We'll see." Ripper laughed with him. "But seriously, before I met you I had no confidence whatsoever, and after a short time of working alongside you, being allowed to kill that copper, and with the drugs and the money collecting side of things, I know I'm capable of holding my own in the family businesses. May I use your gun?"

"I keep my favourite gun with me, but there are two others upstairs, in my bedside cupboard. Take your pick of those."

Beetle offered the dog another handful of biscuits to try to bring some normality into the morning. Together they listened to Ripper bounding up the stairs and the dog looked up from his bowl only once when he heard footsteps coming from directly overhead.

What happened next was more typical of Beetle's luck.

His mug of coffee crashed at his feet and Angus's dog biscuits skittered across the floor. Angus raced to his bed in the corner of the room, made himself as small as he possibly could and lay there trembling.

The dog hadn't liked the sudden, frightening noise, followed by the softer thud, from the place where the stranger had gone. It had rattled his dish and made his master curse and rush from the room.

*

Forbes took the direct call from Martin Jones and immediately dispatched a car. He was furious and didn't care who knew it. His officers were trained on how not to compromise evidence. What had Martin been thinking when he'd opened the letter, let alone when he was heading up onto a moor, in the middle of a snowstorm, to look for a site marked on a hand-drawn map? Anger became frustration. Most roads were clear of snow now but nothing was likely to be gained by searching the moor until the snow sunk to a point where they could see the ground. Until then an area would have to be closed to the public without allowing news of the letter to leak out, and that was going to take considerable organisation. At a time when they already had two missing persons and he didn't have officers to spare, special constables would have to be drafted in, but for how long? His immediate superior, Detective Superintendent Christine Price, would have to be brought up to date with the latest fiasco before did anything, and as usual one of her main concerns would be the budget, or lack of it. It wasn't a good start to the day.

He was mulling over the list of potential problems Martin had caused by his actions when his office door opened and DS Adam Ross's head appeared in the gap. "Sir, I think we might have a break in Ryan's case."

"Come in. Tell me more. I could use some better news."

"Last night, uniformed officers in Chesterfield arrested a teenager – a small-time drug dealer, and apparently, the lad was so afraid of going to prison that they couldn't stop him talking. He claims that the drug scene in the town has been unbalanced in recent weeks by one man, Stevie Hall, who is trying to take control of the streets and of the clubs and public houses. There's been some sort of shake-up among the gangs in Chesterfield and this man, Big Stevie as he's known locally, apparently, has come out on top. It seems he's from a gangland family, originating in Manchester, and he has a fearsome reputation. According to the lad in the custody suite, he also controls a string of prostitutes of both sexes, and there are rumours on the street that his family have several police officers on their payroll, as well as a couple of hired killers."

"A real charmer... so why have we not come across the name before?"

"I've had a quick look at records and that's where it becomes more interesting, sir. Stevie has lived in Preston, along with his father and brothers, for the past decade. While stationed in Preston, our Ryan worked several cases involving the Hall family, and Stevie is known to drive a dark grey Mercedes."

"Like the one seen being followed by Ryan at the end of his last shift?"

"Exactly sir, and Rob's finding out all he can about him now, but I thought you needed to be updated."

"Ryan wasn't a corrupt officer – I'd stake my reputation on it, despite not knowing him for long. Has he paid the ultimate price for doing his job, and if so, where does the woman fit it? Did she set him up, or was she collateral damage?"

"You speak as if they're both dead, sir."

"After what you've just told me, unfortunately, I think they may well be."

"That isn't all the lad had to say. He also suggested a name for the hit-and-run fatality on our patch – a teenager called Tony Murray from the Hurst Farm Estate in Matlock. Local police are out looking for him now."

"Request that they contact us as soon as they have him in custody. We'll drive over there if they haven't got the spare manpower to bring him to us."

"And Jade's just asked, should we call the Preston station to alert them to our interest in Stevie Hall?"

"Good idea. Tell her to ask if they could take him into custody for questioning. Then we'll see which one of them gets pulled in first – young Murray or Mr Hall. If necessary, DI Lang can interview Murray. We need to speak to Hall as a matter of urgency."

Matlock Police Station's interview room reeked of disinfectant, and Tony Murray didn't smell much better. Forbes sat facing the dark haired lad who looked younger than the seventeen years he was supposed to have behind him. "I'm DCI Michael Forbes and this is DS Adam Ross, and we're from the Leaburn Police Station. We'd like to ask you about your whereabouts nineteen days ago, the night Stephen Monks died, to be precise."

"I don't remember," the lad replied without making eye contact, a sure sign of guilt as far as Forbes was concerned.

"We think that you do. We're here to inform you that your car has been impounded and that if the damage to the front of it matches the injuries found on the body of Stephen Monks then you're going to be in here for quite a while. And if forensic evidence backs up what we suspect then you'll be facing a murder charge."

The youth's face couldn't have gone any paler. He looked at Adam and then stared into Forbes's eyes. "It was an accident. I swear it. It was a narrow road and he was in dark clothing. If he'd turned to face me I might have seen him... but he didn't. I wasn't speeding... I hadn't been drinking... not a drop... and I never do drugs... not any sort... you have to believe me... it was an accident... a terrible accident..." The youth flicked his gaze from Adam to Forbes and back.

"It must have shaken you," Adam broke the silence. "But why didn't you stop?"

"I did stop. On my life, I stopped and I got out of my car, but he was dead. His head was all smashed in, and there was blood all over the road. His body had somehow rolled onto the grass verge."

"From the marks on the road he was dragged several metres by your car." Adam confirmed.

"I guess... but I've thought of little else since it happened and I think it must have taken me a couple of seconds to react and hit the brakes. I told you, I just didn't see him until he was half-way across the front of my car."

"But why leave the scene? Why not phone for help as most people involved in an accident would automatically do?"

"I was going to. I ran back to my car, to get my phone, but as I opened the door, I saw another car's headlights in the distance, coming up behind me. I panicked. I was alone on a little-used back road and it suddenly occurred to me that if the driver of the approaching car was on his way to pick up the person I'd just killed, that I might then be in a dangerous situation. It was selfish, I know, but I was in a state of shock. I put myself first. I jumped back into my car and drove off. At that moment I had every intention of calling the police as soon as I got home, but then I bottled it."

"The car behind you – were you able to tell whether or not it stopped?"

"It definitely didn't stop. It was a sporty type of car. It had to have been speeding because it almost caught me up."

Forbes and Adam exchanged a glance. "Go on..." Forbes said.

"Then I saw a second set of lights even further back. I couldn't be a hundred per cent certain, but I think whoever was driving that vehicle might have stopped because I didn't see their lights again."

"Stephen wasn't found until the following morning. Did you touch the body at all?"

"No. On my life, I didn't touch it. I told you – I panicked."

"Could you tell the colour or make of the car behind you?"

"It was too far back and too dark. The headlights were low to the ground and when I saw it gaining on me I floored it."

"While you were on that stretch of road did you see any other vehicles or anyone else on foot?"

"No, and that's why I never called anyone. I know that leaving the scene of an accident is a crime, but I thought that if no one had seen me I might not get caught and so not get the blame. I've only had a driving licence for a couple of months."

"But you talked to some of your friends about the incident?"

"I have three mates I spend a lot of time with, and they saw I was stressing about something. It was a huge deal for me; I needed to talk to someone. Did one of them shop me – I wouldn't blame them if they did? It's a hell of a secret for anyone to have to keep."

"They can explain that to you themselves when you eventually see them again."

"I'm glad it's over, really I am. If it is one of my friends who've shopped me, will you tell them I don't blame them? I've not been able to keep my food down and I've been losing sleep waiting for your knock on the door."

"You've just confessed to the crimes of manslaughter and leaving the scene of an accident. Officers from this station are going to have to search your home and you'll need to accompany them because we require the clothes and shoes you were wearing that night."

"The clothes have been washed since that night."

"That won't matter. We'll also need to see any phones that you have."

"I thought about calling… honestly."

The lad was telling the truth – you didn't need to be a trained psychologist to see that.

*

Beetle stood behind the shop counter, afraid and annoyed in equal parts. Ripper must have tripped. He'd blown his own head almost completely off his young shoulders. The top few stairs were going to take a hell of a lot of cleaning, as if he didn't have enough to do over the next few days.

Ripper's death had been an accident, but Stevie was hardly likely to see it that way. What else could he have done except wrap the youth in plastic, drag him downstairs and out to the log shed, and place him beside what remained of the policeman. At this rate he'd run out of freezer space. And he now had Ripper's car to dispose of and a woman who was still breathing.

It was a stroke of luck that Stevie was sending his nephew to a country where crime and corruption were rife – it could be weeks, or even months, before the lad was missed. By then his trail would have grown cold. He was a minor cog in Beetle's wheel of misfortune, and nothing to worry about really.

He was back to where he'd been at this time yesterday, with a day's work ahead of him, and having to come up with another way of disposing of the lodger in his garage.

He was indifferent to most of the people who walked through the shop doorway, but he did have a handful of favourites and a similar number he absolutely despised. He supposed it was the same for everyone who faced the public every day of their working life. Mrs Forbes was one of his favourites. She liked to chat, but not about things that were of no interest to him, and she showed a genuine interest in his life and in his opinions.

This morning she'd brought him a little jar of her home-made green tomato chutney. "You ought to have the local radio on in this shop, Beetle," her eyes twinkled as she spoke. She had news and obviously wanted to share it.

"The boss would have to apply for some sort of a licence. It would mean him putting his hand in his pocket, Mrs Forbes, and you and I both know that isn't likely to happen," he gave her what he thought was his most conspiratorial smile.

"Oh I'm sure the old skinflint could afford it. This is a good little business, and hasn't he just taken on some sort of new-boy to help him?"

"He's supposedly hired Adrian to come up with some fresh business ideas, but if you ask me, the real reason is that it enables him to spend more time at home with his family. He wants to semi-retire. He's lost interest in the business and lately we haven't been as busy with the new supermarket pinching so many of our customers. So much for loyalty, eh Mrs Forbes, not like your good self."

She beamed back at him and he felt a wave of genuine affection towards her. Why couldn't all his of customers be like this one?

"Are those today's pork pies?"

"As always, Mrs Forbes, and you know I wouldn't sell anything but the freshest of stock to you. Which one would you like?" He leaned forward and let his hand hover over the tray of pies while she decided. He wanted to hear her gossip while they were alone in the shop. "Am I missing something in particular by not hearing the local news today?"

"Only that the police have this morning sealed off part of Stanton Moor..." She gave him a knowing look and then waited in silence for his response.

He leaned into the counter. "Do we know why?"

"Not yet, no, not for sure, but I reckon they've found that missing couple. I reckon that now the snow has melted slightly someone's found their bodies."

He tried not to smile but felt his face twitch. So the letters did arrive – that was the best news he could ever have expected to hear. "That's good," the words tumbled out before he could stop them.

"Not for their poor families, it's not." She hadn't looked surprised at his outburst, but the furrows in her brow were deepening with each passing second.

"No, don't misunderstand me, Mrs Forbes, I only meant that it must have been awful for them – not knowing what had happened to their loved ones."

"Oh yes, I agree. Not knowing must be almost as bad as having the deaths confirmed." She looked suitably impressed with his insight into human nature.

He knew all about not knowing. He'd lived with that spectre for almost a year now. He'd spent much of the past eleven months guessing and worrying, convinced that the truth would come out one day. It was too much to hope that his run of good luck would last until the farce that was his life reached its final days. Until then each day was a bonus, he'd learned how to get through his life one day at a time, and the mess he was in now would sort itself out eventually, he was sure.

"Bodies on the moor... it sounds like the title of an intriguing book, or a film, don't you think?" She handed a tenner over the counter.

"Indeed it does, Mrs Forbes." An intriguing book with himself as the protagonist, he wanted to add. With Big Stevie's blessing, he intended using two of the bodies wisely. The police officer's remains were bulkier than the first two, he'd clearly liked to work out and keep fit but had been losing the battle against the inevitable paunch of middle age. Even sliced and diced he was going to take up more than half of one of the chest freezers in his garage... and he really must remember to label the bags this time..."

"... Beetle... Beetle... my change... Have you fallen asleep at that till?"

"I'm sorry, Mrs Forbes. I was thinking of those poor, cold bodies. If you hear any more news, and you're passing the shop later this afternoon, you will call in and keep me updated won't you? You know I'm always pleased to see you."

"Of course I will, Beetle. Oh, you are such a sweet man. If I'd had a son I'd have wanted him to be just like you." She turned to greet the next customer, the sour-faced, Mrs Booker. "Beetle is a grand young man, isn't he?"

"If you say so, Lilly," Mrs Booker struggled to find a good word for anyone.

She sat at the opposite end of his likeability scale, but as always, he smiled at her. That was, after all, a part of his job. However, recently he'd even found it difficult to look at her and not smile – on account of the additions he occasionally made to her weekly order of mince. There were times, when she was being particularly belligerent with him, when he'd been sorely tempted to enquire whether the human flesh he'd added to her order had altered the taste of her meals at all. It was supposed to taste like pork, or so he'd heard, though of course he didn't know whether that was one of those so-called 'urban myths' or not.

"I'll maybe see you later then, Mrs Forbes," he shouted past Mrs Booker and through the open doorway to her. "Oh, and by the way, I'm not sure you'd really want someone like me as your son."

"You're too modest, Beetle," she shouted back over her shoulder. "Far too modest for your own good..."

"Time will tell, Mrs Forbes. Time will tell," he murmured.

*

Uniformed officers and fluttering, *crime scene – do not cross,* tapes blocked the main entrances to Stanton Moor and the local press wanted to know what it was all about. "Tell them we're working on information received and have nothing definite to report as yet," Forbes told his press officer who'd been waiting for him to return from Matlock. That was perfectly true.

Adam led the briefing in the incident room by running through the interview he and Forbes had conducted that morning in Matlock.

"So we think we've cleared up the hit-and-run," DC Jade Sharpe said, "and if the accused is to be believed, the incident has nothing to do with Gary Jones or any other officer from this station."

"It looks that way," Adam replied.

"However, I don't want us to relax our vigilance," Forbes added. "We may still have someone targeting this station. Rob, is anything back yet from forensics?"

"They've confirmed that the same type of paper and dried flower petals were used in the second letter as in the first. Also that they've found no traces of blood or any other types of body fluids," DI Lang said.

"More snow is being forecasted for tonight, sir, up to an inch," Jade added.

"Then we'll all have to be patient and have our wellingtons ready. Has there been any progress at all this morning in Operation Anchor?"

"Nothing yet, sir," DC Harry Green spoke. "All the wedding guests are saying pretty much the same thing. No one saw either Ryan or Naomi after they walked into the night as the wedding reception was winding down. The guests who did notice them didn't think there was anything odd in their behaviour, and assumed the couple had either called for a taxi or arranged a lift home. The lawns around the house and the parking area were soft. Dozens of sets of footprints were photographed and measured, but I don't know if they'll be of any use. I'm in the middle of logging them into the system now."

"Keep at it... and from the photos and videos of the night, has everyone at the reception been identified as being either a wedding guest or an employee of the company organising the event?"

"Yes sir," Harry answered. "And they've all been run through the police national computer. Nothing of any relevant interest has been flagged up."

*

The snow had sunk a little during the day but as Beetle turned his car onto the track leading to his home enough white slush remained for him to see that no one had used the track since he'd left. That wasn't enough, however, to prevent the familiar wave of apprehension.

Ryan Wheeler's murder had been nothing to do with him – other than the paired facts that it had happened on his property and that a gun in his possession had been used for the killing. And it was unfortunate that most of Ryan's cold corpse was still cluttering up his log shed, he'd been just too preoccupied to finish the dissection, and that Ripper was now lying beside it. But it was Naomi who was his more immediate problem. The wave of apprehension intensified as he pictured shooting her in cold blood, and as usual, the knot in his gut continued to tighten until he managed to visualise something else.

Tonight, the image springing into his mind was that of Ripper, his hand outstretched in greeting and his face beaming, only minutes before his brains split wide open.

He blinked that picture away and instead focused on the depressing condition of the property opening up in the full glare of his headlights. His mother really had let the old place go.

The guttering was sagging and the paintwork was peeling. The garden resembled a graveyard for old flowerpots, terracotta and plastic and in every shape imaginable, and tonight covered in a glistening, ghostly shroud.

He needed more of Stevie's money if he was to fix up the old place this summer. It would prevent his sister complaining about the neglect and poking her nose into his affairs – not that her coming here was very likely, but it was still something he'd rather avoid.

As far as he knew, Sophie hadn't been near the place in over a year. Their mother's death hadn't brought them closer. They met up very occasionally, in a café in Matlock, during his lunch break, and they spoke on the phone about once a month. She didn't enquire about his life and he didn't ask about hers. She'd always been the one to initiate the contact and he sometimes wondered if she was checking that he hadn't died in his sleep, pinned to his bed by one of his knives. In that case, he'd no doubt that a *For Sale* board would be hammered into place at the end of the lane before the lid of his coffin was screwed down.

He switched off the engine, gathered up the leather roll from the passenger seat and pressed the bundle of knives against his chest.

With Angus fed and walked, and the customary meat pie settling in his own stomach, he felt a whole lot better. If Ripper's death had served any purpose, it had been to alert him to just how precarious life actually was. No one knew of Ripper's visit to his cottage, so he was in the clear as far as Stevie was concerned, and although he felt sorry for the lad he also felt gratitude towards him for opening his eyes to the way life needed to be lived – in the moment.

He had a new pack of freezer bags, waiting to be filled, and he had plans for the disposal of Ripper's car.

All was good.

He drained his glass of malt whisky for the third time, paying no attention to the burning sensation in his throat, filled a mug with water, pulled four slices of bread and a lump of cheese onto the plate he'd used earlier and then reached for his coat. If luck was with him he'd find a body, but if not then he'd take that as a sign to do as Stevie suggested and have some fun with the woman, and when he did eventually kill her, it would surely cement his place in Stevie's team. He'd been handed the chance of a lifetime on a plate and he wasn't going to waste any more time in overthinking things and worrying.

Chapter 17

The incubation period for chicken pox, for symptoms to begin appearing, was ten to twenty-one days, Forbes had read on the internet. His sore throat had developed into a minor cold, which was improving already, but it would be a fortnight before he could be certain of not being infected with the typically childhood illness. To his relief, no one in the station had seemed unduly concerned about the virus.

Alison had been tetchy this morning. She'd hardly spoken and when she had it had been with a scowl etched across her face. He hadn't dared ask whether his uninvited presence was the cause or if it was something else entirely. If she was in the same frame of mind tonight he'd have to ask, but until then he must put her out of his mind.

He pulled into his parking spot and murmured a short prayer that today they would find Ryan and Naomi alive.

The wet snow that had fallen overnight was already sinking rapidly enough to hope that they might be able to begin searching Stanton Moor for the spot marked on the map. He had a bad feeling about it.

He walked through the reception area just as officers were responding to a call. Uniformed officers were pulling on their top coats and heading out towards the station's car park. "What's going on?"

"Sir, an accident involving several vehicles is blocking the main Ashbourne to Buxton road. All available officers have been requested to attend."

He continued on, up the stairs to the first-floor incident room.

"Before we head out to Stanton Moor this morning," Forbes addressed his team, "I want you all to keep in mind that although the first letter to Godfrey Jones contained the blood and fingerprints of Paul Biers, the second letter might be a hoax. Keep your eyes peeled for anyone watching from a distance. We're bound to attract interest from anyone already in the area but I want the names and addresses of all those who stop to take a good look. James, you're in charge but I'll drive out to the site as soon as I can." James Haig was a very capable crime scene manager. "I'll notify the CSI that they may be needed."

The moor was a public, very exposed site, so why would anyone want to risk lugging a body up there? If it hadn't been for the damning evidence in the first letter he wouldn't be taking the second letter so seriously and he wouldn't be using up so many valuable man-hours.

Alison's mood was still playing on his mind as he sat down at his desk and he was feeling distracted. Calling her on her mobile might help.

Her phone went straight to voicemail and that was unusual. She should have been in the mortuary by now and there was normally a decent signal both inside and outside the old brick-built building.

Martin Jones's mobile number was the next he tried. That was answered after the second ring. "Martin, you need to know we're acting on information contained in that second letter today. We have officers on their way to the moor but I must insist that you and your father stay well away. I assume there've been no more?"

"No sir. Will you let us know as soon as you find anything?"

"I will, you have my word. How is your father this morning?"

"Not too bad, he's eating better now and drinking less, but he still isn't sleeping well. I heard him wandering around the house in the early hours. I think the idea that we might be about to discover what happened to Gary and Paul is energising him... either that or striking terror into him."

The unspoken problem lay right there, on both men's lips – the fact that Martin remained unconvinced of his father's innocence in the deaths.

Alison's mobile went to voicemail again. Perhaps she'd been called out to an area with poor mobile reception – there were plenty of those in the Peak District. The police were automatically called out to attend all sudden deaths, but occasionally the second opinion and expertise of a forensic pathologist was requested to confirm either that the death was from natural causes, or that the body was in fact at the centre of a crime scene.

Her colleagues would know where she was.

A porter answered his next call. "No inspector, I'm sorry but she hasn't shown up for work yet. Several folks have been asking after her. Can I give her a message when she does show up?"

"Thank you; just ask her to call me." He was ending the call as his feet touched the first two steps of the stairs. "Dawn," he called over to the first uniformed officer he saw. "The accident on the A515 that everyone's rushed out to… can you find out the makes and models of the vehicles involved for me?"

Alison travelled that road on her way in to work.

"Give me a minute, sir. I think one is a taxi but Dave should be there by now. I'll try his radio."

He should have followed Dawn into the radio room. Instead he stood, trying to breathe steadily while clenching and unclenching his fists. Alison used her trusty, almost forty year old green Toyota Hi-Lux whenever snow or ice lay on the road. "Please God don't let a Hi-Lux be one of those involved," he murmured.

What little composure he'd managed to hold onto slipped away as the constable reappeared. "Well…?" His voice cracked.

"A private taxi which Dave thinks is a Volvo, a tractor with a trailer, and a motorbike and two packed minibuses are all that are involved. It sounds a nasty one, with the road possibly closed for the next hour at least. An air ambulance is on its way there now – ETA, two minutes. Was there anything else, sir?"

"Have there been any other RTAs called in?"

"No sir, given the conditions, the roads have been remarkably quiet this morning."

"Thank you." The news that Alison hadn't been involved in that accident didn't loosen the knot in his stomach. If someone really was setting out to terrorise everyone working at this station, then he was doing a damn good job. Could Alison have been abducted as a means of getting at him? If so, the sooner a search was organised the better their chances would be of finding her.

Suddenly he was at the top of the stairs and re-entering the incident room, with no memory of how he'd arrived there. "Emily, could you try to locate the general area of Alison's mobile phone right now?"

"Yes sir; I'll contact her network. Is there something wrong?"

"I hope not." He couldn't voice his fears prematurely. He'd feel such a fool, and so would Alison when she found out, if she'd simply stopped to change a wheel or gone for some shopping because she knew there wasn't a body waiting for her attentions in the mortuary this morning. But she'd been so distant last night, and this morning – was she being threatened by someone and was she too embarrassed to discuss it with him? Had she known she was in danger when she left the flat this morning and had someone carried out his threat?

His phone rang and he snatched it from his pocket. The name of his crime scene manager filled the screen. "Thought you'd like to know straight away, Michael... we've found sprays of artificial blue flowers exactly where the map indicated we would. We're about to begin excavations on the site but it shouldn't be difficult. It's obvious the ground was disturbed not too long ago – in the last week or so maybe. I'll let you know as soon as we find anything other than soil and animal droppings."

*

Martin sipped at his tea. His brain had suffered a jumble of emotions since learning about the start of the excavations, high up on the moor, close to where he'd trudged behind his father. One of the strongest he'd felt, as the news had been sinking in, had been a pull towards the past – a yearning for some sort of a connection to his missing brother. The feeling had brought on a physical pain in his chest. The family had accepted that Gary had been murdered, they'd had no choice given the blood and brain matter found on the headrests and seats, and if the answers they craved were to come from a grave it would still be preferable to never knowing how or why he'd died. Deep down he didn't really believe his father could have harmed Gary, but he'd never been able to completely shake off the idea that he might have known who had.

At times such as these he found it difficult to be in the same room as his father, but he wanted to test a theory. For an hour the two of them sat at the kitchen table, looking over old cases, on the laptop and on the papers Martin had brought home. He hadn't expected any flashes of inspiration, but he'd been watching the old man's body language when certain names appeared in front of them both.

He saw nothing telling – nothing he hadn't expected.

By the end of the hour, the atmosphere in the kitchen was unbearably stifling. He'd had enough. The permanent ache in his chest from missing his wife and son merged with the sharper pain of missing his younger brother. He had to get out of his father's house, just for a while. "I'm going out now, Dad. A shop in Chesterfield has some parts I need for my computer. Keep the doors and windows locked and don't hesitate to call if you need me." He reached for his hat, coat, phone and car keys and walked from the room without a backward glance.

The tarmac was clear of snow over the moors from Matlock to Chesterfield as Martin drove towards the residential outskirts of the town. He'd told his father the truth about the direction he was taking, but the rest had been a lie. The printouts he'd made in the station had mainly been about one family, and one member of that family in particular, Mr Steven Hall, also known as, Big Stevie.

If, as DCI Forbes had suggested, someone did have a real problem with his family, then he could easily have been the one murdered almost a year ago, or more recently, he and his wife might have been the ones to disappear into the night without trace. It was a sobering thought, and one that wouldn't rest.

Of all of the officers in Leaburn station, and to his surprise, DC Ryan Wheeler had befriended him. It was because of that friendship that he was on the road with one name rattling around in his head now.

Ryan had arrived at Leaburn five months ago, whereupon DC Robert Bell had made sure that everyone in the station became aware that the newest team member was a distant cousin of his. Not everyone in the building was as impressed with Robert's long list of family members in the legal profession as Robert would have liked. For several days, and to the amusement of many in the station, Robert had insisted on explaining to Ryan how everything in the station was done, and eventually Ryan had had enough. He'd politely, but firmly, told Robert to *'stay out of my face'*. Martin saw and heard the altercation and winked at Ryan, and their friendship had begun.

Tarmac rolled out ahead of him on the straight Roman road and Martin relived a conversation he'd had with Ryan just two weeks before his disappearance...

It was Saturday night and the team was in the White Lion having an early drink to celebrate the birth of the son of one of the uniformed officers. Martin sipped at his drink, a scotch and water, while Ryan downed his half-pint of real ale in one before leaning in on the bar towards Martin. He spoke quietly. "Man, I was ready for that. Listen, I have to ask you this, and I know the official line, but do you think it's possible that your brother Gary was attempting to break into the pharmaceutical dealing scene?"

"Drugs...?" Martin rolled his eyes. "Witnesses from the college came forward to say that he wasn't, but I had my doubts. When we were young, Dad never gave us any money, always expecting us to stand on our own two feet, and while I was happy to go without certain things Gary was always on the lookout for easy money. I have no real reason to think that he wasn't mixed up in something of that nature. Why do you ask?"

"I have contacts on the street, back in Preston, and in Manchester, and your father's name came up recently. Have you ever heard of a criminal gang led by the Hall family? They've been a force in both cities for over half a century."

"I can't say that I have, but no doubt Dad will have come across them."

"About ten years ago one branch of the family moved into Preston, where I was living and working. I helped in the investigations into of some of their criminal activities but any charges we made rarely stuck."

"Why are you telling me this?"

Ryan hesitated for a moment. "There were rumours at the time of at least one highly-placed police officer being in the employ of the Halls. Unfortunately, I don't have a name."

"I'm listening..."

Smiling, Ryan said jovially, "Don't get me wrong – I wasn't suggesting that your father was a wrong 'un. I just wondered if you'd ever heard of the Halls."

"I don't get the connection between them and Gary?"

"There may not be one, but there were also rumours on the street of some sort of a connection between the Hall family and yours. They're probably just that, totally unfounded rumours, because I haven't yet been able to find out what that connection might be."

"But...?"

"But a great lump of a man called Stevie Hall is the current leader of the Preston based side of the family, and twice last week I saw him driving through Leaburn."

"Why didn't you report it?"

"He may only have been on his way to visit his mother. There are some respectable properties in the Walton area of Chesterfield, and I know that Stevie Hall's old mum has recently moved into a very nice, decent-sized, detached one after being dropped by her husband of thirty years for a younger model. Before I left Preston, there were rumours of Stevie having bought that property, and regularly visiting her, while at the same time muscling his way into the drug scene in Chesterfield. He has a reputation of trampling over, and disposing of, anyone who gets in his way. Do you understand where I'm going with this?"

"You're suggesting that Gary somehow got caught up in that world?"

"You said yourself he'd enjoyed making easy money."

The sensible course of action would have been to relay that conversation straight to DCI Forbes, but Ryan had given him nothing more concrete than rumours. Instead, he'd conducted his own research into the home addresses and businesses of Hall family. They were largely cash-based, clubs and taxi businesses, and he suspected he'd only found those that the Halls wanted to be found.

The widely accepted criminal code was that you never ratted on your own family, but as police officers, they were supposed to be above all that. A deeply rooted sense of loyalty was preventing him from doing the right thing. His father could be one mean bastard at times, but the bottom line was that he was still his father, and after the trauma of losing Gary, if he was wrong and his dad wasn't involved in any of the missing persons' cases, the fact that his surviving son had turned on him would destroy him.

Being a detective meant finding evidence. It was what he'd been trained to do. He couldn't confront Mrs Hall – she was hardly likely to offer up her own son, but he could hang around the area she lived in, just for a short while, in the hope that fate might present him with something worth following up.

He found the street easily enough. "Well, well, Mrs Hall," he murmured while slowly driving past the impressive-looking property with the large front garden dotted with low-level shrubs all tastefully draped with seasonal decorations. "I wonder whether any of your middle-class neighbours realise they're sharing their respectable road with the matriarch of one of the largest gang of criminals in the Midlands?"

Two properties along, a neighbourhood watch poster was pinned to a garden fence and on the opposite side of the road another was displayed in the window of a house. He smiled at the irony of them, but it did mean that parking up close to her property was out of the question. Mrs Hall had landed herself a nice house in a street full of conveniently nosey neighbours.

If her son was in any way involved in his brother's disappearance then the residents of this respectable street were in for one hell of a shock. He'd make sure of it.

He turned his car into the next side street and parked beside a manicured beech hedge. Its golden leaves gave him some degree of privacy. The branches of the other trees and bushes were swaying in the wind and even the garden birds were staying low to the ground. His woollen hat and scarf, together with the collar of his thick coat, would hide his face without arousing suspicion.

He strolled back past the house he'd come to see, making a mental note of every car parked in the area and every passing vehicle, not that there were many to try to memorise. A hundred metres past the property he'd come to see he made a show of searching through his pockets and muttering to himself, as if he'd forgotten something, then he turned and retraced his steps back to the car.

He slung his hat and scarf down onto the passenger seat. He could feel the disappointment written across his face. The woman couldn't have chosen a better property if what she'd wanted was a view of the road in both directions. Every house around hers was set well back from the road and not one of them had a tree or even a decent-sized hedge or fence around their well-tended lawns and tarmacked driveways, and they no doubt all had surveillance cameras fitted to the buildings.

He picked up his phone and took a few photos, then turned his car round and headed back to his father's home.

*

Forbes picked up his phone and when he saw where the incoming call was from, wasn't sure he could trust his own voice. He pressed the accept icon and waited.

"DCI Forbes...?"

"Yes..."

"Oh hello, this is Darren Coates from the Chesterfield Royal Hospital Mortuary." The mortuary had always provided a service to both the hospital and the local Coroner. It also acted as the public mortuary for North East Derbyshire. It was where Alison had been expected to be at nine o'clock this morning, and it was now almost eleven. "I have a note here in front of me to give you a call."

"Alison...?"

"Alison... ah yes, I see the connection now."

"Is she...?"

"Oh she's fine. She's in an area with poor mobile reception, apparently, but a few minutes ago she managed to get through to us. She wanted you to know that she'd witnessed a bad accident on the Ashbourne road and that she'd stayed to assist. That's all I know, I'm sorry."

He'd barely got his breath back from the brief conversation when his phone pinged again. James Haig's name flashed across the screen.

"Michael, you might want to get your winter woollies on and come up onto the moor to take a look at what we've found." James sounded grim.

"Tell me the worst."

"Three sprigs of flowers, all about two metres apart, meant that we excavated three separate sites. We didn't have to go very far down. The ground here doesn't lend itself to digging, so our chummy only managed to dig shallow graves. It didn't take us long to find what appear to be human body parts. We're leaving them in situ for now."

"Any idea of how long they've been there...?"

"Not too long – a week or two, maybe. We haven't found enough to make up a whole body and the cuts appear to have been cleanly made. Because the blood on that letter had been frozen, I'd suggest that someone's been happily preserving dissected bodies. It's my guess that we've found parts of either Gary Jones or Paul Biers. Anyway, I've updated the CSI team and they're on their way."

Alison was safe and they had finally had a break in a double murder case. Things happened in threes, his father often said – if only the third happening could be the finding of Ryan and Naomi... "I'm on my way."

Chapter 18

Beetle's skittering thoughts had already earned him a reprimand from his boss, but he wasn't worried – qualified butchers were hard to come by these days. Young people fresh from school or college weren't interested in learning a real trade, not unless it enabled them to sit at a desk doing nothing more physically demanding than looking at a screen and pressing buttons. He was as good as irreplaceable. But although he'd been happy enough until now working in the shop, Ripper's untimely death had made him realise how much of his life had been stuck in a rut. A new life beckoned, and for however long it lasted, he intended to embrace it.

The shop was always busy on Saturday morning and normally time flew by – but not today. Today, time was his enemy. He was making a name for himself in another world and growing out of this one.

He looked up from his knives and saw three of his regular, least-favourite customers. He ought to be smiling naturally at them, as he usually would, but today they looked and sounded like a group of harpies, cackling away with their heads together, taunting him with their wild guesses as to what the police activity on the neighbouring moor was all about. He pictured them wearing floor-length, hooded, black capes.

He wished he was back at home, listening to the facts of the news properly while surrounded by the peace and tranquillity of the frozen moor, but most of all he wished he'd woken in time to check on Naomi properly this morning. He'd thrown her a sandwich and a bottle of water but not checked her bindings. What had happened with Ripper had also shown him just how quickly and unexpectedly events could change everything in his life. Twice already this morning his blood-stained hands had slithered along and then off the handle of the knife he was using, ending in both raw meat and one of his precious blades landing at his feet.

He wiped down the counter top and forced a smile, hoping his nerves wouldn't leave his face looking like a demented clown. He couldn't continue like this. He had better things to do than stand at a counter being force-fed gossip. "Good... good morning ladies," he croaked. His morning was deteriorating rapidly and he was in real danger of giving himself away.

The harpies' shopping lists were still of secondary importance. They alternately stuttered and stammered their orders between wild guesses and half-truths of what the police were up to, and all while his heart hammered in his ears and his cheeks blazed like the centre of a bonfire on November the Fifth.

They barely made eye contact with him while they handed over their money and accepted their change, then they wobbled out through the doorway, with their shopping bags swinging and their heads still only inches apart. He pictured an articulated lorry barrelling along the road out of control, mounting the pavement and crushing them into silence.

He really hoped his powerful imagination was something he would never lose.

Maybe he could even use it as an asset – use it to his advantage.

The fastest way to regain control of his situation would be to kill the woman in his garage. It would be one less thing to worry about. The dead couldn't escape, or shout for help – he'd been a fool to keep her alive for so long.

Any fool could turn killer. All he had to do was desensitise his naturally soft nature. If he could picture himself carrying out the act, visualisation he'd heard it called somewhere, it might just work. He'd give it a try. The next person to walk through the shop doorway would be his first guinea pig.

He rearranged the pies and wiped the counter top again. Shadows passed by the window, but as though they could read what was in his mind, none materialised inside the shop.

More sausages were needed from the storeroom; they always sold well on a Saturday. He turned to fetch them but some deep instinct, some primal anticipation, stopped him dead.

He sensed her before he heard her. She… and it was a she, he felt certain… was padding up to the counter. His breath caught in his throat.

When he turned, he saw a healthy-looking young woman, with a dazzling smile, dressed in running clothes and with a black sweat-band across her glowing forehead.

His chest was in turmoil.

He looked her body up and down. Her feet were in damp-looking running shoes, and her hair was a mass of strawberry-blonde curls. Her chest was heaving, gulping in air. The sausages could wait.

When his eyes settled on her face, she was looking directly at him. She was perfect – the same height and slight build as Naomi and with the same startled *rabbit in the headlights,* expression.

…and her timing was impeccable.

He looked past her. No one else was hovering around the shop window. No one was about to come through the open doorway to spoil his first attempt at the visualisation technique which might or might not work.

"Take your time, love." He smiled at her and hoped he sounded sufficiently calming. "There's no rush. I'll just tidy up this counter while you catch your breath." He wanted her to stand for a minute or two longer without speaking while he allowed his imagination free reign.

And what an imagination he had when he let it loose…

He locked the shop door, dragged her by her strawberry-blonde curls behind the counter and into the cold store and within seconds had her trapped in the unrelenting grip of the muslin gag and the ropes he'd left ready. Her eyes no longer smiled at him. They pleaded with him, just as Naomi's eyes had when he'd first taken food to her, and when he'd aimed the gun at her. They no longer bothered him. To hell with his out-dated morals. He'd been reborn and he fully intended to take her and enjoy every second of the experience. With his boning knife, he cut off every shred of her clothing. Then he ran his hands over every inch of her body until he could stand the pressure no longer and had to enter her. She was fully conscious, and there was nothing she could do to stop him.

When he was ready, he pulled out of her and without speaking walked to where the rest of his knives were waiting. Beside them sat his favourite pistol. He walked back to her, pulled back the slide, took aim at the unruly mass of curls, and fired.

The once-smiling eyes were gone in a split second, her head slumped forward and the bouncing, shining curls were a tangled mass of sticky, red threads. He picked his boning knife back up, easily cut through the ropes that held her, and then lifted her onto a meat hook, ready to slice up some time later.

There… he'd done it… he'd actually killed a female, and more importantly – he'd enjoyed doing it…

He looked up and the young woman's eyes were still smiling at him, her mass of curls were still a glistening, strawberry-blonde and her hand was holding money out towards him.

"I ran further than intended and now I need something to give me the energy to get home," she was saying. "Do you think I could have one of those delicious-looking salad cobs?"

He glanced at the clock. In his fantasy world he'd taken his time with her, he'd savoured every second. He felt an almost painful pressure against the zip of his trousers. In reality only two minutes had passed. No one else had entered the shop, and although his pistol was still at home, his precious knives were ready and waiting to work. His boss never came in before cashing-up time on a Saturday and ponytail-man never worked weekends...

What if he were to take his fantasy one stage further...?

It would take no more than five seconds to pick up his largest knife and then move to lock the door... maybe another ten seconds to force her into the rear of the shop...

No... no... no... Beetle, don't go there. You're in enough trouble. You'd ruin everything. He shook the image from his head.

"Are you all right?" Blondie's smile had slipped.

Had she read his thoughts?

No... how could she? She was looking concerned, that was all. "Sorry, I was daydreaming. One salad cob coming up and I hope you enjoy it."

Fantasy time was over.

The young woman would never know how lucky she'd been on this cold, but fine Saturday morning. He certainly wasn't about to follow her out onto the street to tell her, as much as he'd like to.

He watched the sway of her body as she moved across the front of the shop, along the pavement, then he stepped over to his knives, selected one he hadn't used since the previous day, and began sharpening it.

Would one fantasy be sufficient visualisation to work for him? It might have to be. There was only an hour left until the shop shut. All that was left then was to call in at the supermarket on his way home for a bottle of bleach and some liquid courage – in case his nerves failed him at the crucial moment, and he'd be ready.

*

Michael Forbes reached down into his desk drawer for some chocolate. It was his treat to himself. He'd never smoked and only drank the occasional pint of real ale, and he hadn't had one of those in over a week. The wine Alison kept in her fridge didn't appeal. She'd been her normal cheery self after her customary Friday night get-together in a coffee shop in town with her friends and her improved mood had continued into this morning. He hadn't enquired about what had upset her and hadn't dared tell her how close he'd come to making a fool of himself by turning her into a missing person. She'd have found it hilarious, and would no doubt have teased him about it for a long, long time. They made a good team. He felt whole when he was with her, and it wasn't just the sex, amazing though that had always been, but they could talk for hours and simply enjoy each other's company, and they didn't have to be in a large house to do any of those things. He was enjoying being in the cramped flat far more than he'd expected.

The hit-and-run investigation was back with the officers downstairs. It had been nothing to with the Jones family after all.

He'd recently learned that the case against an elderly man, who'd claimed self-defence last summer in the killing of one particularly nasty character, had officially been dismissed. He hadn't believed the self-defence story for one second, but he was pleased for the old guy and his dependant mother. As far as he was concerned, the courts had acted correctly.

The moor remained closed to the public while a more extensive search was carried out, the body parts having being taken to the morgue late last night.

He was scanning through the latest in the case notes of Ryan and Naomi when Alison's number lit up the screen on his phone.

"OK, Michael. I've had a busy morning. Are you ready for this?" She was getting straight to the point and sounded serious.

"I'm listening."

"The majority of the body parts are from one person. A DNA match is needed to confirm the identity but the blood group suggests that they are from Paul Biers. They've been sliced up neatly, with a small-toothed hacksaw or a mechanical saw, I'd suggest. In front of me now I've got two complete legs and feet, about half a torso, and part of a right arm."

"No head or hands...?"

"No hands... no face... no fingers... and..."

"And...?"

"And... this needs to be confirmed by the labs of course, but four slices of the flesh are not of human origin."

"Come again...?"

"We think they're slices of pork."

He almost laughed into the phone. "You're not serious."

"Deadly – if you'll excuse the mortuary joke. Everyone who's looked at them so far has agreed that they appear to be slices cut from a leg of pork."

"No apple sauce...?" He shouldn't be joking but he couldn't help himself.

"Are you feeling hungry?" She continued with the humour. It was what people in their respective professions often did to help cope with the grim realities.

"Fish for tea tonight, I think. It's my turn to call at the chippy."

"I'll hold you to that. I'm stripping the flesh from the sections of bones with the most definitive saw marks, and slices of those bones will be parcelled off to forensic specialists in London who can examine the saw marks in more detail for patterns."

"There must be thousands of saws in this area."

"Yes, but from the way this one's been used we may gain relevant information. Usually when a person is sawing through bone, they are also sawing through flesh. This causes the blade to go through at differing angles, because the flesh is moving. And of course it depends on whether or not it's being held down. Body parts aren't things that can easily be held in place in a vice. Usually the sawing takes place on a table, on the floor, or in a bath, and it isn't easy to cut smoothly and evenly in those situations."

"Were the pieces frozen when cut?"

"We're fairly sure the body was dissected first, and then the pieces individually wrapped in plastic before being frozen."

"Nice..."

"Paint and other materials often snag in the saw marks, also many blades can be identified by the colour, or the make, of the paint which can be found in the form of either tiny flakes or smears. Even more interesting is the fact that both new and well-worn tools can be confirmed as being the implement used because of microscopic imperfections found on the surface of the bone. The bottom line is, every blade is different, and every blade is theoretically identifiable."

"If we can find it...?"

"You have my contribution to the enquiry. The rest is down to you and your team, so I'll see you later, and don't forget to call at the chippy for our tea."

He switched off his phone, walked to the incident room and then felt a wave of revulsion as he relayed the news. He was hardly surprised at the shudders and raised eyebrows from his team as the implications of it began to sink in.

"Pork..." Adam was the first to speak. "Someone had to have been in an odd mental state to consider storing human body parts alongside edible food."

"It's yet to be confirmed..."

"Even so, sir," Jade Sharpe had found her voice, "someone's had Paul, and presumably also Gary, chopped up and stored in a freezer for almost a year. What do you think's made him take them out now and then let us know where they can be found?"

"Guilty conscience, maybe," DC Harry Green offered, "or maybe he thought they'd passed their used-by dates. How long is meat supposed to be frozen for before it spoils – does anyone know?"

"... not funny..." Jade snapped.

"Jade does have a valid point. Why now and why involve Godfrey Jones? I think we need to dig more deeply into the work life and personal life of Godfrey, so let's get onto it."

There were three more still to be found, two of them hopefully alive, and now an unidentified pig had been thrown into the mix?

They had finally found one missing person, or at least parts of him, and it was slow and very strange progress, but it was progress none the less.

*

The winter sun cast a feeble glow on Jane Ross and the two children as they made the most of their Saturday morning out. Weekends off had been cancelled for all officers at Leaburn station, and as a result Adam hadn't accompanied them to the Santa's grotto in Chesterfield as previously planned. It did however, mean that she could leave the two youngsters in the car while she popped into the supermarket in Matlock on her way home, for an extra bottle or two of wine.

Feeling slightly guilty, she waited in line at the checkout.

"Excuse me, but I do believe I recognise you," the little man standing behind her in the queue was leaning to one side, trying to get a better look at her face.

She turned and stared back at him. Nothing clicked, "...I don't think so."

Oblivious to her discomfort, or just being plain rude, he leaned closer, forcing her to take a step back and bumping her into the woman ahead of her in the queue.

"Yes, I do," he continued as if she hadn't spoken, or wasn't glaring at him. "You're the lady who married that policeman in Leaburn last summer, aren't you?"

"I'm sorry, but I don't remember you." In a sudden wave of panic, she tried to picture the day. Perhaps she was being unnecessarily rude to a friend or a distant relative of Adam's.

"No you won't. We've never actually met. I can recognise most of the officers at that station. I have an excellent memory for faces."

"You're in the force?"

"No, no, it's nothing like that; I like to watch. I follow all the local news."

"I'm sorry...?"

"I people watch. You must have heard of that."

"You don't know anything about me."

"I'm right though, aren't I? You did marry that police officer, didn't you? You make a lovely couple, and you have two beautiful children between you. Do you think you might have a child together?"

"Who are you?" Her instinct was to tell him to *go to hell*, but her police training was kicking in. She'd already noted the brand of whisky and the make of the dog meat he'd placed on the conveyer belt and she offered him the hint of a smile, hoping to draw out more information. "I see you have a dog – do you live in Matlock?"

"I'm a nobody… I blend into the background wherever I go." He looked past her. "I believe the cashier's waiting for you to pay for those bottles."

She felt her face burn as she turned to the cashier.

Ignoring the cold, she stepped into the shadows alongside the stone wall of the modern building and hugged her two bottles of cheap wine into her coat. The weirdo was smartly dressed and purchasing a quality brand of dog meat and a one litre bottle of expensive malt whisky. She felt there ought to be some subliminal message in the comparison. There'd been no whiff of alcohol on his breath – if anything the odour coming off him had reminded her of old-fashioned, pine disinfectant.

She quietly cursed the fact that she'd left her phone in the car. The creep's face was fixed in her memory but she wanted to record as many other details about him as she could.

The black winter coat she'd never really liked after arriving back home with it, was now working in her favour. From her vantage point she watched him in the shop's foyer, standing for a moment and looking around.

When he hurried, his posture changed. He had the slightest of gaits. Her own feet were freezing but she stayed as still as she could in the shadows.

A car pulled out of the disabled parking area at precisely the wrong moment. The weirdo's registration plate was obscured but she'd seen enough to know that he drove an old car, possibly a Vauxhall, and that it was grey. The sky was clouding over, the world had grown monochrome beyond the lights of the shop, and the little car vanished into it.

*

Beetle entered his home in a calmer frame of mind than when he'd left it. For years, he'd portrayed the friendly face of the local butcher in the local shop. Who was ever going to suspect him of anything so vile as drug running, kidnapping and murder? He smiled at the fact that he could so easily shake off the persona of master criminal and turn himself back into a regular person.

His experiment with visualisation had had an unexpected side effect, and during the short journey home, he'd decided he might as well keep the young woman alive for the remainder of the weekend and do as Stevie suggested – enjoy having her in his garage to use whenever he felt the urge. Thanks to the blonde jogger who'd trotted into the shop at exactly the right moment he could now visualise using and then killing the woman whenever the mood took him. The scenes were almost on a loop in his brain. He was desensitised all right, if that was the right term, he was desensitised to the point where he was actually looking forward to holding Naomi's gaze as he squeezed the trigger and ended her suffering. By Sunday night he'd probably have tired of her anyway and be more than ready to carry out the final moments of his fantasy. He'd been worrying over nothing.

He was looking forward, in a way that he'd never before thought possible, to the sexually uninhibited Saturday evening that lay ahead of him. And tomorrow could be one long, glorious repeat of tonight, if he was up to it. He might even sleep beside her, but that was a decision he'd save for later, after he'd fed and walked Angus, and hung up his knives.

If boredom set in on Sunday he'd throw caution to the wind and compose the third letter. The first two had reached their target and, despite the underlying risk of awakening the real killer, he was finding the idea of finally making contact with Godfrey Jones to be quite addictive.

According to the news, they'd been Paul's remains he'd buried up on the moor. He'd never known which body was which, although he'd kept them separate, and it pleased him to finally be able to put names to them. They'd been killed together and the message to Godfrey remained the same – REMEMBER ME?

He'd done his best not to leave anything of himself on Paul's remains, or on the letters, but even if he had, he'd never been in any trouble with the police. His DNA wasn't on any databases anywhere waiting to be matched up to the crimes, and Godfrey was highly unlikely to say that he might know who was sending the letters – it was more than his pension was worth.

He'd waited a long time to come face to face with Godfrey again; he could wait a little while longer.

Even so, he had to remain cautious. He wasn't stupid. His spotless record had to be one of the reasons why Stevie Hall had selected him to do his bidding, and he didn't care what any other reasons might be. A man who he'd heard could be capable of great violence had shown an unexpected level of faith in him, and he wasn't about to let him down.

He'd previously thought of himself as a good man, boring but undeniably good. Very occasionally, the cautious part of his brain begged that he return to his past way of life, and reminded him that, with his luck, a giant heap of shit could land on him from a great height at any time.

He placed the dish of dog meat on the floor and then unscrewed the cap of the newly purchased bottle.

*

Before leaving the station, Forbes had again reminded everyone not to go out unaccompanied and to try to ensure that their family members did the same. If, and it remained a big if, there was someone out there with some sort of a grudge against his station or his officers there was no sense in making another strike easy for them. After a short protest,

Adam had agreed to accompany him on a Saturday evening visit to the home of Godfrey Jones.

Returning from the Jones household both men were exhausted from the strain of an investigation that they felt unable to leave. Forbes broke the silence. It was time to bring up the subject of Adam's first wife. "Godfrey Jones must have had a soft spot in his heart at some time if he'd agreed to be Erin's godfather."

Adam snorted before he replied. "About thirty-five years ago he would probably have considered it good for his image and promotion prospects to have an extended family. I know he hoped Erin would eventually be a high-flyer with a six figure income. He told me that on more than one occasion. He'd been expecting to bask in her reflected glory, and marrying a lowly copper wasn't on his bucket-list for her."

"Nevertheless, you did well tonight."

"Godfrey's never going to be a fan of mine. So tell me, why did you insist I accompanied you — apart from the safety in numbers theory?"

"I wanted you there with me as a distraction. He clearly still dislikes you and I thought that maybe if he was wasting energy by focusing on you then he might let his guard down when answering my questions."

"And did your ruse work?"

"Honestly… no. He's a hard man to read."

"He admitted to knowing Stevie Hall, but we expected that. And we still have no proof Stevie is connected to the disappearance of Godfrey's son, or even if he's connected in any way other than a Morrison's car park, to Ryan and Naomi."

"Stevie's gone to ground, the Preston and Manchester stations have both commented on that, and that in itself is suspicious. I'm wondering whether someone might have tipped him off about being wanted for questioning."

"Erin didn't like him very much either…"

"What… Stevie…?"

"No… Erin disliked her godfather — Godfrey."

"You never mentioned that."

"She didn't like people knowing. I feel I'm being disloyal to her by telling you this now."

"Not too many people do like him. Do you know of her reasons?"

"No, but I can ask her parents."

Chapter 19

Beetle's most pleasurable weekend ever ended all too soon. At five a.m. on Monday, his alarm silenced with a thump, he rolled out from under the stinking duvet and headed for the shower.

He had just one task to complete before deciding whether to give Naomi the pleasure of his body once more before he went to work. He removed one white envelope from the kitchen drawer and one larger brown one. Then he removed a picture from the smaller of the two before placing it back into the drawer.

He'd spent the whole of Saturday night next to Naomi and, never having spent the entire night with a woman before, been surprised at how much warmth had come off her. That wasn't all that had come off her, and at times he'd almost gagged at the rank odour from her body and from the damp covers, but it had been worth putting up with.

On Saturday night, he'd had difficulty falling asleep, until a blinding revelation had hit him and the reason for his insomnia made him laugh out loud. He was missing his knives – he never slept without closing his eyes on at least one of them. He'd leapt up and fetched one from his bedroom. Through the tiny window, moonlight had glinted on it, hung on the rusty nail just inside the garage door, and a peaceful sleep had washed over him. It had been the kind of deep, dreamless sleep that he'd always assumed must follow intense, physical, sexual exhaustion.

They'd then shared a pleasant Sunday morning breakfast of toast and cornflakes and at midday he'd taken her a steak pie and some mushy peas that she hadn't eaten very much of. He'd wondered whether she was thinking of her figure – not that she needed to worry about that now.

He'd left the knife where it hung for the remainder of the day, amused to see her glancing at it, knowing she saw it as an aid to her escape, so near and yet so far. She'd slept for most of Sunday afternoon, and again been sound asleep when he'd crept from the garage into the cold, Monday morning air.

He'd already decided to delay killing her until later in the day. She'd suffered in relative silence in his garage for over a week. Another twelve hours was neither here nor there.

He'd enjoyed the sex, and might indulge again later in the day. The act of abusing her had served its purpose. By depersonalising her, by seeing her as an object only to be used until no longer desired, he knew he'd be able to dispose of her as if she were just another faceless carcase whenever the mood took him.

Exactly how best to word the third letter had been playing on his mind for much of the night – it was why he was still sitting in his draughty kitchen now instead of being cuddled up to a soft, warm body.

Finally he'd finished it and was happy with it. He wiped it down, sealed the envelope with tap water and was all set to place it in his car, ready to post on his way in to work. While serving Monday's customers he'd be able to fantasise about the effect it would have on Godfrey Jones.

He looked at the clock. If he didn't hang about he'd have time for another quick bunk-up and another shower.

*

Martin Jones hadn't slept well. He missed the feel of his wife's body against his more intensely with each passing hour. Just the touch of her soft skin and the smell of her Nivea face cream would quickly send him into the deep sleep his system craved. What was making it worse was that no one was forcing him to stay with his father. He felt torn. The alternative to baby-sitting a bad tempered, ungrateful old man was to move back home and then drive away from his wife and son every morning at the crack of dawn to intercept his father's post and check on him — although even that was more appealing than what he was doing now, which was pretty much nothing.

There couldn't be many other police officers who'd ever felt the kind of pressure that he was feeling. There were only two weeks left until Christmas Day and so much needed doing, at home and at work. It was 6 a.m. He kicked off the bedcovers, walked to the window and shook his head in despair before heading for the shower.

More snow was beginning to fall.

He'd speak with his father first thing this morning. Unless there was another letter, or unless his father could provide a valid reason to keep him here, then DCI Forbes or no DCI Forbes, snow or no snow, he was going to be sleeping in his own bed with his wife beside him and his son in the next room, by ten o'clock tonight.

*

Michael Forbes walked into the Leaburn Station incident room and cleared his throat. Hoarseness seemed to be the price he was paying for the ten-minute brisk walk that he'd taken, in almost white-out conditions, between Alison's flat and the station. Once road conditions improved, he'd stretch his legs again and fetch his car. "Operation Anchor is failing to make enough progress." He didn't like to hear the dissillusionment in his own voice. It was his job to keep the team motivated. He cleared his throat again but the room remained silent — the atmosphere needing no explanation. "Two people cannot just disappear from a crowded location without someone seeing something of use to us. I want everyone who attended that wedding reception to be contacted, and re-interviewed. The first rounds of statements then need to be cross-checked against the second." He paused, expecting a rumble of complaint but none came. "It's our job to uncover what happened and if we have to trawl through those statements and pictures a hundred times to find one clue then that's what we'll do."

"Yes sir," a murmur rippled round the room. One of their own had been missing for over a week now and the feeling was that Ryan and his date were longer alive.

*

Beetle opened his eyes and blinked at what seemed to be unfamiliar surroundings. He'd slept heavily – too heavily, it was still dark – or was it? The light level was strange and his feet were ice-cold.

He placed an arm over Naomi and felt her shiver, her cool, but living body lay beside him. He breathed a sigh of relief and smiled. Yes, he was in the garage... they were in the garage... together. Everything was all right.

He turned over and squinted, his eyes, as always, drawn to the source of the light. The cobwebbed window seemed to be glowing. Car headlights... a torch... no... the dull light was too constant to be either... was it moonlight? He picked up his wristwatch and swore.

Everything was very much not all right.

Continuing his success in his after-hours career depended on him behaving normally and keeping out of trouble during daylight hours. Except that, this morning, he'd slept his way into trouble. He should be on his way to work already. Daylight was struggling to shine through the little window that appeared plastered with snow, or ice, or both. It hadn't looked like that earlier, he was sure.

Lady Luck had just had to go and dump on him once more.

There was no time for a shower so he pulled on his damp, crumpled clothes.

Before stumbling out into the snow, he turned to take a last look at Naomi. Her eyes were locked onto his, and burning with hatred, but she was still. There was no time to check her bindings. The knots had held for a week and only tightened on her swollen wrists. It was a shame, but she wouldn't have to suffer the discomfort for many more hours.

His weekend of bliss was being chased away by a morning from hell. Breakfast was out of the question and Angus would have to make do with a handful of dry biscuits and a cupful of water. Already late, it was likely to take him half an hour longer than normal to get to work.

Why did these things keep happening to him?

His rollercoaster of a day continued. One minute he was happily remembering the sealed letter in the glove box of his car, and the next he was roaring with rage as he realised he'd left his best knife suspended on a rusty nail in the garage. For once, he wasn't caring about the wary looks from his boss, or the customers.

He tried to put Naomi out of his mind. Any gossip, which might have helped take his mind off his problems, was thin on the ground, as were the customers. That wasn't unusual for a Monday morning, but it was frustrating all the same.

At lunchtime, he used his twenty minutes out of the shop to post the third brown envelope. He noticed how the other pedestrians were all too busy holding onto their hats and watching where they were placing their feet to look at him. It was the first thing to go right for him all day and he offered up thanks to the snow-gods.

The shop had been closed for an hour, powdery snow was falling again and due to his late arrival, his boss was still finding cleaning jobs for him to do. He was annoyed at his boss's obvious slight on his skills as a trained butcher, and at his disregard for the problems that he knew he'd face just to get up onto Beeley Moor tonight, but as the old man had provided him with a steady job since he'd left school he could never harm him. Unlike his shadow, the weasel-faced Adrian – the creep who always looked so smug these days that when he spoke Beetle felt an almost overpowering urge to carve the sneer from his pointed face.

That wasn't going to happen today, but the thought reminded him of his best knife, still hanging on a rusty hook, and of Angus who'd only had biscuits and water. Then he pictured Naomi, who'd had nothing at all to eat or drink since yesterday.

He couldn't risk getting stranded in Matlock. He had to get back onto the moor.

He wiped the paintwork around the store room door one last time, tipped the bowl of grey water down the sink, brushed past weasel-face who was pretending to be engaged on some important phone call or other and stepped into the back office. "I'll have to leave now, boss." The words came out sounding like a challenge. It was how they were meant.

"You haven't tidied the store room."

"Adrian can do that. Road conditions are deteriorating and if I don't get back soon the dog will think I've abandoned him."

"I've told you before, Beetle, you shouldn't leave the poor thing alone all day. You ought to find him a new home."

"I intend to. I just haven't got round to it yet." Angus was too useful to him now. The dog served as an excuse to get away from work as well as an early warning if anyone was his property uninvited.

"Well make sure you're not late in tomorrow, or I'll be advertising for your replacement."

Yea... right... he wanted to reply... *as if...*

The roads weren't as bad as he'd feared. For once the council had gritted the side roads as well as the main ones and the wind was whipping waves of dry snow off the tarmac and up onto the grass verges. Thirty minutes after leaving the shop, and without once skidding on his way up the notorious Sydnope Hill, he was once again turning onto his own snow-covered lane. The wind had worked in his favour on the hill, but on his lane, it was a different story. It had blanketed everything with the white dust. His tracks from the morning had all been smothered, as would anyone else's. His tyres spun and the dry snow crunched. Ten metres from the house he stopped and sat for a minute, peering into the shadows, trying to see through the flurries and imagining what could be beyond the reach of his headlights. Fingers of cold air whistled through the gaps around the car's doors and then around his legs and he pictured Naomi – cold, hungry, desperate Naomi.

He wondered at how his life could have changed so drastically in so short a time. He could only go with the flow and let it take him where it would.

He drove the final few metres and a minute later, with his longest blade held out in front of him, he rushed through the door of his house only to be greeted by Angus.

Confident no one had been inside his home, and after opening a tin of dog meat and making a mug of instant coffee, he set his incomplete row of knives out on the kitchen table and took a loaf of bread from the cupboard.

The coffee tasted bitter and he spit it into the sink. In his haste to get home he'd forgotten to buy milk. Nothing would be right until his precious babies were back to being a full set, back to their full glory, rowed up and gleaming and in their correct order. Without bothering to reach for a coat he walked back outside, with the faithful dog at his heels.

He felt for the light switch, flicked it on, and froze.

His life really was the stuff of nightmares – of repetitive, unending, smothering, black dreams. Why, and how, for pity's sake, was this happening to him?

He'd checked the knots yesterday, hadn't he?

They'd been secure enough then. He should have checked again this morning. He should have reset the alarm. Late or not, he should have run through his checklist.

His heart hammered against his ribcage.

He'd intended killing her yesterday. So why the hell hadn't he?

He pictured her breasts and answered his own question.

He'd heard of men holding women captive for years, but he hadn't been able to keep his for a fortnight. He wasn't a complete idiot – he wasn't a full-blown head-case with a death wish – so why did everything go so spectacularly wrong for him? How many fates had conspired against him... the weather... his boss... his tiredness? It couldn't all be down to him – luck had to play a massive part in his misfortune, didn't it?

He blinked hard, but the nightmare remained.

The creased duvets looked as if they were grinning, the dark stains resembling human features staring back at him. He swallowed down burning-hot vomit and leaned against the door surround. His breathing was rapid and shallow. He had to get that under control or risk falling to the floor.

His left hand brushed against the rough, breezeblock wall – up and across, until it touched the rusty nail – the empty, rusty nail. He shook his head to clear his vision and rattle his thoughts into some sort of order. One of two things had to have happened. Either Naomi had freed herself or someone had been onto his property and found her. There was no third, more hopeful option – they were all there were.

Naomi, or whoever had freed her, could be waiting in the shadows, holding his knife, ready to strike him down, or maybe she was on her way off the moor, heading straight towards the arms of the law. If the police had already found her then the place would be crawling with people and he'd be languishing in a police cell.

Oddly, that thought felt more appealing than the alternatives that were beginning to spring into his mind – alternatives which all involved Stevie Hall.

Either way, someone was out there, in the snow.

Angus sat at his feet, looking up into his face. At least he was fed and safe. He wondered whether the animal had picked up on his terror. The only thing he dared do was lock the two of them in the garage for the night. The window was too small for anyone to climb through and with a bit of effort he could push both chest freezers in front of the door.

If only he'd brought his mobile phone outside with him, he might call someone... but no... that would be really dumb. He couldn't let Big Stevie Hall know that Naomi was missing. None of his men were likely to have taken her without calling into the shop to let him know. His sister was hundreds of miles away, and he could hardly call the police.

Two stained duvets and a dog would have to be enough to keep him warm, and what little appetite he'd had had vanished along with the woman. If he could make the garage safe they'd be all right together until morning, but he had to work quickly.

He pushed himself away from the doorframe, locked the door and staggered to the freezers.

Chapter 20

At seven a.m. Martin Jones was back in Leaburn station, in front of his DCI, explaining why he'd felt compelled to return home. "My wife and son need me. We belong together, in our own home, especially at this time of the year. And I'm sorry sir, but I've reached the point where I can no longer stay for any length of time with my father." Martin was embarrassed, and it showed.

"It was never my intention to make you stay where you felt uncomfortable." Forbes said.

"I thought I should call in and explain. I'm on my way over to see him, to make sure there hasn't been another letter, not that he's forced to tell me, but I'll keep doing that for as long as you think it's necessary. Do you still want me to take the rest of the week off?"

"You're on sick leave, so go and make the most of your time. This station won't fall apart without you."

"I'd like to add, for the record, that although I can't prove it, I feel that my father knows more about the letters than he's saying."

"This hasn't been easy for either of you. For a few hours last week we thought we might have found your brother and that's bound to have had an effect on your father."

"I know, sir, and I'm taking that into account. But I'd still like my concerns to go on record."

"As you wish, but just remember that whatever he says, he needs you in his life right now."

*

Beetle checked his watch for the sixth time in as many hours. The east-facing window was still in darkness, but the longest and coldest night of his life was ending. The police hadn't hammered his doors down, as would have happened if Naomi had escaped all by herself, so that only left the more terrifying of the two alternatives – someone had taken her. Some scumbag had come onto his property when they knew he was working, and was now having a piss-take at his expense. Someone, somewhere, was laughing at him, mocking his failed attempts to do the bidding of hard-man, Stevie Hall.

What they obviously didn't realise was that the old Beetle had now sold his soul to the dark side.

Who the hell did they think they were, messing with him like this?

He pushed the damp duvet from his legs, ignoring the whining from the dog, and struggled to his feet. The officially longest night of the year was only a week or so away, which meant that until it was light enough to see outside Beetle had the advantage over his tormentor, assuming he was still on the property.

The guns were all in his house; in his bedroom to be exact. If he'd only had one of them downstairs with him last night he might have thought to have picked it up. Armed, he could have been outside by now instead of cowering in his own garage like a whipped dog. He promised himself that, assuming the weapons were where he'd left them, he was going to take at least one of them with him everywhere, even to the toilet, from now on. Someone was going to pay for the suffering he and Angus had endured over the previous night.

Yesterday's snow meant that anyone, including himself and a dog, would be unable to move around outside without making a sound. He walked over to the window and listened. Not even the birds were awake yet.

He scanned the room, a pointless exercise because he knew exactly what it held, and that nothing in it remotely resembled a weapon of self-defence. The axes, picks and shovels were all hanging in the log shed. The freezers held the only objects that might be of use. He lifted the lid of the nearest one, peered in, and for the first time regretted having sawn the corpses into such small pieces. A frozen arm would have come in handy. He smiled at his own joke, wishing there was someone with him to share it.

With the lid of the freezer propped open he tugged off his woollen top jumper and his thinner, cotton, polo-necked one. He then quickly pulled the warmer one of the two back on and tied knots in the ends of each of the sleeves of the thinner garment. His frozen fingers made the job more difficult than it should have been. Finally, he'd manoeuvred the knots down to the ends of the sleeves, and was tying a larger and bulkier knot at the base of the garment, leaving only the neck-hole open. He held it up and looked at his work. It would have to do.

He quietly cursed the plastic wrapping sticking to his hands as he pulled the largest lumps from the freezer and stuffed them through the neck-hole of the garment and into the sleeves and the body.

The resulting, three-pronged object was surprisingly heavy. He swung it around his head and was pleased with the reach provided.

The dog had stopped whining. He was watching the food whizzing through the air.

The jumper had stretched but his knots held firm. Some of his ideas were better than others, and this could be one of his more inspired ones. Luck would determine whether it would stop a bullet but it would be adequate defence against anyone wielding a knife.

He allowed himself another smile. There had to be some sort of irony in what he'd just achieved – making the frozen remains of a man he'd been credited with killing, into a weapon with which to defend himself and Angus from the next person he intended to kill. Because he was going to kill them, whether it was Naomi or his tormentor, he was going to make them regret having messed with him.

"If we come out of this alive," he said to the dog, "then I promise you that you and I are going to start living for the day."

Angus gazed into his eyes and winked.

It is true what they say about dogs, he thought. They do understand. He winked back.

With the stuffed jumper on the floor, and the slobbering dog pushed away, he heaved the freezers just far enough to open the door and peer through the crack.

A blackbird somewhere was waking, but other than from that there were no sounds. "Wait there, Angus," he whispered. "I'll let you out in a minute." Again, the animal was going to come in useful. He was a naturally friendly dog and his nose would lead him straight to anyone lurking on the property.

*

Martin Jones was never going to beat his father to the post every morning. He wasn't even going to try. It didn't matter that the traffic in Leaburn was so slow that he'd have made better time by parking up and walking. If his father didn't trust him enough to be open and honest with him, then why should he put himself out to help him? He could see the logic of DCI Forbes's suggestion that he should spend time with his father, but he really didn't want to be in his company any longer than he had to.

He parked on the roadside, blocking his father's gateway, and saw footprints pointing to and from the front door. The post had already delivered something.

Exactly one hour after leaving it, Martin was back in his DCI's office on the first floor of Leaburn Police Station. With an evidence bag in hand, he was for once making excuses for his father. "He's so desperate for news of Gary that he's doing things he ordinarily wouldn't dream of. This morning's letter held more blue petals and another map of the moor, this time with the arrow pointing to a spot close to the village of Stanton-in the Peak, about two miles from where the body parts were recovered."

Martin looked pale and Forbes felt guilty for putting pressure on him by sending him to check on his father. Physically he was recovering well from the previous week's attack but his mental well-being was another matter. "If he'd already opened it when you arrived... can you be sure it didn't contain anything else?" he asked gently.

"As sure as I can be... Father was wearing the latex gloves I'd left for him, and he had an evidence bag ready on the table. I believe he intended to call the letter in, but that he couldn't resist opening it. He didn't look in any condition to be lying."

"He still should have known better." Forbes stated the obvious, but only out of frustration and concern for Godfrey's safety. The words were out of his mouth before he could stop them. "It could have contained an incendiary device, or something of a toxic nature. As it is he may have destroyed vital evidence."

"I told him all that, but I really don't know how much of it sunk in. When I got there he was just standing; staring at the latest map as if he recognised something, or was committing it to memory... or... I don't know. He looked strange. That's the only way I can describe it. A full minute passed before he acknowledged that I was even in the room with him. I asked, but he wouldn't tell me what he was thinking. His behaviour worries me but I'm at a loss as to what to do."

Forbes bit back his anger at Godfrey and slid on a pair of latex gloves. "None of this is your fault, Martin. As the letter has already been opened we'll photograph its contents before it goes off to forensics. Then while we wait for them to come back on it we'll see if anyone on the team has any new ideas."

Technology sometimes worked in their favour, rather than in the favour of the criminals. It was a rapidly changing playing field, in which he frequently struggled to keep up. He didn't mind admitting it.

DC Ryan Wheeler had been proving his worth on the computers.

He swallowed down a lump in his throat.

Within minutes, photos of the letter, the envelope, and the map were uploaded onto every working computer in the incident room, the letter was winging its way to the laboratory and Forbes was back where he felt most comfortable, facing his team in the incident room. He was silently praying for a flash of inspiration from one of them.

"The first envelope was posted in Chesterfield, but the second and third letters were posted in Matlock." DC Robert Bell commented. "Did road conditions prevent the sender from travelling? If so he may live in or around the town of Matlock. Stanton Moor is only about six miles from the town's centre."

"The postal area of Matlock must have dozens of post boxes," Forbes said. "But we can request the station there to check for CCTV coverage for as many as possible, then when we do have a suspect it may come in useful. I think we should assume there may be more body parts."

"Is the moor still closed to the public, sir?"

"It is, and as soon as we start sending more officers there the press will want to know why. They're already milking the story of Paul's body parts for all its worth and they're likely to assume that we've found Gary, and they may well be right. Until the roads are clear enough for us to access the moor and until the CSI team is ready, I don't want news of a second dig to be made public, and I still don't want news of any of these letters to be leaked out. Is that understood?" He turned to Martin. "I want you to go home."

"To be honest, sir, I'd like to take another crack at getting my father to tell me what the hell is going on. This morning I just wanted to get the letter off him to bring here."

"You did right. We can bring him in for questioning, using the excuse that it's for his own safety, if you'd prefer? Come to think of it, that might not be such a bad idea."

"He won't come in voluntarily, I know he won't, and we can't arrest him for anything more serious than tampering with evidence, in which case you'd have to arrest me as well. His solicitor would have him home again in no time. No thanks, sir, if you don't mind I'll have another go at him on his own ground."

"All right, but get home to your wife and son sooner rather than later, and let me know how you get on."

*

Beetle was going to be seriously late for work, but that was the least of his problems. Angus had bounded through the drifts before spending a long minute relieving his bladder. Mission accomplished, the dog was now making a beeline for the front door of the cottage, with his jumper-wielding master behind him.

No footprints other than his and the dog's had broken yesterday's blanket of drifted snow. That was one fear he could dismiss. No one had been creeping around his yard or garden since he'd landed home, and no one was likely to have been hiding out overnight in the log shed – they'd have been sleeping beside one and a bit dead bodies and been even colder than he had been in the garage. If anyone was still on the property, the odds were that they were waiting inside his house.

He felt as if his senses were grinding up through gearing in his head. The song of the lone blackbird was deafening. A plane, which was so far overhead that he could only see only pinpricks of flashing lights, thundered in his ears. The crunch of frozen snow vibrated up through his feet and legs. He could smell the ice, the sweat from his own body mixed with the smell of Naomi and the damp duvets, and the musky odour drifting from the fur and the hot breath of the dog.

His body tensed as he reached for the door handle, ready for Angus to rush in, but something caused him to glance down. What he saw sent his brain spinning even further off kilter.

He hadn't thought it possible for anything to make him feel worse than on the previous, long night, but his missing knife, partly buried in the snow, winked up at him and proved him wrong.

His heart was pounding at his ribcage again. He was in danger of passing out. "Get... a... grip... Beetle," he gasped. "Pick... up... the knife..." Using the wall for support, his knees folded and his back slid down the stonework. "My baby..."

His frozen fingers lifted it, very gently, from the snow.

His breathing steadied.

It left no reddish traces in the knife-shaped whole. He was no wiser as to whether Naomi had escaped or been taken. She could be anywhere – out on the moors, frozen to death – back in the clutches of Big Stevie and his minders, or even walking into a police station at this very moment. Each one of those scenarios was outside of his control, but if she was inside his house brandishing any of his other blades... or his guns... and alone... then that was a different matter entirely. Then he had a chance of recovering the situation.

"Only one way to find out," he flung open the door. "In you go, Angus."

The road ahead sparkled in the weak, morning sun. "No one has been in my home," he recited as he pressed his foot too firmly onto the accelerator.

Had his knife been lying beside his front door the previous night? Had he walked past it without noticing? He couldn't be sure. It was quite possible. Back then, he hadn't been looking for anything on the ground, and if it had been partially buried in the snow, he could easily have walked passed it.

He was driving too fast for the road conditions but below the speed limit. The road was unusually clear of oncoming traffic.

He glanced across at the contents of the passenger seat and smiled, but their soothing effect lasted barely a second. The sound of a siren pierced his thoughts and the sight of blue lights flashing in his rear view mirror sent his blood thundering into his chest.

"Oh crap, no, no, this can't be happening!" His stomach lurched and his hands shook.

He wanted to throw up.

For one mad moment he considered flooring the accelerator – but in his old Corsa how far was he likely to get? He was out of options. A convenient layby presented itself and he pulled off the road, stopped his car and tucked his hands under his thighs.

With only an inch of snow on the pull-in, he'd have no problem setting off again – his problem was going to be in holding his nerve.

"Just keep calm… keep calm… keep calm…." He exposed one hand just long enough to wind down the window and then tucked it back into the warmth. Flashes of a television program he'd seen recently about Peter Sutcliffe, the monster known as the Yorkshire Ripper, played through his mind. Sutcliffe had been caught as the result of a routine traffic stop, but only because of false number plates and because his behaviour alerted the officer who'd stopped him.

His false plates were well hidden in the boot and if he could keep his cool, the police would have no reason to look there.

They couldn't possibly be looking for him.

He was about to find out.

"Morning sir," The uniformed officer sounded friendly enough. "Do you know what speed you were doing back there?"

"I wasn't over the limit, was I? I didn't think I was speeding."

"There's been an accident on the hill ahead of you. I've been dispatched to close this road and I had trouble catching up with you." The officer's eyes were scanning the contents of his battered vehicle while the rest of his face wore the expression of someone looking for something objectionable at the bottom of a rubbish bin. "You were below the limit, but not by a lot. With so much snow and ice still on the road, sir, it isn't wise to drive at anything close to the speed you were doing. Where are you going in such a hurry?"

"Matlock... I'm already late for work... at the butchers... on this side of town."

"Well you're going to be even later, I'm afraid. You'll have to make a U-turn here and take a detour. If you take the next right and then turn right again at the crossroads you'll get off this hill."

"I know it. I can find it." Time was ticking away. *'Just move, officer. Get out of my way.'* He wanted to yell through the open window.

"What's that you've got on the passenger seat?" He sounded friendly, but Beetle knew it was a ploy used to make people drop their guard.

Beetle shifted in his seat but didn't answer and didn't move his hands. He watched the officer walking around the front of his car and saw his hand resting on the bonnet for support. The metal barrel of the pistol pressed into his side. This was the first morning he'd taken the gun to work. Wasn't that just typical? If he had to get out of the car, and if he was frisked the way he'd seen it done on the television, he was finished. He needed a massive dose of good luck right now.

The officer's line of sight showed him what the problem was. A gleaming metal tip was protruding from the roll of leather.

His blades were innocent... but then... Peter Sutcliffe had tried to hide his knives. Might the officer be having similar thoughts to himself?

He had to speak, and he had to sound convincing. He couldn't afford to give him a reason to search further. He took a deep breath. "Knives, officer, but they're hardly weapons... they're the tools of my trade. I take them home with me every night... in case the butcher's shop gets broken into. I'm very careful. Do you need to see them?" Now he was prattling... time to shut up, Beetle.

"I know you now," the face below the hat creased in recognition but the owner of it opened the passenger door anyway and leaned in. "I call into your shop for a meat pie at least once a week."

Another deep breath…"Yes, I work on the front counter. Our pies are some of the best around. But I'm going to get the sack if I don't get moving."

"On you go then. You must keep people like me fed, especially in this weather. Just mind how you go and remember to watch your speed." He slammed the door and stepped back into the snow.

"I will do, and thanks." He'd stayed cool and it had worked.

It took a supreme effort to hold his car at an even speed as he pulled away. His hands squeezed the steering wheel and his lungs fought to keep a balanced amount of oxygen in his bloodstream.

The emotional roller coaster of the last twelve months was showing no signs of slowing – if anything it was accelerating, and whizzing him along with it. All he needed today was to see Naomi walking into the butcher's shop and his head would explode.

His one consolation was that Godfrey Jones's head should by now be in a similar condition.

*

DCI Forbes risked a small detour on the icy roads on his way in to work to revisit Naomi's basement flat. His gut feeling was that the young woman whose life he'd only seen a snapshot of would never again occupy the comfortable, but cluttered space. As well as her laptop and tablet, she'd left hand-written notes and opened text books on almost every flat surface – books covering topics such as midwifery and paediatric nursing. Her unwashed underwear lay on the bathroom floor, her washed clothes were drying on a wooden, freestanding rail in the hall, and a pile of dry and neatly folded clothes covered an ironing board in the small, but clean kitchen.

Victims of sudden deaths left similar scenes all over the world, and in most cases, they wouldn't be how they'd want complete strangers to be forming their opinions of them.

His opinion so far of Naomi was of a clean living, law abiding and hardworking young woman.

Ryan's bedroom had been in a less tidy, but similar condition, with clothes randomly piled onto chairs, and books and magazines about computers, law, and police policy lay on the bedside table and underneath the bed.

Forbes had seen no signs of police corruption, no signs of drugs, no stashes of cash or anything else of an illegal nature – not that he'd expected to.

The couple might have had a future together, but with each passing day, it was looking less likely anyone would ever know.

He dragged his thoughts into the present and reached into his desk drawer for a square of chocolate. Was Naomi's abduction simply collateral damage in a revenge attack on a police officer, or had she been the target with Ryan attempting to protect her? Assuming they'd both been killed, what was the actual motive? Deaths without some kind of reason were the worst kind, for the detectives and for the victims' families. So what was it that his team was missing?

Ryan had almost certainly been following Stevie Hall when he'd called in on the Friday afternoon of his last shift, and over the last few days several of Naomi's friends had reported knowing she'd recently dumped a violent boyfriend. Yesterday one of them suggested the boyfriend may have originated from the Preston area.

Stevie Hall was from Preston.

While Ryan had been following Mr Hall into the Morrison's car park, had Hall in turn actually been following Naomi?

Was that too much of a co-incidence?

Could Hall have been the mystery boyfriend?

Was that the link he and his team had been missing?

It was tenuous, but feasible. Could they be looking at a crime of passion? Had Ryan and Naomi really only met recently, and by chance, as his team had been led to believe?

There hadn't been a single sighting of Stevie, and that was frustrating. He dearly wanted to make eye contact with the man.

His office door opened and DS Adam Ross walked in. "The snow's sinking nicely," he said. "Everything's in place and we're ready to move up onto the moor as soon as you give the word. I've informed the Matlock Station of our plans."

"Go as soon as you like, but before you do, just answer me a couple of questions."

"Sir...?"

"Could Naomi have been Stevie Hall's girlfriend?"

"We've been hearing he has a long-term girlfriend, of about fifteen or twenty years, and Naomi's too young to fit that bill. Besides, the woman from the checkout insists she introduced her to Ryan. She took them to be complete strangers, but it would explain why Naomi asked for someone to escort her to her car. Until now, we've assumed she felt ill, as she'd said, but she could have been afraid. I'll certainly look into the theory."

"Taking that a step further, were Ryan and Naomi merely pretending not to know each other? They were in the same supermarket at the same time, and at the same checkout."

"Ryan's shift was ending and Naomi had come straight from work. They both needed shopping and there was only one checkout free at that time. I think it could have been a co-incidence, sir."

"An unfortunate one, as it turned out."

"Yes sir."

"Let's assume we're right, and they were on a first date as Ryan's flatmate seemed to believe, how did anyone know to pick them up, thirty-six hours later, from the roadside, at the end of a wedding reception? We've checked their call logs and neither Naomi nor Ryan phoned anyone for a lift home."

"The lift was pre-arranged... or one of them had a phone we're not aware of..."

"The taxi firm Naomi used to take her to the wedding was expecting her to call them back, and no one's mentioned a missing phone. No, they walked to the roadside expecting to be picked up."

"One of them must have spoken to another guest or an employee about getting home."

"Or someone who knew that Naomi would be attending the wedding was there with Stevie Hall's blessing, and watching and waiting for their opportunity."

"It's worth taking a closer look at the photos and videos from the night, sir. You could be on to something. What else did you want to ask?"

"Truthfully now, do you consider there to be a real threat to people associated with this station, or do you think I'm overreacting when I keep reminding the team to be on their guard?"

"It never hurts to be overcautious in this job, but if Stevie Hall is behind Gary's and Paul's deaths, because of a drugs war, and also behind whatever's happened to Ryan and Naomi because of Ryan's work while he was stationed at Preston or because of jealousy, and considering that we now know the hit and run to be an unfortunate accident, then no, I don't think we need to be too worried."

"But why is Godfrey being persecuted by the kidnapping of his other son and by the sending of letters? From what we've uncovered on Stevie Hall he heads up a criminal network comprising of scores of legal and illegal businesses. I can't see him sanctioning the sending of cryptic messages which allow body parts be found in shallow graves. Someone else has to be behind that. Of course I could be wrong."

"I don't know, sir, but Hall has to turn up sooner or later. There are no warrants out on him but Interpol have him marked as a person of interest and we're to be alerted if he tries to leave the country. We'll get him. Are you staying in Alison's flat for the rest of the week?"

"Yes, and next week too, always assuming she doesn't throw me out," he smiled and hoped Adam couldn't see his words were a long way from being a joke.

"But you're feeling all right, aren't you? You're looking a bit pale this morning."

"Thanks for that. I was feeling OK until you pointed it out. As well as avoiding the chickenpox myself, I don't want to be responsible for passing it on to others."

"I shouldn't worry too much about that, sir."

Chapter 21

Martin Jones entered his father's house with a determined stride. He'd left the station as some of his colleagues were getting into their vehicles for the return visit to Stanton Moor and he'd bet a month's wages on them finding more body parts. Between grief, anger, and sheer mental exhaustion he was in no mood for his father's excuses or temper tantrums. He wanted answers and wasn't leaving until he'd got them.

The scene in the living room was as unexpected as it was distressing – his father crunched up in the corner of the sofa, sobbing noisily into a cushion.

He could have turned and walked away, but he didn't. After a moment's hesitation, he sat down and placed one arm around the bony, heaving shoulders.

For the first time in months, he felt like crying. "It's all right, Dad."

"I'm so sorry, Son, I haven't been straight with you," his father mumbled.

"I thought as much, and that's why I'm here. I'm owed some answers, don't you think? I'm suffering too."

"I've let you down – all of you."

"Whatever it is, Dad, we'll get through it. I'll make us both a cup of sweet tea and then we'll talk it through, but please, please, don't clam up on me. I deserve to know everything that's been going on." His eyes narrowed. A creased, black and white photograph had fallen from his father's hand and landed face up on the floor at his feet. He retrieved it and smoothed it out.

From the clothing worn by the smiling figures, he guessed the picture had to have been taken twenty or thirty years earlier. He didn't recognise anyone. Two young children and a woman had been photographed, standing on a bleak moor, with a large rock formation as the backdrop.

"Tip some whisky into mine and I'll explain everything. And have some yourself. You might feel the need of it after we've talked."

"Your mother wasn't the only woman I've ever loved," his father began. "I'm sorry Son, but I married your mum when you were on the way because, at the time, that was the right thing to do, but by then I'd already been incredibly stupid."

"I know things weren't always easy between you..."

"We thought we'd hidden it from you and Gary, and your baby sister. I'm sorry again for upsetting you all. People look at me and see a strong man, but underneath I'm weak. For years before you were conceived I'd been in love with a woman who was married to a bully and a crook – a small time burglar who selected the elderly as his victims, and you know how everyone in the force feels about those types of criminals. I know that's no excuse for what I did, but I did it out of love."

"It's time to get it off your chest, Dad."

"You think you know everything," he snapped, "but you've no idea of how I felt back then. I was a beat copper, doing as I was told and keeping my head down. I gathered evidence from crime scenes which I didn't hand in and I bided my time."

"For what... are you telling me you set her husband up?"

"An elderly lady had been mugged and robbed in her own home and been pronounced dead before I was sent to act as a scene guard. The scenes of crimes officers hadn't arrived and it wasn't difficult for me to plant small items bearing his fingerprints and a button from a coat he normally wore."

"He went down for murder...?"

"Worse than that," he shook his head sadly, "he was stabbed to death by another prisoner while still on remand. It seems there is honour among thieves — or at least there used to be. I'm not so sure about now."

"So... what happened?"

"My deceptions were never uncovered, and after a break of a couple of months, to make things appear innocent, I prepared to move in with this woman and her two children. They weren't mine, you understand, but I'd known them since they were babies and I couldn't have loved them more if they had been. This must be difficult for you to hear, but you asked for the full story."

"And Mum...?"

"I'd been dating your mother as a smoke screen. I was still nervous back then of my planted evidence coming to light, but it never did and as far as I know no one ever suspected me of anything dodgy."

"It's a bit more than dodgy..."

"The day I'd planned to move in with the ready-made family that I loved was the day your mother chose to announce her pregnancy. It was also the day her father punched me in the face and insisted I do the decent thing and marry her."

"But you did, and you said you loved her... and us. Are you saying weren't we enough?"

"I loved both women, and that was my trouble. Your mum was clever and intuitive. I couldn't hide my true feelings and so of course she found out. She was six months pregnant with Gary when she first threw me out. I should have fought for her then, but I didn't. I returned to my other love."

"I don't remember that. How long did you live with this other family?"

"Only a year; I'm pathetic, I know, but I missed seeing my children growing up and so I went crawling back to your mum. I begged her forgiveness. After a few months she took me back on condition that I never saw the woman again, but like I said, I was weak."

"I'm finding this hard to believe."

"Your mother was the strong one in the relationship. She threw me out a second time and filed for divorce. It was only when she began to fall ill that she allowed me back into your lives."

"Did I ever meet this other family?"

"No, never, and after I left the woman for a second time she ordered me never to contact her again. She told me she intended moving away from the area. Then after your mother passed away I was too busy raising the three of you and furthering my career to go looking for her."

"Doesn't she have a name – this other woman?"

"Julie… her married name was Julie Becket and her children were Ian and Sophie. Years later, I considered trying to trace them, but then when you joined the force I was afraid that if Julie was holding a grudge she might decide to bring my past to light. I was afraid it might impact on your career."

"Very noble of you… to consider my career…" Martin didn't try to hide his sarcasm. "Even when Gary went missing – you couldn't tell me all of this…?"

"I didn't connect the two events at that time – not for one second. Why would I, after so long? I even told myself that the spot you were found in last week, near one of Julie's favourite walks, and the location of the first set of body parts on one of our favourite picnic sites had to be coincidences. But then the second map pointed to another of our picnic sites."

What could he say, he'd had no idea. "We'll sort this out together, Dad. You might still be mistaken."

"I fear the worst. This photograph, as well as the map, arrived in the third letter. It was wrong, I know, but I kept it back. I should have told you all of this after the second letter arrived, when I began to piece things together before we went to the moor, but you must try to understand why I didn't."

"I'm trying, Dad, really I am. How old were the children when Julie finally binned you?"

"Ian was twelve and Sophie was nine."

"I could search the Police National Computer for you, now that we have names to work with."

"You don't want to take everything I've just told you to DCI Forbes?"

"Not yet Dad; not until I've had a nose around. I told you, we'll sort this together, and if I can see a way to keep your past mistakes out of the enquiry then that's the route I'll take. Michael Forbes has been a good friend to you and I know he'll not want to see you disgraced, but the longer I can keep him in the dark, the better the chances are of no one finding out." Martin rocked his body back and forth on the sofa. The movement helped him think. "The woman you loved will be too old by now to be lugging bodies about, but her two children will be in their late thirties, and it was a male who abducted me and coshed me over the head. We need to find them, all of them, and we have to know one way or another whether they're behind the letters... and everything else."

*

As Forbes considered whether or not to insist Martin Jones attend at least one counselling session, his phone rang. "More body parts, Michael, as expected, again marked by blue silk flowers, and again in three small, separate graves," James Haig, the crime scenes manager, sounded chirpy. "Do you want to come up and take a look before we begin exhuming them? The sun's melted most of the snow but the ground's still pretty hard."

"I'll be with you in an hour."

"We'll make a start then. It'll take a few hours and I'd like to get them inside before dark. Tomorrow I'll bring my dog up here and the two of us will have a nose around for any other recently disturbed areas, not that I expect to find more in this particular area. Your man has an obsession with blue, or an obsession with flowers. He'd marked these sites very conveniently for us, so maybe he's marked more."

"Good idea." He ought to make a quick check on Godfrey Jones on his way to the moor to tell him first-hand about the discovery. There was a chance Gary's remains would be in the second round of graves – unless of course James had uncovered the remainder of the pig.

On his way out, he was surprised to see Martin Jones about to climb the stairs to the CID area. "Has something else happened, Martin?"

"No sir, but is it all right if I do a bit of digging on the Police National Computer?"

"Digging seems to be the order of the day today, so help yourself. I was on my way to see your father to tell him of the discovery of a second set of remains. Do you want to be there with him?"

"He'll be all right with you. He's been expecting that news since he opened the third letter. I'll only be half an hour or so and then I'll follow."

*

For once Beetle couldn't wait to get home. The realisation that he hadn't thought to check the log shed last night or this morning, had come to him while he'd been slicing some particularly pink boiled ham. It had given him a glimmer of hope, and he'd been clinging to all afternoon.

Thank goodness he'd thought to keep young Ripper safely hidden away at the rear of that shed, under a tarpaulin and a dozen uncut logs. No one entering the shed was likely to bother looking beyond what was left of Ryan.

If Stevie or one of his henchmen had disposed of Naomi, then they'd probably have dumped her in the log shed with her boyfriend, ready for slicing up and freezing. They'd have expected him to look in there first, wouldn't they? Of course they would. And they'd have left his knife beside his front door, expecting him to see it when he arrived home. Why couldn't he have had all these thoughts last night?

The comforting idea had even softened the impact of seeing Martin Jones driving past the butcher's shop in his fancy sport's car. Martin Jones — the man who's charmed, financially-secure life had been laid out before him, the man who was living a life a million miles removed from that of a bored butcher and shop assistant, and now, *killer for hire*.

Snow was only visible under the hedgerows now, not that there were many of those up on the moor. The strips of white were what his mother used to call *'snow bones'*. His car rumbled and bumped along the metalled track to his home. Excitement and dread, in equal measures, clawed at his stomach. Either his fears over Naomi's disappearance were about to be blown out of the water, or he was in for a second night of living in what was becoming a familiar state of terror.

He ran to the log shed and yanked the door open. As quickly as his eyes adjusted to the gloom, his heart sank. "Damn it... so now what... where the hell can she be?" Like the fool that he was he'd convinced himself that everything was under his control when actually it was anything but. Ryan's legs lay alongside an oak branch, waiting for his special treatment, and a mouse scurried for cover between some ready-sawn logs. But nowhere in the shed was there a lifeless body of a young woman. "Where the hell are you?" He began to sob. He couldn't stop himself. He sank to the floor and tears streamed down his cheeks. Oblivious to the cold and wet, he crawled on his hands and knees out of the shed and into the night air. "I can't stand not knowing." He muttered as he turned his face up towards the full moon in the centre of the star-speckled sky. It was days since he'd last seen a shooting star. "I can't take any more, do you hear me? I can't take it."

Angus's excited bark pulled him back to reality. One living creature was waiting for him, even if it was only his mother's dog. He hauled himself upright and brushed the wet gravel from his trousers.

Angus expected his evening meal as if nothing were wrong and Beetle stroked him and then placed the dish of food down on the kitchen floor. The familiar routine calmed him slightly. The animal had many uses and the thought of rehoming him, although he knew it was the right thing to do, shot another wave of panic through his guts. Angus wasn't the only living thing in his life that he cared about, but he was the only thing he was totally in control of. And that was a scary thought.

The next best things under his control were the letters. He would compose another. Decision made, he felt calmer. Two mugs of coffee and one ham sandwich later, he walked to the drawer containing the envelopes and pulled out a small white and a large brown, just like before. This time he tipped the contents of the white one onto the kitchen table and with an open palm slid the photographs around until they were all lying separately. He slumped down into the wooden kitchen chair and dropped his head into hands – so many happy memories, all permanently tainted by a handful of bad ones.

Until last week, he hadn't seen the pictures in almost thirty years. He'd blotted out their existence. Memories stirred and hazy images formed in his mind.

There wasn't much to choose between the pictures. He'd already posted his favourite one – the one he'd found first. He selected another at random, turned it over, grabbed a pen and scribbled a few words on the back. Then he stuffed the picture into the larger envelope and scribbled an address. He reached for a first class stamp, thumped it down onto the corner of the envelope and shoved the letter into his coat pocket ready for morning. Finally, he reached for the only bottle of alcohol he had left in the house, a sweet sherry, and headed for the living room. The only way he would sleep through tonight would be curled up on the sofa with Angus, and with a loaded gun at his side.

Chapter 22

"Sir, Stevie Hall's surfaced," Adam's voice crackled from his car phone.

"Where is he now?" Forbes smiled despite himself. He knew such a big player in the criminal world wouldn't be able to stay out sight for too long.

"In Preston nick; they want to know how soon we can be there."

"Tell them a couple of hours, traffic permitting." He briefly wondered why Adam was in work so early on a dark Wednesday, then he focused on Stevie Hall. Not that he needed to think much – he had a list of questions buzzing around in his head. He felt his pulse quicken as he squeezed down on the accelerator. As long as they were ahead of the rush-hour traffic around Manchester, two hours should be ample.

Preston Police Station formed part of the Lancashire Constabulary and was a modern, brick-built building set close to the centre of town. He'd been before but still felt intimidated by the size of the place. Hopefully, it had a similar effect of some of the low-life passing through its portals, though from what he'd learned about Stevie, he didn't think the man would be easily frightened.

A uniformed constable was waiting and he guided them through the corridors. "This way, sirs, we've taken Mr Hall into interview room four. He's repeatedly stated he doesn't require the services of a solicitor." They followed like sheep, past walls lined with posters meant to remind the officers of their obligations to the public, and of procedure, and of crimes solved by this station and crimes yet to be solved. Preston had at least two more dedicated interview rooms than Leaburn, and obviously spent more of its budget on posters.

Stevie Hall was a well-groomed man in his early forties. As Forbes and Adam entered the room, he looked them over, stood up and stepped to one side. He appeared strong and incredibly fit, if somewhat overweight, his tailored suit showing off his broad shoulders and a solid frame. He oozed presence and poise, and by standing was presumably hoping to impress or intimidate. Forbes imagined him greeting every new acquaintance in this way. He was well accustomed to people he met showing their respect.

"Sit down please, Mr Hall. You've been informed as to why you're here?"

"Please, gentlemen, call me Stevie." He was smiling as he spoke but Forbes detected an underlying seriousness in his tone. "I was asked, very politely, to come in and help clear up some queries that you have. I can offer you another thirty minutes of my time and then I really must dash. I have many businesses to run and hundreds of loyal staff depending on me for their livelihoods. I'm sure you understand."

"Then I'll get straight to the point, Mr Hall. Exactly what was your relationship with Miss Naomi Proctor, and how well did you know Detective Constable Ryan Wheeler?"

"Naomi… sweet Naomi… I dated her for a few weeks… on and off. She was a bit of a mouse, if you know what I mean, not at all my usual type, and I ditched her completely about a month ago. As for DC Ryan Wheeler… the name rings a bell, but I'm not sure that I actually knew him."

"Naomi's friends and colleagues claim you behaved violently towards her, and that it was she who ended the relationship. They claim she was left living in fear of you stalking her."

"That's rubbish. Look at me. Look at my bank balances and my assets, if you must. Look at the people I associate with. Do you really think a man of my standing would go chasing after a lowly nurse when I could have practically any woman I snapped my fingers at? Really Inspector…"

I think you're an arrogant arsehole who gets decent people killed, Forbes was close to saying. He took a slow breath. "We have you on camera appearing to be following her into a supermarket car park on the afternoon before she disappeared."

Hall sneered. "Appearing... a supermarket car park... can you hear yourself? How many thousands of people pass through those places every hour of every day? I may have been checking on any one of my employees. I like to be seen. It keeps my people on their toes. I certainly wasn't checking on Naomi and I'm afraid that you're wasting your time if you're following that particular line of enquiry."

"We believe DC Wheeler knew you from his time at this station. He specialised in drugs related investigations."

"Then I may have crossed paths with him. I own and run several nightclubs and public houses, both in Preston and in Manchester, as I'm sure you're already aware. I operate a zero-tolerance policy on drugs, as anyone associated with me will tell you, but there will always be some slips through the net. I may have come across your officer on one of the many drugs awareness talks I organise for the staff. And yes, I have young cousins who in the past have got a little excited at the prospect of earning large sums of money through drugs, and who, under my instructions, have pleaded guilty to their mistakes and accepted their punishments. But I'm sure you're also aware of all of this."

"Ryan and Naomi have both been missing for eleven days. The day before they disappeared you were caught on camera in the vicinity of both Ryan and Naomi."

"We're back to the car park... really... is that all that these questions are about? Didn't I see where the couple in question went missing after a wedding reception? I have proof of my whereabouts for the Saturday night and Sunday morning in question, and I'll provide that proof if and when it becomes necessary. Now if there's nothing else I can help you with I think we're about done here."

Half way across the car park Forbes regained his composure. Until then he'd wanted to punch a wall, or a tree, or even better, the smug face of Stevie Hall. "I mean," he growled at Adam, "what a pathetic, whimpish name for a gangland leader – Stevie. Why not Steve, or Big Steve, or plain Mr Hall if you want respect, but Stevie…?"

"We didn't achieve much in there," Adam sounded in a similar frame of mind. "I feel we've just wasted a morning."

"Far from it, although we may not be leaving here with anything a court would accept, I'm now more convinced than ever that he's behind the disappearances."

"Did I miss something in there?"

"When I said that he'd been seen in the vicinity of both Ryan and Naomi, he straight away assumed I was talking about the supermarket car park. Assuming they were a couple, Hall could have crossed paths with them accidentally just about anywhere. Ryan and Naomi had parked well away from the entrance, where Mr Hall parked his Mercedes, it was raining, and it was dark. He must have seen them both on that Friday afternoon, and to me that suggests he was following Naomi and subsequently saw them together."

"So how do we go about proving it, and assuming you're right, how do we ever find them? If we're talking about organised gangs then they'll have been taken out by professional hit-men, surely?"

"We search harder and deeper for a motive. We need all of Naomi's electronic communications dating back to the month before she met Stevie Hall. And we need all of Ryan's communications, personal and work-related, from his days at Preston and since he's been with us at Leaburn. We'll dig deeper into Mr Hall's activities and take a closer look at his family. There has to be more of a link somewhere, or something else that we're missing. Naomi may have stumbled onto something she shouldn't and when seen with a detective paid for it with her life."

*

Beetle had better things to do than wait for fate to strike him another, below-the-belt blow. So Naomi had gone – so what, there was absolutely nothing he could do about that now. It was out of his hands. Life had thrown him another curve ball and, good or bad, fate would determine what happened to him next. The best thing he could do, in fact the only thing he could do if he expected to retain any sort of sanity, was to push her to the back of his mind and concentrate on Godfrey Jones and his oh-so perfect son.

During his lunch break he posted the fourth letter, and after that, when no one was looking, he prepared some special mince for his least favourite customer. A warm glow spread through him every time he imagined her and her stuck-up husband tucking into it.

The shop was empty and he was muttering to himself and his knives. "Just wait till I find out who's been messing with my mind. I'll feed that person their own most tender body parts before gutting them and then pushing their boned limbs through the mincer. And then, for good measure, I'll make them into burgers and put them on special offer, you see if I don't." He giggled his way over to the mincer.

*

The front entrance door to Leaburn Station buzzed and Forbes pushed it open and stepped inside, almost bumping into Martin Jones in the process. "Are you here again? What part of 'take time off work' don't you understand?"

"I needed to look something up on the PNC again. I hope that's all right, sir. I'm on my way home now."

"I should think so. What were you looking for?"

"It's nothing important – just a name Dad thought he'd remembered, but he was mistaken. It's nothing."

He let it go. He was better at reading his officers than they realised, and Martin was definitely hiding something.

In the incident room, one head looked up from a computer station.

"Sir," DC Jade Sharpe, the latest recruit to his team, appeared to have news. "Alison Ransom's been trying to reach you on your mobile."

"I'd left it in my office."

"She was phoning to confirm that yesterday's body parts were almost certainly from Paul Biers and that there appear to be traces of animal fat on parts of the packaging. She'll be able to say for definite by this time tomorrow. They'd been in the ground a week or two longer than those we found first, but because of the cold weather she doesn't think the lab will be able to give us a more accurate timeline. She's put it all in an email but she asked me to draw your attention to it as soon as possible. And she said she'd try calling you later."

"Still no signs of Gary then?"

"No sir, and Martin was here when the call came in. He's relaying the news to his father."

"Did he now? I was speaking with him only a minute ago and he didn't mention it. Jade, could you find out what Martin's been researching? I believe he was using the PNC."

"I'll take a look."

His team was desperate for any sort of a break in the case. He couldn't decide whether to have Stevie Hall brought to Leaburn for more intense questioning, or to let him carry on believing he'd nothing to worry about. His few remaining squares of milk chocolate were calling to him from his desk drawer – they helped him think, or so he liked to believe. His sore throat was a thing of the past and so he pushed the cough sweets to one side. With any luck, he'd escaped the dreaded chickenpox virus and not passed it on.

"Found it, sir…" Jade burst into his office holding up a scrap of paper and looking smug. "He made two searches, one yesterday and one today, both related to the same family."

"I knew he was hiding something. Who are they? Do we know them?"

"They're Mrs Julie Becket, who's been dead for just over a year, and her two children, Ian and Sophie. Julie was the widow of Keith Becket, who was arrested several times in the nineteen-eighties for burglary, and then again in nineteen-ninety for aggravated burglary and the manslaughter of an elderly woman. While on remand, a few months later, he was stabbed to death in a prison cell."

"Why would he be interested in them? How old are the children now?"

"Ian will be thirty-eight and Julie's thirty-five. Ian's lived in this area for most of his life and according to this year's electoral register has now moved into his late mother's house on Beeley Moor."

"Beeley Moor... that's midway between Matlock and Chesterfield, isn't it?"

"Yes sir. Sophie moves around, but largely within this area, and today Martin spent most of his time tracking her down."

"We'll leave that puzzle for tomorrow. It's getting late and the roads are freezing over. Get off home and I'll see you tomorrow, Jade. And well done."

"Yes sir, thank you. There's one other thing I thought I ought to mention," she hesitated. "I happened to glance over Martin's shoulder while he was accessing the internet on his own phone, and I can't be sure about this, but he appeared to be searching for private detectives."

Chapter 23

At six o'clock on a dark Thursday morning, in the dead of December, the snow had sunk into the wet ground and two stumbling feet and four bouncing paws crossed from the front door of Hill Top Cottage to the door of the log shed. Beetle flung open the door, flashed the torch beam around the small space and breathed a sigh of relief. The skin of Ryan's legs appeared greyer, but other than that everything was as he'd left it. The dream that had woken him hadn't been an omen after all, but it may have been a warning. The longer he left Ripper under a pile of timber, and what was left of Ryan alongside a pile of chopped logs, the greater the risk was of someone stumbling across them. He'd bring more large-sized freezer bags home with him from the shop tonight.

Without Naomi to entertain him he'd have a few free hours on Saturday evening, after his drug collection and distributions, and again on Sunday morning before he finally came face to face with Godfrey Jones. And there was still the not-so-small matter of Ripper's car, hidden away in the barn. Ripper's phone and sat-nav were already in the River Derwent, and although it was a crying shame to destroy a decent car, that also needed to be one of his priorities for the week ahead. He couldn't risk dumping and torching it — Stevie's contacts were far too widespread for that, so he planned on taking a sledge hammer to the interior and then taking the seats and as much debris as he could manage to various skip sites. He'd bought a new angle grinder to cut through the metalwork, leaving only the chassis and wheels which would soon become grown over in the neglected corner of the garden and would eventually rot away.

For once, he'd arrived at the shop early. The woman who came in daily to help with the morning pie baking was still up to her elbows in flour. She smiled at him through a haze of dust and steam and he smiled back, determined to behave normally, and so far, he thought he was making a reasonable job. Today was just another day to get through, to take him one step closer to seeing Godfrey's expression and to finally having his life complete a full-circle.

The panic attacks of old had haunted him through the darkest hours of the previous night. He'd thought about abandoning everything and starting a new life somewhere. Things were becoming too complicated and too dangerous. He'd considered throwing a few bare essentials, plus the cash, into his car and driving off into the unknown with Angus for company. He had enough used notes to keep him going for a year or two and three guns and his knives for personal protection. Then the winter wind had rattled his bedroom window in its frame and made him pull the duvet up around his chin. Where would he go at this time of the year? Where could he go? It might be the season of goodwill to all men but who was likely to give him a bed to sleep in – certainly not his sister, wherever she was, and all his new friends had hotlines to Stevie.

He couldn't remember the last time he'd heard from Sophie – it had to be two months ago, at least. If he did a bunk, as soon as she realised he'd gone for good she'd come to the house and find the bodies, and from that moment on he'd be a hunted man, by both Stevie Hall and the police.

No, he had to stay strong and trust to his luck.

In the feeble light of day, things seemed not quite so bad. For the first time in his life, he had a place of his own and it felt good. He'd no wish to return to the days of spending all his money on a smelly flat with noisy neighbours. Then there was the small matter of a new identity and employment.

Fear gripped him once again and he was back on the roller coaster.

Maybe that would be preferable to a prison cell – or an unmarked grave if Stevie realised that he hadn't killed Gary and Paul, that his beloved nephew, Ripper, was dead, and that he knew nothing at all of the whereabouts of Naomi.

He stepped over to his knives and stroked them.

*

The previous evening Martin had helped put his son to bed, watched television, made love to his wife and finally settled down for some much-needed sleep. Enjoyable as those familiar things had been, through most of them he'd felt his brain had been under a cloud. He knew Sarah would never approve of him hiring an investigator and that he'd have a real battle on his hands to talk her round. Depending on what the private eye uncovered, his father's reputation could be ruined, but it was his own career that was likely to be the biggest casualty. By going outside the force, he was breaking some of the most fundamental rules he and his colleagues lived and worked by.

The man he'd chosen had offered to do a preliminary check on Sophie Becket overnight and then phone him back this morning with his findings. He must have been short of business, and maybe that was a bad sign, but it was too late now – he already had a hundred pounds of Martin's money as a retainer. Sarah would argue that he'd been scammed, so he'd decided to keep the whole sorry business of his father's adultery and the need to look into the Becket family from her, at least for now.

When he arrived at his father's house, he expected the postman to have already been. He wasn't in his usual worried state – he was apprehensive, but feeling more hopeful than over the last few days. They were on the verge of finally getting some answers. He had a current address and a place of work for Ian Becket, and as soon as his father was ready the two of them intended visiting both locations.

He hadn't even considered the possibility of another letter.

"Take a look at that." His father looked up with a forced smile on his drawn face. "It came in this morning's post… in a fourth letter… turn it over… read the back."

Martin took the faded photograph from his father's trembling hand and flipped it over. He read the short note once to himself and then out loud. "Meet me somewhere close to these rocks at midday this Sunday. I know you'll remember where they are. Bring no one and I'll tell everything I know about Gary's disappearance. Don't tell the police or I promise you we're both screwed. From your loving would-be stepchild."

Martin dropped the photograph onto the kitchen table, picture-side-up. They'd both handled it without wearing gloves. "This should be in an evidence bag, Dad. Come on, you know better than this."

"I can't hand it in."

It was time for the gentle approach, even though the note terrified him and he'd no intentions of going along with its request. "OK, Dad, but where is this place? I'll support you. We'll go together."

Godfrey had the grace to look sheepish. "That cluster of rocks is close to where you were found. It's also where I used to take Julie and the children for picnics. It's known as Robin Hood's Stride. The two roads closest to it are a five and a ten minute walk away."

"You're not seriously thinking of going...?"

"Why not...? With the bracken lying flat at this time of year and the majority of the trees bare, there's little to no chance of an ambush."

"For us or for him...?"

"For either of us – and you're doing as I did at first – assuming it to be Ian. It could just as easily be Sophie sending these letters."

"Dad, listen to yourself... the letters are from whoever killed Gary and Paul and moved their bodies... during a snowstorm. A woman couldn't have done that without help. The letter says step-child – not step-children. It has to be from Ian."

"Well we've just over seventy-two hours until we find out."

"Come on dad... this is good. It gives the investigator extra time and it gives us the upper hand. It offers us the opportunity to strike first and ask questions later."

"The last time I saw them they were children." His father stared at the faded photograph and looked close to tears. For the first time since Gary had been an infant Martin felt a stab of jealousy. "Well they're most definitely not children now, Dad."

"The day I walked out on them they weren't much older than they are in that picture. I remember the afternoon it was taken."

Martin didn't try to hold back a scornful snort. "We were children too, when you and mum were tearing lumps out of each other and Gary and I were lying in our beds believing it was because of something we'd done or not done."

"This is too much. Gary... your mum... Ian... Sophie... Julie... you. I need to make this pain stop."

"Thanks for putting me last on that list, Dad."

"You know what I mean. The others are gone from me. You're here."

"Then come with me to Ian's house today, like we planned. He'll be at work. We can make sure of that on our way over there by looking in on the shop. We can get a feel for how he lives. We won't break in, but we'll check the layout of the place in daylight and then return after dark. We'll confront him together, tonight. One way or another we'll either get the answers we need from him or we'll know it's his sister that we have to find before Sunday."

From looking beaten and vulnerable, his father straightened his frame and puffed out his chest. "I'm doing this *my* way. If it is Ian, why has he handed himself to us like this? Why would he make himself so easy to find? He wants to talk to *me*. I let him down in the past but I won't do it now."

"He could be setting a trap, or simply playing mind games."

"He was a normal little boy when I left."

"Then he must have changed. Why else would he torture us like this?"

"I loved him and his sister... I still do." Tears trickled down.

"Calm down, Dad. There is still a third option. I could hand that photo in and tell Inspector Forbes everything. It might be for the best."

"No, I need to see this through. I need to know why he's doing this."

"Then let's go there tonight. I'll set my phone to speed dial the station in case anything goes wrong, or if I feel uncomfortable. Please, Dad?"

"I'm the one he wants, but not until Sunday. Today and tonight we stay well away, have you got that?"

"I think you're making a mistake, but I'll do whatever you want." He hoped his relief wasn't conveyed by his voice.

"For a long, long time I treated that boy and girl as if they were my own. It should be me who confronts him or her, alone, and on the letter sender's terms."

He wanted to see things from his father's perspective. He had tried, but never quite managed it. He was a hard man to understand. Had his father's behaviour caused irreparable damage to two other young children, but even if that was the case why would either of them kill Gary? And why wait so many years?

They moved through to the hallway and Martin was thinking of his mother as he reached for his car keys, of how she must have experienced such isolation, with two small children, that she'd taken her straying husband back for a second time. He was finding it almost impossible to stomach that, even now, after sharing his story of betrayal, his father was still claiming to feel something for two children who were nothing to do with his real family. He flinched when he felt his father's hand on his shoulder.

"We've got visitors. You get the door and I'll put the photo away."

Rain hammering at the kitchen window had hidden the sound of DCI Forbes's Mercedes pulling up on the driveway.

From the kitchen, the outside world hadn't existed, but now he was watching a familiar figure through frosted glass and waiting for the doorbell to ring.

A wave of dread washed over him. Had Alison made a mistake with the blood types? Had Gary's remains been found yesterday? Why else would his boss be calling at his father's house this morning?

He slipped his car keys into his pocket and moved through the hallway. His legs felt heavy. Before opening the door he took a deep breath to steady himself for bad news.

"May I come in Martin? Your wife said I'd find you here. Is your father around?"

"He's in the bathroom. He'll be through in a minute. I haven't told him yet that more of Gary's remains were found on the moor. He's in a rather fragile state."

"Would you like a family liaison officer to come round and help break the news?"

"Thanks, but no. It's best if I do it."

"All right, but that's not why I'm here. I'd like a brief chat about your use of the police database yesterday. What haven't you been telling us, Martin? Where does the Becket family fit into this investigation, or have you been using police resources for something else entirely?" He saw Martin hesitate.

"I'm sorry sir; I know I took a bit of a liberty. Dad remembered the name from the past and thought he ought to run it past you, but I considered it to be such a long shot that I decided not to waste your time with it."

"Your father was a police constable at the time of the Becket case. Why would that family concern him now?"

"He's been recalling old cases which went badly and he remembered speaking at length with Mrs Becket and her two small children after Mr Becket was killed while on remand. I told him I'd try to trace the family – to check whether they'd gone on to have any history of trouble. I only did it to set his mind at rest, but they had no motive that I could see to make them want to terrorise an old man."

"And did it...?"

"Did it what...?"

"Did what you found out about the family set his mind at rest?"

"He was sorry to learn of Julie Becket's death, but the fact that neither Ian nor Sophie had a criminal record and that they were both gainfully employed allowed him to put their names to bed."

Forbes turned to see Godfrey Jones shuffling into the living room, looking more like a down-and-out than a retired senior police officer.

"Good morning Godfrey, no more letters today, I take it?"

"We'd have called you if there had been, Michael. Have you anything new for us this morning?"

He ignored the question. "I wanted a quick word with Martin. Did you hear any of our conversation just now?"

"I heard enough to know that you've had a wasted journey. I dredged those names up from the distant past but I wasn't honestly expecting anything to come of them. Martin was doing what he thought was best so please don't reprimand him. We're both having rather a rough time of things."

"Is there anything that either of you aren't telling me, because if so, now is the time?"

Godfrey answered while Martin hesitated again. "Trust me we're as much in the dark as anyone else, Michael."

He picked up the exasperation in the man's voice. If he continued they were bound to fall out, and he didn't want that. "Well if you're both all right I'll leave you in peace."

*

Forbes slid into his driving seat, convinced he'd been lied to. Martin had hired, or was considering hiring, a private investigator, so why the hell hadn't he bothered to mention the fact when he'd had the chance. Either he hadn't told his father of what he was planning or the two of them were colluding and were taking the Becket name seriously enough to throw money at it.

He'd always demanded openness and honesty from his team. That everyone had complete trust in everyone else, and in him, he believed was vital to the smooth running of his team. If any of them ever needed help, support, or guidance, in their private or their work lives, whatever they'd become involved in, he expected them to know they could always come to him. Either Martin was being bullied by his overbearing father, or there was more to this new development than they were saying. Back at the station, he'd task someone to urgently do a more detailed check on the Becket siblings.

On a positive note – if Martin and Godfrey were right in their thinking, it would mean it was far less likely that someone was targeting his station, or his team. It narrowed down the investigations considerably – hopefully to the Beckets and the Halls and no further.

His eyes switched to the car's radio as it crackled into life.

"Sir," it sounded like PC Katie Brown on the switchboard, "I've a message just in from traffic. Naomi Proctor's car was taken last night from the street in front of her flat. It was spotted by officers in an unmarked car and after a very short chase was brought to a halt without injury or damage to either vehicle. Two seventeen year old youths escaped on foot but were both arrested an hour ago after a call to the station by one of their parents. They're in the cells now."

"I'm five minutes away. Find Adam and tell him to meet me outside the interview room."

"Will do sir..."

*

Godfrey Jones's face had changed from the colour of ashes to the colour of bleached parchment, his voice barely more than a whisper. "You should never have logged their names into the police computer."

"It's too late for recriminations, Dad," Martin snapped back. "You seem to forget that all of this could well be happening because you couldn't keep it in your trousers thirty-odd years ago."

"Talking to me like that doesn't help."

"So tell me Dad, what will help? And while you're at it, please, tell me – just what do you plan on doing now?"

"Be quiet a minute and let me think. Michael Forbes is no fool. He'll check out both Ian and Sophie and sooner or later he'll want to question them. But without more than we've already told him he won't get a search warrant. I still say we shouldn't go anywhere near Ian's place of work, or his home, and that I should go to meet him on Sunday as he asks. We know that Sophie stays somewhere in the area so you must tell your investigator that we need to find her before the police do."

"I'm not sure we can risk waiting until Sunday. To have any hope of saving your reputation and pension, not to mention my career, we need to know what Ian's playing at and what he intends to tell police when he is questioned. It's called damage limitation. There's nothing to stop us going up to Beeley Moor tonight. I can check the layout of his property on Google Earth and you can prepare your speech. It will be dark for well over an hour before the shop closes and we can be waiting for him. He may be expecting us, but that's a risk we'll take."

"Have you conveniently forgotten that Gary and Paul were both shot? We don't know what sort of an arsenal either of the siblings might have inside that property. No, I insist that we do this my way. We'll do as the letter says and wait until Sunday. He wants to meet in a public place and I can live with that. After eleven months I can wait three extra days to hear what he has to say about my Gary."

"You're making a mistake... a dangerous mistake..."

"It's my mistake to make, Son, and as you so cruelly pointed out a few moments ago, I am the one who created this mess. It's therefore down to me to take whatever risks are involved in sorting it out. We wait until Sunday, and that's my final decision."

*

"We didn't break into it." Forbes looked at the youth with the mop of hair flopping down over his eyes. He didn't appear remorseful. He was just another cocky teenager. "Why would we? We've been walking around the streets of Matlock and Leaburn flashing those car keys for days and no one's challenged us." The lad stretched and yawned noisily.

"Well you're being challenged now, Andrew." Forbes leaned towards the table.

"All right, chill, we didn't know whose car it was, did we? And I was driving OK. I've had lessons. When that cop car came gunning down the road it scared the shit out of us. That's why I floored it – I panicked. I should be due some sort of treatment for the trauma."

"You panicked... but what else did you expect to happen after you'd taken a car without permission?"

"We were gonna take the back roads to Longnor, hang out with some mates for an hour or two and then return the car to where we'd found it. We were having a laugh."

"Not quite so funny now, is it?" He saw Andrew's hands trembling. Reality was setting in.

"As soon as Gavin yelled at me to slow down I pulled up. I wasn't speeding for more than a few seconds. It's not as though we set out to deliberately cause damage like some of those council estate twats who pinch cars for fun. We would have looked after it, I promise. Look, I'm telling you the truth. We didn't steal those keys."

"All right, so let's assume for a minute that I believe you, shall we? How, and when, did you come into possession of them?"

"Gavin picked them up from the side of the road... from the layby at the top of Sydnope Hill... honestly... he'll tell you the same. We guessed someone had dropped their spare car keys into the snow because it was melting around them. They hadn't been run over or anything and the battery was still working, so everywhere we've been since then we've been pressing them and looking for a car's lights to flash. We were fooling about."

"You didn't think to hand them in?"

"Like I said, we were fooling. We were going to hand them in when the battery went flat, we'd said as much to each other. We hadn't seriously expected to find the car they belonged to but then last night we got a result. The temptation was too much, but we would have returned the car, honestly. How were we to know it belonged to that missing woman? You can't think we had anything to do with that, for Christ's sake?"

"I can think what I like until I'm convinced you're telling the truth. You may have found those keys in an area where a serious crime was committed, and at the moment I don't know that you're not involved."

"I am telling the truth." He looked from Forbes to Adam and then back again several times. "We found them in the snow in a layby. We've never taken a car before and I've only had three driving lessons. If we hadn't been chased by your lot we'd have taken the car back and locked it up and no one would have been any the wiser."

"If we show you a map you could you pinpoint the layby for us?"

"Yeah... no problem... then can I go? I'm late for a college class."

"You can forget about college for today. You're being charged with taking a motor vehicle without consent and you've yet to be processed. And then, if you co-operate, and if your friend confirms to us exactly where you found the keys, we might consider letting you go."

"Phone the Matlock station," he instructed Adam as they left the interview room together, "and request that they seal off that layby as a matter of urgency. In the unlikely event of any useful material still being there we need it to be with forensics as quickly as possible. I want boards at the roadsides in both directions asking for anyone who used that road around or shortly after midnight on the date of the abductions to come forward, and if anyone has dash-cam footage that hasn't been recorded over we need to see it. I want an appeal to that effect on tonight's local news and on the front pages of all the local newspapers."

"Let's hope the lads are telling the truth."

"Naomi had a handbag at the wedding which hasn't yet turned up and only one set of car keys was found in her flat. Most people have a spare set and keep them in two separate locations, don't they? I know I do."

"That layby must be fifteen miles from the wedding venue." Adam couldn't help thinking back to his own wedding earlier in the year. That had begun as a far smaller and far quieter affair, but had also ended in dramatic style when early the following morning he'd found himself standing beside DCI Forbes staring down at a blood-soaked body.

"The kidnappers may have changed vehicles in that lay-by, or Ryan or Naomi may have attempted an escape and forced the driver to pull over. Whatever took place happened alongside a main road and so someone may have noticed something. If nothing positive comes out of this in the next twenty-four hours then we'll request that it be featured on the main national news, and then on Crimewatch."

In the incident room, Forbes took a mouthful of lukewarm coffee and swallowed it down quickly. The layby had been sealed off, as a potential crime scene. Officers from the CSI team were on their way over there now and his immediate attendance wasn't necessary. There was work to be done at Leaburn while he waited for news of anything being found.

No suspects had yet surfaced for either the Matlock or the Bakewell shootings. He was the Chief Investigating Officer of both incidents; overseeing the work of the two smaller stations and he wanted them to feel they were making progress, but so far there had been very little. He studied the white board featuring the first of the two deaths and then did the same with the second. The only similarity, apart from the obvious that both victims were male, was that they did voluntary work with local youngsters, although in different towns and in different ways.

He stared at the photographs. Gun crime... young people... possible but unproved drug use... was a link to the deaths of Gary and Paul really out of the question? It had been considered, but no evidence had been found to support the suggestion. He studied the boards for another minute. Since the two shootings, several new names had surfaced. What he was considering was a long shot, but in the absence of any other new information coming to light it had to be worth pursuing. "Adam, re-contact these two youth groups. Get hold of the organisers and as many of the volunteers as you can. It doesn't matter whether they're at work or not – I want answers. Run the names of Ryan Wheeler, Naomi Proctor, Stevie Hall, Julie Becket, Ian Becket and Sophie Becket past them and find out whether anyone knew any of them."

Chapter 24

On the dot of five-thirty, car lights bounced along the short, rutted lane to Hill Top Cottage. Godfrey Jones stood alone in the shadows. He was tired tonight; tired and nervous, and waiting in the cold for a face that he hadn't seen in over a quarter of a century. A pounding headache was coming on and he attributed it to the stress. The car began slowing and he stepped into the beam of its headlights and watched in silence while the driver pulled to a halt, gathered up a bundle from his front passenger seat, stepped from his car, fumbled with a set of house keys and began walking towards him.

"Godfrey... I had a feeling you'd come. No... I knew that you'd come." Beetle tentatively offered out his right hand for a formal handshake but then seemed to think better of it and retracted it nervously. "I'll leave the headlights... one minute... are you alone?"

"Hullo Ian, yes, I'm alone. It really is good to see you. How are you? How have you been?"

"It's been a long time since anyone called me Ian. Everyone calls me Beetle. Even my old mum used to call me by that name."

"I remember. I was very sorry to learn about your mother. You'll always be Ian to me. I never stopped loving you, you know."

Beetle snorted, but said nothing.

"It's cold out here. Do you think we could go inside and talk?" He wasn't looking forward to entering the house, if he was honest, but as Ian hadn't already swung at him with a right hook, a conversation seemed a possibility. For that to take place properly, he needed to be out of the night air.

"I have to feed Angus and let him out." Beetle calmly turned away from him.

A key clicked in the lock and Godfrey heard scrabbling from the other side of the door. "Yes of course, Ian, whatever you want."

Light flooded a tidy hallway and he stood and watched an overweight black dog bounding around in circles and making full use of the space. There was a distinct smell of bleach. The police officer in him thought *crime scene clean up* – bleach was the substance most commonly used where blood was involved. But there was a dog, left alone in the house all day presumably, and likely to make a mess more often than not.

He'd seen no signs of malice in Ian's eyes – no burning resentment or flashes of hatred, in fact, the soft, expressive eyes he'd recognised from all those years ago had looked remarkably friendly, and even rather sad... or apologetic?

"Go into the living room, Godfrey. There's brandy on the sideboard and glasses in the cupboard below. Help yourself and pour a large one for me."

He'd felt physically sick while waiting in his car – that feeling had gone but as he entered the large, high-ceilinged living room he could feel his headache worsening. He blamed the cold December air for compounding his stress. Maybe a generous measure of brandy would help, it would certainly be more than welcome, but he wanted to keep his thoughts lucid.

He found two expensive-looking lead crystal glasses and filled them anyway.

The dark sideboards, chairs, and side-tables all appeared to be original Victorian and the room was as clean and tidy as the entrance hall. The smell of bleach had followed him and now mingled with the smell of lavender polish. He knew this had been Julie's family home for generations and guessed that most of the furniture had been handed down. He selected the armchair furthest from the door, but facing it, and gratefully sunk into it. His legs had suddenly felt like jelly.

Ian was talking as he walked into the room. "This is a difficult meeting... for both of us... but firstly I need you to believe that I never harmed a hair on your Gary's head." The dog traipsed into the room and without taking its eyes off the newcomer lay down in the centre of a worn rug in front of the unlit, open fire.

Godfrey leaned forward in his chair and looked up intently at the familiar face. "But you know who killed him, don't you… and why he was killed? I deserve to know that much at least."

"Not really, no. I know what was supposed to happen, and talking to you now I'm hanging my head in shame, but… it's a long story."

He was so close to the answers. He felt light-headed at the idea of someone finally giving up a part of the puzzle, however small that part might be. He sipped at the brandy and felt the burn in his throat. "I've got all night, if necessary. Sit down, Ian, and start from the beginning. I promise I won't judge you because I accept that I've no right to do that. We've all made mistakes, God knows, I've made some whoppers in my time, so you can tell me anything… anything at all, but before I leave here I need to hear the truth from your lips."

Beetle perched on the edge of the adjacent armchair, leaned forward and shot out his right hand. "Put it there, mate. Tonight, we clear the air…?" he suggested hopefully.

Godfrey accepted the firm handshake but the lump in his throat prevented him answering.

"I loved you, you know." Beetle said respectfully. "You were the father I'd always wanted. I need you to know that when you came into my life, as young as I was, I instinctively knew it was the best thing that had ever happened, or was ever likely to happen, to me. You gave my life meaning and joy. I still love you and you'll be a part of me forever."

"Ian…"

"Please… let me talk. I need to say this to try to make you understand. My real father beat me… regularly. He did things to me that I didn't understand and he beat mum almost every night – but then you knew all about that, didn't you? I was a child who was happy to hear about his father's death in prison. How sad is that?"

"I don't…"

"That day I knew it meant that the monster would never return. I also thought it meant that you'd never leave."

"I didn't want to, Ian, but I was torn. The woman I'd been intending to divorce had become terminally ill and suddenly I had three children younger than yourself and Sophie to take care of. Your mum couldn't forgive me for returning to them, and in all honesty I couldn't blame her for that. After I'd been widowed I would have come looking for you all but your mum made her intentions very clear. She was moving away and was adamant that she didn't want me to find her or follow her. I should have tried, I know that, and I never stopped thinking about you and wondering what you were doing, but I was busy with the children and with my career. I know it's a poor excuse, and I'm desperately sorry for abandoning you. I loved all three of you and it broke my heart to cut all ties, you must know that."

"We've all suffered. Sophie became impossible after you left. She turned all her frustration and all her hurt onto her memories of you. She could go for days without eating or speaking to anyone. The doctors were no help and the schools frequently sent her home early. She was difficult to live with."

"I never knew that. I'm sorry if I was the cause of Sophie's unhappiness and if I made life hard for you."

"I loved you then, and to this day that feeling has never died. Sophie hated you and could never accept or understand that I didn't feel the same way."

"Do you still see her?"

"We meet up occasionally, in town, in a café. She doesn't come to the house any more – she hasn't been here since the funeral, despite having a half-share in it."

"So what was your connection with my Gary, and Paul Biers, and what made you begin sending those letters?"

"Straight to the point, eh Godfrey? You sound like the no-nonsense police officer that I remember. I didn't have any connection with them before that fateful night. Incidentally, I didn't kill Paul either."

"I wasn't suggesting that you had. I'm sorry; do you want to return to your story?"

"You may not like what you're about to hear."

"I want to hear the truth, however terrible it is."

"Mum hit the bottle after you left. She became a lush, and a whore. One man after another came through our front door, but to give her credit she tried her best to keep them away from us. As I grew I realised that must have been how she'd afforded to feed and clothe us. I guessed that her drinking was a means of coping. I never stopped wanting you to come back to us, to take care of us properly, so that mum wouldn't have to do the disgusting things that she did."

"If I'd known, Ian, then I would."

"Mum inherited this house and a few years later Sophie and I moved out. She found employment in the cosmetics retailing industry and I trained to be a butcher. Then about eighteen months ago mum fell ill and Sophie returned here to nurse her. After she passed away Sophie moved out again and I moved back in."

"You moved back here a year ago...?"

"I moved back in on the night of Gary's death. Until then I'd been renting a poky little flat in Matlock, but because the shop had lost so much trade to the new supermarkets I was only receiving the minimum wage and half of that went on paying the rent. I'd built up some serious debts. I'd begun taking drugs, nothing heavy, just the odd puff of weed to blot out the boredom of my life, and I'd been over-spending. At the time of mum's death, I'd got creditors coming at me almost every day of the week. Then one day, out of the blue, a turn of events that I could never have imagined, happened. A man approached me as I was getting into my car to drive home. He knew who I was and he knew all about my debts. He stood there, under a street light, with people passing by, and he offered me a contract... a very lucrative contract... a contract to kill someone and then make their body disappear for a while."

"And you took it...?"

Beetle smiled faintly. "Not straight away... no... well would you?"

"I guess not." Godfrey felt anger rising up through his chest.

"I was shocked. I was left speechless. The man said to consider it but not to tell anyone or I'd regret it. He said he'd be back for my answer in a few days and then he just walked away. I thought of little else during those days. I was preparing to move out of the flat, so getting rid of my largest monthly bill, and I didn't think I'd be capable of taking another person's life, so I was on the verge of deciding to tell him to *'go fuck yourself pal'*, excuse the language. But then one morning the old car wouldn't start and I didn't have the money for a taxi in to work. In the hope of a lift from a Good Samaritan, I set off walking, in the rain, but not one vehicle even slowed down. I walked seven miles that morning, only to be told off by the boss for being late. So I suddenly thought – *why not, Beetle, why not do something life changing and outrageous?* I felt had to be due a change of luck, and a change of fortune, and I'd been told the target was supposed to be a no-good drug dealer. I'd been assured that, because I'd never been in any trouble and because I'd had no prior contact with the victim, there was next to no chance of me getting caught."

"My Gary was never a drug dealer."

"I wasn't to know that, and I swear to you that I'd no idea it was your son I was meant to kill or I wouldn't have had anything to do with it. In fact, I'd probably have gone to the police. Anyway, when the man came up to me a week later I accepted the gun and the verbal contract. I was given a photograph and a mobile phone with one number loaded into it. I was to arrange a meeting in a remote location and execute any passengers who happened to be in the vehicle with the target. I just had to provide the time and location of the intended hit to the people on the other end of the phone."

"Who was paying you? Who is responsible for my Gary's death?"

"I'd rather not say... not yet. You might go charging out of here and I might not see you again. I'm talking about some very dangerous people."

Godfrey sighed in annoyance. At this moment, he didn't feel he could charge anywhere. "Well I'd gathered that. So what went wrong?"

"What didn't go wrong? The weather was against me, for a start. I was late arriving at the arranged meeting place and not expecting anyone to still be there. But the victim's car, your Gary's car, was there. Through the snow I saw two figures, sitting... waiting..., or so I thought."

"My Gary...," Godfrey's mouth was dry and his throat felt parched. He swirled the brandy around in the glass and wished he'd asked for some water with it, but he couldn't tear himself away from the story, not after waiting to hear it for so very, very long. He was horrified and mesmerised in equal measures.

"I parked up and walked to the car, but there were two bodies inside it. I'd been a bag of nerves driving to the site and what I saw totally threw me, I don't mind telling you. I stood and stared at them for I don't know how long. I'd only had a photograph to go by, and... I'm sorry... but I wasn't even sure which youth was which. Finally I realised I had to get away from that place, and I reasoned that if I carried out the second part of the contract and removed the bodies from the vehicle that I might still get some of the money I'd been offered."

"Where did you take them?"

"I brought them home... here... as I'd originally planned, and with the snow on the roads I only just made it. I swear to you that I didn't know the names of the youths until I heard them on the local news the following afternoon. By then I'd chopped and sawn them up. I have most of the body parts still bagged and stored in the freezers in the garage. I really am sorry."

"Gary's here, now, on this property?"

"Yes he is."

Godfrey finished his brandy in a few deep gulps; all of them swallowed drown in anger. He spluttered and then managed to growl out a few words. "So who did kill them?"

"I have absolutely no sodding idea... you must believe me on that. The thought of an unknown killer out there, walking into the shop maybe, turned me into a nervous wreck for months."

"I need another drink." Godfrey rubbed at his temples. He felt as if knives were being jabbed into his brain as the revelations sunk in.

"I'll get the bottle. You look as though you need it."

"If you didn't kill them you could have gone to the police for help. You could have got out of it at that stage."

"That's easy for you to say. Did I mention that the man I'd dealt with was one mean-looking fucker? No one without a death wish would have considered crossing him. Anyway, the next day, while I was cowering behind barricaded doors, in fear for my own life, a car pulled up outside and bundles of used twenty pound notes were shoved through the letterbox. The car drove off, I counted the money, and when I realised I'd been paid in full I was even more shit-scared. Some dangerous people were crediting me with a double killing and I was too scared to tell them otherwise. The days and weeks passed by, and the longer I kept quiet the more trouble I knew I'd be in if they discovered what had actually happened."

Godfrey flinched as another searing pain shot across his temples but he stayed quiet.

Beetle carried on talking. It was if he was talking about the weather, his voice was so steady. "Someone out there had to know I'd taken the credit and the cash for something I hadn't done but I had no idea who that someone might be. For two weeks I stayed home. I locked myself in and I stayed clear of the windows. I told my boss I was ill, and it was the truth. He kept phoning and threatening to replace me and so in the end I returned to work. I didn't know what else to do. But I was a complete wreck. Hardly a day went by when I wasn't threatened with the sack, and I didn't dare touch the money which by then I'd hidden all over the house. After a couple of months I was offered more jobs by these people – lucrative jobs, delivering drugs and collecting loans, and I accepted them and began to pull myself together."

"Where does Sophie fit into all of this? Does she know what you've done?"

"Hell no, she'd go crazy, although on our first meeting after I'd taken the bodies I almost broke down in front of her. We were in a café in Matlock and she shoved the local newspaper under my nose. Gary's picture was in the centre of the page with a smaller picture of you beside it. That was the first time I realised I had your son in my freezer. I'd seen his picture often enough on the television but I hadn't seen yours. I was appalled, and I didn't think the moment could get any worse, but it did. Sophie had recognised you and saved the page to deliberately upset me, and it worked. On seeing my reaction, she burst out laughing. You've no idea of the stress I was under not to blurt out what I'd done there and then."

"You were stressed...?" Godfrey exclaimed.

"Again, I'm so, so sorry. I would never knowingly do anything to hurt you. I always knew you'd have come back and taken care of us if you'd been able to, or if you'd known what we were going through."

"What made you begin sending the letters?"

"Two things... your son, Martin, came into the shop. I recognised him from the local paper and as I watched him driving away in his fancy sports car I got to thinking that his life, the way he was living it, should have been mine. I looked him up on the internet and I followed him and some of his friends and colleagues on Facebook. I began to think that, if you'd stayed with us, I would have been the one to be financially supported and encouraged to go to university. I would have been the respected officer of the law with the interesting career and generous pension to look forward to, instead of having to leave school early and accept the first job offered to me to help pay mum's spiralling bills. I began to follow his car occasionally."

"The assault on Martin... that was down to you, wasn't it?"

"For a policeman, your son isn't very observant. He only noticed me when I became careless one evening and drew too close to his car. I've been in his garden and around his property on numerous occasions. I've even stopped his wife in the street and asked her for directions. She's a beautiful lady and you have a perfect grandson. If I'd wanted, if I'd really been consumed with jealousy, I could have destroyed them all. I was jealous, but above that, I was lonely and I felt unloved. I set out to scare Martin but not seriously hurt him, although I could easily have maimed or killed him if I'd wanted to. Do you understand what I'm saying? I would never have hurt his family... your family. I know all too well how it feels to have your life torn apart. Martin's abduction was a way of grabbing your attention; it was simple as that."

"Why didn't you just come and see me?"

"I thought about doing just that, but I was too afraid of rejection. I convinced myself that if you gradually began thinking about me, remembering the good times we had as a family, that when we did finally meet up again you'd be ready to accept me as your son once more."

"And... the letters...? You said there were two reasons you started sending them."

"It only took a few days for the fuss over Martin's abduction to die down. I felt the need to do something more dramatic. I'd become torn between a desperate need for you to notice me again and an overwhelming desire to make you suffer."

"Did you not think I'd suffered enough?"

"Things were jumbled up in my head. At times, I wanted to inflict more anguish into your life. I wanted you to experience some of the fear and the dread that I'd lived with on a daily basis for so long. I was going through some of mum's personal things when I found old photos and old love letters from you. Some of them were very revealing. Anyway, because of them I hit on the idea of sending letters. I'm sorry now for how I must have upset Paul's family when parts of him were dug up – truly

I am. Life should be about family, shouldn't it? That's something I feel I've missed out on. Can you understand that?"

"I'm trying, Ian."

"Now that you've come back into my life... and you're not too angry with me... maybe we can be a family again? You don't have to answer now. I realise it's more than I've any right to expect."

"Why bury parts of Paul up on the moor like that?"

"I chose our favourite picnic sites. I had hoped you'd recognise them and remember."

"I did, but why Paul?"

"Until the police dug up and identified the remains I'd no idea which of the bodies was which. I kept them separate. Gary's in one freezer, in the garage, and I have what's left of Paul in another."

"Along with some pork...?" Godfrey's voice was clear despite the waves of horror and revulsion surging through him.

"Well yes... that wasn't deliberate. The pork was some I'd brought from work for mother, before she became ill. I should have labelled the bags before the layers of ice formed. Can I get you another brandy? I know I could use one."

"Why not...," he held out his glass and grimaced. The brandy seemed to have revived him a little but was doing nothing for his headache.

Only the dog's snores broke the silence while Beetle refilled the glasses and while Godfrey's body prickled with fear at what he might learn next.

But he was here, and he had to keep Ian talking. "What was the significance of the flower petals?"

"Mum liked having displays of dried flowers about the place and blue was her favourite colour. I thought you might have remembered."

"No, Ian, I didn't. You didn't need to go to those extremes. You only needed to contact me and I would have welcomed both you and Sophie back into my life. The police have your name now and they'll be investigating you. When they learn what you've done I don't know how much I'll be able to protect you."

"I don't fear the police, or the courts, or even prison – not if I know I've got you in my corner. I've done some bad things that I'll gladly hold my hands up to but with you on my side I shouldn't be locked away for long. Together we'll make people understand. I'll be forever in your debt, and that will be a good thing. I'll spend the rest of my life repaying you in whatever way I can."

The fire wasn't lit but some form of heating must have come on in the room. Godfrey felt sweat forming on his back. "We'll sort out this mess together."

"I've never actually killed anyone. Can you believe that – employed as a contract killer for almost a year now, and yes, people have died as an indirect result of my actions, but I've never been the direct cause of anyone taking their last breath?"

"What do you mean…?"

"I was contracted to take out some undesirables – that's how they were described to me and, as with your Gary, I never asked for names or reasons. The two local shootings… the other week… did you see the reports on the news?"

"Yes…"

"I was the one who pulled the triggers. I winged both men – can you fathom that? They both died simply because they were incredibly unlucky. Can't you see what a strange turn of events that was for me? For once I was the lucky one – and despite messing up I still received the credit and full payments."

"You were such a good little boy…," Godfrey needed air but didn't want to stop the flow of confessions.

"I was an unlucky little boy. The best thing that ever happened to me was when you set my scumbag of a father up for a murder he hadn't committed."

"You knew…?"

"Not until a few months ago, when I read the letters you'd sent to mum at the time. You shouldn't have put any of those details in writing you know, and she shouldn't have kept them."

"You're not trying to blackmail me, are you, Ian?"

Beetle shook his head and looked shocked. "No... never... all I want in return for my silence is your support... and your love if you can find it within yourself to feel that emotion towards me again. Blackmail is the furthest thing from my mind. I want you in my life because that's where you choose to be, not because you feel forced. I want to feel I'm still important to you, and I want you to feel you can trust me. I want a dad. All I've craved for years is to have you back in my life. If that sounds soppy then I apologise for embarrassing you, but it's the absolute truth. I'll be able to cope with prison only if I know you still think of me as one of your sons."

"You'll always be a son to me. I can see now how much I've harmed you and for that I'm genuinely sorry. I'm back in your life, Ian, and this time I'm going nowhere. I promise you that whatever happens, you'll have my emotional and financial support. It's the least I can do for you after all this time, but won't Sophie have something to say about it?"

"She's far too busy with her career to bother about me. I expect she'll be so ashamed she'll cut all ties with me. That's not what I want, but we've never been particularly close. It's a shame really. She travels from Newcastle to London most weeks and she has a rich boyfriend in one of those cities, I'm not sure which. She's rarely in this part of the country anyway."

"No, that's not right. Yesterday Martin began searching for her. She lives and works in Preston and has done for years. From what he's found out so far she's had the same boyfriend for at least a decade, maybe more, and he too lives in Preston. He is rich but he's a nasty piece of work descending from a long line of career criminals. I know because I dealt with many of them when I was in the force."

"Miss goody-goody's been dating a criminal – well, well, who'd have thought it?" Ian's face lit up with a mischievous grin for the first time that evening and Godfrey saw the boy he'd once thought of as his own.

"Maybe that's why she kept him from you."

"Are you absolutely sure?"

"Yes…"

"Oh my God. I love it. Wait till I see her next. Do you know his name?"

"Oh yes, he likes to be known as Big Stevie, but his name is Stevie Hall."

Beetle's glass hit the threadbare carpet and bounced. Angus raised his head, looked mildly concerned for a second, and then lowered it again.

"Nooo!" Beetle's breath left his body and like a deflated balloon, he sank back into the armchair and closed his eyes. "Stevie… no… no… Stevie Hall… Preston… no… it can't be… can it…?" He knew he sounded melodramatic, even to his own ears, and for a short while nothing about his life made any sense. He opened his eyes again. Godfrey was still sitting opposite, watching him, and in a jumbled fashion and with remarkable speed, events, people, and random conversations began slotting into place in his brain. "There's more," he gasped. "I have to tell you… so much more."

Chapter 25

Michael Forbes sank into the sofa, watched Alison Ransom pouring the last two glasses of wine from a chilled bottle and reluctantly accepted one. "I phoned my GP this afternoon," he told her, "and he said it's safe for me to return home. There have been a few cases of chickenpox in the district but the virus is officially extinct in the Forbes household and as far as I'm aware I haven't passed it on to anyone. I'll get out of your long, gorgeous hair this weekend."

"Shame," she replied, a cheeky smile lifting her face. "And just as I was getting used to having you hanging around the place all the time."

"That's a *slight* exaggeration. I've barely had any time off work since I moved in. If you'd like I could stay a little longer."

"I'll help you pack," she replied, far too quickly. "Are you working Saturday and Sunday?"

"With three investigations running I've no choice."

"Where are you with them, can you tell me?"

"The investigations into the shootings in Matlock and Bakewell aren't making much progress. The bullets were fired from different guns but considering how rare gun crime in this area is the same person could be responsible for both incidents. As for Ryan and Naomi..., I believe a career criminal, Mr Hall, had something to do with the couple's abduction and I'm afraid that we're now looking for two bodies. Motives could be jealousy or revenge – take your pick. The murders of Gary and Paul last year and the brief abduction of Martin Jones just over a fortnight ago could have something to do with a brother and sister duo, Ian and Sophie Becket, and that case is the closer of the three to being solved. The motive may have a connection to Godfrey Jones's distant past – at least that's what Martin seems to believe. We're hoping to learn more about the Becket siblings tomorrow."

"Well I wish you luck. It sounds like you need more officers."

"We're coping... just. If I could get one of the three cases wrapped up over the next day or two it would ease things. Let's sleep on that note, shall we?"

"I have a better idea."

*

Martin and Sarah Jones settled their five-year-old son back in his own bed for the third time in as many hours and then climbed back into their own bed together. He'd told her about the first three letters to his father and in his comfortable state he felt he ought now to tell her everything. "I have a confession to make," he whispered, "and you're not going to like it. A couple of days ago I hired the services of a private investigator."

"I know," she replied.

"What... how...?"

"When you were in the shower yesterday your phone rang. I didn't recognise the number so I didn't answer it, but I saw that the caller left a message. I dialled the number on my own phone. Don't look at me like that... I worry about you... and you don't think I could be married to a detective for all these years and not pick up a trick or two, do you?"

"Why didn't you say something?"

"I knew you'd tell me about it sooner or later."

"I can explain."

"You'd better. Go on, I'm listening."

"Dad likes to do things his way, as you know, and because of that almost thirty years ago, when he was in uniform, he acted illegally. He told me something, which when it comes out, could cost him his pension. DCI Forbes now has the names of those involved but he doesn't have the full story. The problem is that another envelope arrived yesterday containing a photograph of three people. It was taken almost thirty years ago and he's refusing to allow me to hand it in. It has a message on the back, requesting a meeting with him on Sunday at some rocks where the photo was taken."

"You can't let him do it."

"I don't intend to. I'm taking the whole sorry story to my DCI tomorrow and he can decide what to do about it."

"Can you tell me first?"

"Of course, but before I do can I have a cuddle? On top of Gary's death this business has really got to me this week."

"Can I tempt you to share a mug of cocoa with me, and then we can have as many cuddles as you want while we talk it through?"

*

Jane Ross had been sleeping on and off for an hour when Adam climbed into bed beside her. "Snooker match finished?" she mumbled.

"No, I couldn't keep my mind off work so I thought I'd come up to bed. Did I wake you?"

"Kind of – I've been waiting to talk to you."

"Sounds ominous – what about?"

"It may be nothing, but with the children, and Christmas, and everything else I kept forgetting to mention it. Almost a week ago, last Saturday actually in the Matlock supermarket I had a strange encounter with a funny little man."

"Were the children with you?"

"They were in the car. I only wanted milk," she lied. "A man standing behind me at the checkout suddenly leaned in and began talking as though he knew me. He mentioned our wedding, said he'd seen it in the newspaper, and he knew about both our pasts and our two children. He even had the cheek to ask whether we intended having a child together. And he said that although he didn't live in Leaburn he followed the lives of everyone at the Leaburn Police Station. He reeked of pine disinfectant."

She felt his body go tense.

"I can't believe you haven't said anything sooner. We're all meant to be on our guard."

"I do have other things to think about," she snapped back.

"The safety of this family should be your number one priority."

She saw anger in his eyes and understood his thinly veiled accusation. Her drinking worried him, but she had it well under control these days. "…says the man who's employed in a job where he faces real danger on a daily basis! Where would this family be if you failed to come home one day?"

"All right… point taken… I'm sorry… would you recognise this man if you saw him again?"

He was right. She should have put the children's safety first and mentioned it straight away, and if that was all that the flash of argument had been about she wouldn't still be seething. She took a deep breath before answering. "I would. He was right in my face, you know. I watched him leaving the shop and when he tried to rush, I saw he had a slight limp. He drove an old grey car, but because of other traffic leaving at the same time I couldn't see the make or model, or the registration plate."

"I wonder whether the shop might still have the CCTV footage. I'll find out tomorrow. At what time did all this happen?

"Early afternoon; we were on our way back from the Santa's Grotto."

*

Godfrey closed his eyes and wondered how his life had come to this. He swallowed down tears – they served no purpose. Over the last half an hour he'd listened to Beetle's account of how Ryan had been brutally murdered and how Naomi had been beaten, raped and starved, and then abducted again and how Stevie Hall's nephew had met his untimely, but accidental end.

How could Ian claim to be a victim of circumstance after such revelations?

"Well that's all the brandy gone," Beetle held the empty bottle out at arm's length and stated the obvious. "I'm off to bed. Are you sure you'll be all right sleeping on the sofa? You're welcome to my bed. I can sleep down here."

"I'll be fine. When I'm this tired I can sleep just about anywhere," Godfrey answered. In truth, he thought he was probably too drunk to climb the stairs.

"It feels wonderful to have you sleeping under the same roof as me. You're welcome here any time. I'll fetch a pillow and duvet. I've got plenty."

"Whatever happens, I won't desert you again," his words slurred together but they made Beetle smile. It wasn't just that he had too much alcohol inside him to move from where he was comfortable, but that he felt he couldn't leave the resting place of Gary now that he'd finally found it. He hadn't seen it – he didn't want to, at least not tonight. Parts of Paul were still on the property, and now, the missing detective, Ryan Wheeler, was also in a dismembered state and in bags in the same freezers, and Stevie Hall's nephew, who hadn't yet been reported as missing, was in the log shed.

Was he out of his mind to want to spend the night here, given that there were three hand guns on the property, that Gary's killer was still out there and that Naomi remained unaccounted for? Almost certainly he was, but he felt that, one way or another, everything was about to come to a head. And the old policeman inside of him was telling him that he still had a part to play.

Chapter 26

Michael Forbes was surprised to see a traffic officer from the Matlock station waiting for him in reception at six a.m. on a cold Friday morning.

"I live about five miles from Leaburn," the officer explained, "and when I spoke with my sergeant late last night he suggested I come straight here this morning to speak to you face-to-face."

"Follow me to my office... PC...?"

"PC Philip Watkins, sir."

"Take a seat, Philip. Now what can I do for you?"

"This may not be important, and it was something so minor I hadn't written it in my notebook, but when I remembered it last night I knew I needed to bring it to someone's attention."

Forbes could see the young officer was hoping he had something of significance. Everyone in every station up and down the country could relate to that feeling. "I'm listening."

"On Tuesday morning the roads were treacherous, if you recall, and a traffic accident on Sydnope Hill, between Matlock and Chesterfield, had closed the road. I was dispatched to divert drivers onto neighbouring roads but I had to chase down one who was driving far too fast for the conditions. When I finally persuaded him to pull over it was into the layby that's now the focus of the CSI." Philip paused.

"Any small thing you noticed there could be vital."

"I spoke to the man about his speed and he seemed nervous. Something didn't seem right about him, he kept glancing to his left, so I decided to investigate further. I remember that there was a good layer of snow on the gravel of the layby when I walked around the car. I opened the passenger door and on the seat was a rolled-up leather pouch containing several, lethal-looking knives. He explained that he was a butcher and they were the tools of his trade that he took home with him every night. He said he worked on the shop counter of the butchers on the A6 to the north of Matlock, and at that point I realised I'd been in his shop and seen him behind the counter. I was happy enough with his explanation and allowed him drive to away. But last night in bed I was churning things over in my mind and I thought that if anything had fallen from the passenger door-well that morning that I wouldn't necessarily have seen it. I was thinking of the missing woman's keys, sir. And… I know this might sound a bit off the wall, sir…"

"Go on…"

"Well, I was half asleep and… strange thoughts can come to me sometimes…"

"Spit it out, man."

"I began thinking about the body parts recovered from Stanton Moor. As I understand it they were expertly dissected, possibly by someone skilled in cutting flesh and bone, and that some of the graves contained pork…"

Forbes felt his pulse quicken. Had they really missed a connection between the two most prominent cases they were working on right now? "Are you suggesting what I think you're suggesting?" The question sounded stupid, even to his ears, but he'd been thrown by the idea.

"I know you'll probably think it's too much of a long shot…"

If the traffic officer standing in front of him was proved right then he was about to become the hero of the hour. "Do you know this man's name?"

"No, but I know where he works. I buy a pie from his shop at least once a week. Behind the counter, he's a bit of a comedian. I believe he goes by the nickname of Beetle. More than once I've heard him describing himself as 'the jovial butcher with a limp', to which I've heard his female customers responding, 'a limp what?'"

"…you are joking?"

"No, sir, but some of his female customers find him amusing."

"Would you care to work here today with CID?"

"Yes please, sir, but I'll have to ask my sergeant back at the station."

"Someone here can do that for you. Grab yourself a coffee and then go and wait in the incident room for the rest of the team to catch up."

"Err…"

"Down the corridor, then third door on the left."

"Thank you, sir."

*

"Are you all right, Godfrey? You look like death warmed up."

Godfrey closed his eyes and fought back another wave of nausea. "Thanks for that, Ian. I drank too much brandy last night, that's all. My head is pounding, but we do need to talk some more."

"As a guest I should have insisted you slept in my bed."

"Forget about that. I want to talk to you about Stevie Hall. I know you're wary of him, but last night I don't think I got across to you just how much of a psycho he really is. I knew his family, back when he was in his teens and his twenties, and even they couldn't control him and were nervous of him. Men like that don't improve with age."

"I've know he has his mean side, Godfrey, but he's always treated me well enough."

"That's because he thinks of you as his obedient little puppy. What do you think will happen to you when he finds out you've taken his money under false pretences?"

"Once I've been arrested he won't be able to touch me. I still have most of the money. I'll tell you where I've hidden it and if you like you can get it back to him somehow."

"Just like that…?"

"Why not?"

"Because those people exist in a different world to the rest of society, and I'm sure you think you've been inducted into it, but trust me, you won't have seen a fraction of what they do or what they're capable of. Before my face was known, I worked undercover for a while, gathering evidence against Stevie and his family and that was the last time I ever volunteered for anything like that. I've seen outsiders being used exactly as you have. I've seen Stevie seriously pissed off, I've been in the room with him when he's lost his colossal temper and I've witnessed him incapable of listening to reason." He was annoyed. Ian's understanding of things was a joke. He felt sick. "May I have a slice of toast or something, to settle my stomach?"

"Of course, you can. You look terrible. Are you sure that you're fit to drive home today? I have to leave for work in half an hour but you can stay on here as long as you need. Angus will welcome the company."

"Thanks, I might stay a while longer. I'll try to sleep off this hangover. You just go to work and behave normally while I try to think of a way to minimise your punishment."

"I'm about to be arrested, aren't I?"

"Yes Ian, it's the only way forward for you. If you tell the truth I'll support you, I promise."

"I'm so glad to hear you saying those words. You've no idea how much your support means to me. I just want this all to be over and done with. I realise now I was never cut out for the sort of work Stevie expects of me."

"What are you going to do about Sophie? Have you given her any more thought? You're going to be in the news and she ought to hear your side of things before the press get a hold of the story."

"I texted her last night – told her I wanted to see her. It's laughable isn't it, that she's so consistently lied to me about her glamorous job and her amazing life? And all the time she's been dating a man who buys and sells people as if they're commodities and who I wouldn't have had anything to do with if I hadn't been in such a desperate, financial pickle."

*

"Adam, what are you doing?" Forbes rarely saw his detective sergeant looking flustered, especially while staring at a computer screen.

"I contacted the night staff of the Sainsbury's supermarket in Matlock first thing this morning to make sure they didn't record over last Saturday's film footage of their checkouts and car park. They've just sent these over."

"What are you looking for?" he leaned into the desk.

Adam described Jane's run-in with the creepy little man at the checkout. "I've got eight camera angles here to check through."

"She definitely said he walked with a limp?"

"When he rushed; yes sir."

"Show our new recruit...? Sorry I've forgotten your name."

"PC Philip Watkins, sir."

"Show Philip a picture of Jane and let him check some of the footage with you. If it's who I think it is then he should recognise him." He stood straight. "And the rest of you, you all know Jane, so pick a camera angle and start searching. This could be a vital new development. One of you can check the social media sites. I want to see a picture of this man as soon as possible."

"Sir, on the phone, I have a witness," DC Jade Sharpe raised her left hand while holding her phone in her right. "Mr Wright, one of the organisers of the Matlock youth group, claims to remember Sophie Becket. He says she was a volunteer with the group for a short while just over a year ago. They had to ask her to stay away after several of the girls complained about her showing an unnatural interest in them."

Forbes hurried across the room and took the phone. "Mr Wright, this is Detective Chief Inspector Forbes, just what sort of an unnatural interest do you mean?"

*

Martin Jones was fed up. He hated leaving his wife and son in their warm and comfortable house so early each morning, especially when the outside world was dark, cold, and where, until half an hour ago, it had been raining heavily. He was supposed to be recuperating, after all, and he was expected to be back at work after the coming weekend. He'd made an error of judgement offering to check on his father on a daily basis. The man was more than capable of taking care of himself and quite capable of using a telephone.

He strode up the garden path, feeling so hacked off he failed to notice the house was in complete darkness. And despite the security light, he didn't notice that his father's car wasn't where it should have been, and that the ground where it was normally parked wasn't dry, as it would have been if his father had just popped out for his morning paper.

He let himself in, switched on the lights, strode into the kitchen and flicked the button on the kettle. After putting instant coffee into two mugs and sugar into one he reached into a cupboard for a packet of biscuits. Then he turned to set the biscuits down and froze.

His father was obsessive about leaving the kitchen tidy at night, yet the crumpled, black and white photograph from the previous day was sitting there, staring back at him from the centre of the table. Why would he have left it there to be seen as soon as he arose the next morning, and why would he have been looking at it last thing at night, before retiring to bed? The kettle clicked off and he poured boiling water into both mugs. The rumbling sound made by the bubbles in the kettle subsided. Coffee-flavoured steam caught in his throat and filled his mouth and nostrils. The house was too silent.

He reached into his pocket for his phone but left it there, ashamed at how easily he'd been panicked by a silent house. He'd feel stupid calling for assistance if his father had simply overslept.

The hairs on the back of his neck were telling him that wasn't likely. The cupboard next to the cooker was where his mother had kept her rolling pin. It was one of several items his father had steadfastly refused to dispose of, even though it hadn't been used in years. He bent down and saw it was still there. It wouldn't be as effective as a truncheon but the weight of it in his hand felt reassuring.

If his colleagues could see him now...?

Moving as silently as he could, he checked the living room for intruders, the downstairs bathroom, and the cupboard beneath the stairs. If a killer was lurking in the house, waiting for a chance to get away, he wasn't about to oblige him or her.

He crept up the stairs.

If his father was here he might be unwell and in need of medical attention. The alternative was unthinkable. He stepped forward and flung open his father's bedroom door.

The bed hadn't been slept in.

He repeated the sequence at the doorways of the other two bedrooms. Satisfied he was alone in the house he walked to a bedroom window and looked down on the driveway. "Son of a bitch... the stupid old sod took the car out last night after all."

He ran back down the stairs, gathered up the photograph and raced to his car.

*

Footage from the supermarket's outdoor cameras in Matlock were disappointing – all they had so far was a grainy picture which PC Watkins said could possibly be the man he'd stopped at the top of Sydnope Hill, leaving in a grey Vauxhall with very dirty registration plates. The cameras at the checkouts focused mainly on the tills and the cashiers. Two uniformed officers had been drafted in from downstairs and James Haig, the crime scene manager, was flitting between desks and co-ordinating sightings.

"Everyone, things are moving rapidly this morning," Forbes kept a lid on his emotions as he addressed the packed incident room. "Ian and Sophie Becket can be historically linked to Godfrey Jones and there is a chance they were responsible for Martin's abduction as well as being involved in the murders of Paul and Gary. The unidentified DNA samples isolated from Martin's car should confirm that. If this morning's breakthrough, courtesy of PC Watkins, is as good as we hope it is then we're in for a busy day."

"So there was someone with a grudge against Martin's family?" DC Emily Jackson asked.

He didn't answer. "Thanks to information dug out by Martin, we know that Sophie has been in a long-standing relationship with Stevie Hall and that throws up another link to the abduction of Ryan and Naomi."

"The man on the supermarket tapes – is he the brother – the one nicknamed Beetle?" Emily tried again.

"Yes to all questions, Emily. Now until we have proof that Ryan and Naomi are no longer alive that side of the investigation will take priority." Forbes spoke with more emotion in his voice than he'd intended. "We know where Ian lives and that he works in a butcher's shop on the outskirts of Matlock, but because firearms are involved I don't want him becoming jittery."

PC Gary Rawlings looked up from his terminal. "Sir, I've found something in the forensic reports from the wedding venue. The last people to see Ryan and Naomi that night stated that they were walking, hand in hand, down the driveway towards the road. It was assumed they were looking for a taxi, or a lift. Hundreds of footprints were isolated, far too many for casts to be taken of all of them, but one set did stand out because whoever made them had walked out alone onto the grass verge by the side of the public road. Again it was assumed that person had hailed a taxi or been given a lift because the prints stopped short just beyond the farm's entrance. The report states that the footprints were uneven – possibly made by someone who walked with a limp."

"Have the guest lists and employee lists been checked for Ian's and Sophie's names?" Forbes asked no one in particular.

"They're not on any of them," DC Bell answered. "If either of them were present, then they used an alias."

"Show PC Watkins pictures from the wedding reception – he's the only one of us who's seen Ian close to. We can't yet positively link Ian to Ryan's disappearance, other than the fact that his sister is dating our main suspect and he was stopped in that lay-by. I'd like something more concrete to work with before we go to arrest him. We can't allow him to go to his home tonight but I don't want any officers anywhere near that shop until I give the word. Who's searching for Sophie?"

DI Rob Lang raised his hand. "The declaration she needed in order to be accepted as a volunteer working with young people checked out. She's never been in any trouble and the address she gave at the time was correct but she's since moved. I haven't found a current address for her yet."

"Keep digging. Stevie Hall has managed to keep her record clean. I wonder why? At the moment we can only guess at why she wanted young girls from deprived backgrounds to be accompanying her on nights out."

"She was grooming them, sir," Jade answered, quite unnecessarily. Everyone in the room was thinking something similar. "We know the Hall family runs working girls. Stevie will want young flesh for his customers and I heard a rumour that British, English speaking girls were commanding more money in the brothels these days than their Eastern European counterparts."

"Are you saying the punters are racists?" DC Bell exclaimed in mock horror.

"Well we all know you're turned on by just about any…"

"Enough!" Forbes stopped the banter. "Concentrate on the job in hand."

"A poor choice of words," someone in the room muttered but no one owned up to.

Forbes let the comment slide. Everyone was feeling the tension and the occasional banter was inevitable. "Once it's confirmed that Ian Becket has arrived at his place of work this morning we'll have it under surveillance, but before the end of the day I want him in my cells, and I want as much information on him as I can get. We'll search his home as soon as he's left for work."

"Don't you need a warrant for that…" Philip Watkins asked, "…sir?"

"Not if we say we're working on the possibility of Ryan and Naomi being held prisoner in his home, we don't. I know it isn't very likely, but we can always hope."

"An e-mail's just come in from the Bakewell youth group," Adam Ross said. "They've been trawling through their records and Sophie Becket did apply to join the volunteers about six months ago. She was turned down."

"Does it say why?"

Adam was reading while summarising the e-mail. "It seems she offered to be a beauty consultant to the girls' football team – hair and make-up, etcetera, whatever the etcetera was. She was interviewed but later informed through the post that her services were considered unnecessary for girls of that age."

"That must have stung," Emily Jackson said.

"And… get this… the man who signed the 'dear John' letter was none other than the second shooting victim, Darren Reed, who drowned after being shot at beside the river in Bakewell."

Chapter 27

Martin Jones broke every speed limit on his way to the station. His immediate thoughts on leaving the empty house had been to drive up onto Beeley Moor, to find his father, but he'd quelled the impulse.

He had a wife and son depending on him, and a father who'd told him a big fat stinking lie when he'd said he wouldn't be making contact with Ian before Sunday.

And not least of all – firearms were involved. He'd no desire to be a dead hero.

He took the station stairs two at a time and burst into the incident room. A blur of faces stared back at him but he only saw DCI Michael Forbes. "I've been a fool, sir. Dad's missing, his bed's not been slept in, but I think I know where he is."

"Calm down Martin. Take a deep breath and talk us through what you know. We've had some developments here this morning. Let's see how your news fits in with ours before we do anything that might make a bad situation worse."

*

Beetle's world was about to implode, yet he couldn't remember ever experiencing such a state of sublime calmness.

He was going to be arrested — that was a given, and in some ways he welcomed it. He was ready to wipe the slate clean and start life over as part of a family, even if it was from a prison cell. He was about to be charged with manslaughter, or attempted murder, but he hadn't actually killed anyone, and with Godfrey accepting him as his son once more, and providing him with a character reference and a first-rate lawyer, as he'd promised, he shouldn't be looking at too long a prison sentence.

The only blot on this rainbow-coloured landscape was his sister. If only he could be sure that the reason Sophie had lied to him about living so far away, for so many years, was that she was ashamed of her boyfriend — ashamed of her long-term association with a family of criminals, then he'd feel less worried.

She hadn't answered his calls or texts for a week now, but that was nothing unusual. For probably the first time in his life, he was longing to see her. If he had to wait until he was in prison to receive a visit from her, then so be it — just as long as she gave him the opportunity to tell her he could never be ashamed of her, and that he loved her.

Family was everything. He had his surrogate father back in his life and all he needed now was his sister's love and support. Nothing could ever be more important than those two things. Stevie Hall could have his money back, and the world could throw whatever it wanted at him and he wouldn't mind, just as long as he had the love of his family to fall back on.

For a Friday morning, the shop had been busy, with more male customers than usual popping in for sausages and burgers. Maybe there was a major sporting event coming up on the television because it certainly wasn't barbeque weather. Beetle didn't do sports.

A suited, middle-aged man and a harassed-looking, but smartly dressed younger woman entered the shop, each carrying a black, A4 sized file, and his heart pounded. Even Mrs Harris, the customer he was serving, looked round, looked the couple up and down and then turned back to him and raised her eyebrows. Two other men, in dark overcoats, stood on the pavement. They were pretending to examine the display in the shop window but Beetle saw their eyes taking in the layout of the shop.

He was ready.

If they wanted to take him now – he was prepared, and for Godfrey's sake, he was determined not to make a scene. He took a deep breath, straightened his posture and addressed the odd couple. "Can I help you?"

"Is the owner or the manager of the shop on the premises? We're immigration officers from the border control agency. We'd like a quick word – nothing to worry about."

"He's in the back. Go straight through." He shook his head, as if trying to clear it.

The two men in overcoats walked into the shop. He felt every hair on his body standing on end. If this was what they meant by an adrenaline rush, he thought, then they could keep it. His body screamed at him to run, but people were blocking every exit. He took a deep breath and tried to slow his hammering heartbeats. For Godfrey's sake, he couldn't throw out his plans to stay calm. He turned and studied his knives.

When he turned back, instead of flashing their ID cards as he'd expected, the taller of the two men pulled out an ordinary-looking, leather wallet.

"Eight pork sausages, please..." Their faces were giving nothing away.

Maybe he was being paranoid.

He relaxed his shoulders and forced a smile. They smiled back. What was it with people and sausages today? At this rate, he was going to have to give up half his lunch break to make more.

He leaned into the chilled cabinet and wished he could hear the conversation in the back room. His hearing, like his eyesight, had always been first rate but he couldn't quite catch any of the words. Foreign workers weren't employed in this shop, and had never been, so what were the couple really here for? What was in those files?

He counted the change into the customer's hand and heard the fire door at the rear of the shop being opened and closed. Seconds later, he was glaring at the rear of Adrian, the little creep, jogging across the road away from the shop.

He swallowed down his annoyance.

There was an hour and forty minutes to go until the shop closed for lunch. What gave him the right to go sloping off when more sausages needed making?

*

"Right, listen up again everyone," the incident room fell silent. "In the last few minutes Ian Becket's identity has been confirmed by his employer, who is now with Emily and Robert and being brought back to this station. I had hoped to keep the arrest low key, but unfortunately the shop's other employee disappeared shortly after Emily and Robert arrived. His whereabouts is unknown, and that's a concern, but for now we know that Ian is the only worker in the shop, which should close for lunch in about an hour and a half and is under heavy surveillance. Our priority this morning, before we move on Ian Becket, is to locate Godfrey Jones."

"What about Sophie Becket?" Jade asked. "She could be anywhere."

"You've all seen her photograph, taken about a year ago, so study it but keep in mind that she may have changed her appearance. An armed response unit is on its way to Beeley Moor – to Hill Top Cottage, where Martin believes Godfrey went last night. An ambulance is also on its way there and if we don't get a move on we'll be the last to arrive. Is everyone ready?"

Coats were shrugged on and car keys rattled.

"Once we're through Matlock I don't want sirens used. Until then, let's cover the ground as rapidly as we can. Are you going to be all right, Martin?"

"Yes sir. I just want to get going."

Forbes led the convoy onto the rutted lane to the cottage. A white, armed response unit vehicle was already parked half way along, blocking the remainder of the way. One of its officers rushed to meet the convoy. "We've been here five minutes, sir. We've located two heat sources from inside but one's been identified as canine. There's only one person visible on the thermal imaging camera."

"Any movement...?" Black dog hairs had been retrieved from Martin's car – another box ticked.

"Nothing yet... we're about to try to make contact."

Martin jumped from the second vehicle in the convoy and ran towards the white van. "That's my dad's car over there. What are you planning?" There was rising panic in his voice.

"Officers are trying the landline now, and your father's mobile. So far, we've had no response from anyone in the building. Using the loud speaker is an option, but as there's only one...."

"If it's Dad in there he may be injured. Can't you just rush in?"

"We're preparing for that eventuality, sir. You need to trust us. If your father is in there we have to minimise any risk to him as well as to ourselves. Give us one more minute to try to establish contact, to make sure he's alone and that the place isn't booby trapped."

"But he must be hurt if he isn't he answering his phone. Where's the ambulance?"

"Ambulance two minutes away," a voice from inside the white van answered.

Forbes placed his hand on Martin's shoulder. "Any second now..."

A radio crackled, 'All clear... preparing to enter premises now.'

"Everyone ready..."

"Go... go...go..."

Noise and movement exploded simultaneously.

Forbes held Martin back. "Let them secure the building."

"Paramedics needed...," a voice echoed through the house, followed immediately by several barks. "...one male, alive but unconscious."

Martin rushed ahead of Forbes and through the door of the cottage. "What's happened? Is it Dad? What's wrong with him? Let me through." He pushed aside an officer who tried to block his path and ran through the hallway, into the living room. Then he stopped as abruptly as if he'd hit a wall. His father was lying on a sofa, with a pillow under his head, apparently sleeping peacefully.

The two paramedics seemed to come from nowhere. One dropped to his knees and began feeling for a pulse while the other busied himself with the equipment they'd carried in.

"Rapid pulse, shallow breathing, possible fever," the one on his knees said quietly. "Giving oxygen..."

Martin felt helpless. The paramedic unfastened four of his father's shirt buttons and Martin noticed a hesitation, followed by exchanged glances. He felt his stomach lurch. "What is it – what's wrong...?"

"Has your father been unwell over the last few days?"

"He's had a headache occasionally. He's been under a lot of pressure."

"We'll get him to Calow as quickly as we can, sir. Have you been feeling all right?"

"I'm fine. Just get him some help."

"That's what we're doing now. Do you want to come in the ambulance with him?"

Forbes stood watching the ambulance bounce down the lane, its blue lights flashing. He was quietly fuming at Godfrey and if the man hadn't been so ill he'd have caused a scene by telling him exactly what he thought of him.

"Well... that's one out of two accounted for," he said to Adam.

"The old idiot put himself and us in danger."

Forbes nodded in agreement then turned to the officer in charge of the armed response unit. "I'd fully expected Sophie to be at the cottage. She's still unaccounted for but that doesn't mean she isn't somewhere close by. I want two armed officers and two uniforms to remain here until we can get back to do a full search. Is that all right?"

"Yes sir."

"The rest of you – we have a shop to raid and a suspect to arrest."

He climbed into his car as his radio crackled. "Sir, we have a situation at the shop. A woman who resembles Sophie has entered by the front door. There are no other customers inside. Within seconds of her arrival the female suspect locked the front door and turned the sign to show closed."

"We're on our way now... ETA ten minutes..." That news solved two potential problems – the risk of customers wandering in off the street and alerting Ian to the presence of so many officers in the area, and the possibility that Sophie Becket could be the more dangerous of the two siblings and could go even deeper into hiding after Ian's arrest. The road would need closing to ensure the safety of the public but with both suspects in one building the situation should be easier to contain. "Remain as you are. If either suspect leaves then arrest them the moment they're out of sight of the shop."

*

Beetle looked up and for a second thought that he'd lapsed into one of his old fantasies. There she stood, in her calf-length, fake-fur coat, her blonde curls tumbling over her shoulders and her face made-up as if she was on route to a glamorous photo shoot. "Sophie... what the... you shouldn't be here. Why didn't you answer my text?" She flashed her artificially whitened teeth at him. Her whole persona was stunning, as always. She'd lightened her hair since he'd last seen her and it suited her. "Never mind... you're looking well." Beetle thought he saw a momentary softness in his sister's eyes, but maybe it was wishful thinking.

"I think the police are outside," ignoring his comments, she smiled as she clicked the lock on the door and turned the sign to read *closed*. "I think you've been a naughty boy."

"It's wonderful to see you but I'm about to be arrested. I'm so ashamed, and I've been worrying about how to explain everything to you. But I shouldn't be closing the shop now and you shouldn't be here. I couldn't stand it if you were dragged down with me."

"Oh do stop whining on. You normally close at lunchtime, don't you?"

"Not for another ten minutes... you must go. We can talk properly later... if they'll allow us. But before that I want to tell you that I know about your boyfriend, Stevie Hall. You didn't need to keep him a secret from me. What you do with your own life is your business. I only want us to be close again, like a proper family."

"Shut... up...!"

Sophie hadn't seemed surprised at anything he'd said. He felt his guts move and he went quiet.

"We need to talk." She spoke calmly. "You've made a mess of things and Stevie isn't best pleased."

"You know...?"

"Let's go through to the back, shall we?"

He held open the wooden hatch and invited her behind the counter. She brushed against him and his lungs filled with her expensive perfume.

"Ever the considerate big brother... God, how I've hated you... you and your oh-so-perfect memories of the man responsible for the death of our real father...!" Her eyes flashed a look of hatred before she stepped towards the door leading to the rear of the shop.

Like a lamb to the slaughter, he followed. "How much do you know? Why are you really here, sis?"

"I'm here to witness your downfall, *big brother*. Adrian kindly phoned to tell me the police had visited the shop. I thanked him and gave him a little job that would keep him well away from here. You see... I just couldn't resist watching your face when the penny finally dropped in that stupid head of yours."

"What visit from the police? I know they're outside but..."

"Are you really that gullible… immigration officers in Matlock… really?"

"I did wonder, and don't call me stupid. What do you mean by the penny finally dropping? What are you talking about?"

"You're going to prison for a long, long time, and your precious Godfrey Jones and his real family are finally getting what they deserve for the false arrest and untimely death of our dad. Have you not worked it out yet? Have you really not worked out yet that Stevie Hall and I have been an item for many, many years?"

She was smiling again – that superior, smug smile he remembered from childhood. "Godfrey's family… Gary Jones…?"

She threw her hands up into the air. "Finally, he gets it! Yes big brother – I shot Gary and Paul because I didn't think you'd have the guts to go through with the executions. And do you know what else…?"

She was visibly shaking with emotion. He could see she was desperate for him to ask what else, and why. He knew then, with stunning clarity, that she was lost to him. Sadly, the years hadn't changed her.

"Tell me," his words came out more calmly than he expected.

"I set everything up for that night. I was the one who told Stevie about rumours concerning Gary Jones muscling in on his territory and selling large quantities of drugs. And I was the one who suggested your name as a possible new hit man. I must say I was a little surprised when you accepted the contract so easily, although I suppose I shouldn't have been, the money was good and you always were a greedy little sod. But after you'd accepted the contract I couldn't risk you bottling it – my reputation was on the line, and so I drove up to the woods on my motorbike, parked well out of sight, and I waited. The rest you can work out for yourself."

"I was terrified that night. I've lived in fear of the real killer coming after me. You could have said something."

"What... and spoil my fun... not likely." She was having fun now.

A small part of him still wouldn't believe what he knew to be true. "Please tell me you're having a laugh, sis? Tell me this is all one big joke. I won't be angry with you. Tell me you're not the killer."

"Oh, and another thing, the gun I used that night was passed on to you a few months later. You were told to use it to shoot at one of those pompous youth workers. The police will discover that for themselves when they recover the bullets from Gary's and Paul's corpses."

His mouth opened but no words came. He stared at her and she nodded.

"I orchestrated Gary's death to get back at Godfrey. An eye for an eye – we lost our father because of him and so he had to lose a son."

"I didn't know that Godfrey had set up Dad until after Mum's death. How long have you known?"

"When I moved back home to nurse our mum she told me the story. She was so pitifully grateful to Godfrey that it made me physically sick. She asked me to try to trace him, so she could make her peace with him for ending their relationship. And so I did. I had no trouble finding him. Of course I told her he'd emigrated. I couldn't have him coming to the house, could I – not when I was making plans for him to suffer."

"But why involve me in your revenge?"

"Because for so many years, all the time we were growing up together, you thought the sun shone out of that man's sodding arse... that's why. I had hoped the police might trace your car to the murder scene. I'd intended for you to take the blame, but you took the bodies and the snow worked in your favour and no one saw you."

He digested her words. The news, crazy though it was, almost felt a relief. The burden of not knowing who the killer was had finally been lifted from his shoulders. But there was something he didn't understand. "Why the others...? Why those two men?"

"Well I thought that as you'd been quite prepared to kill for money once, you might be prepared to do it again. I thought I'd make use of you to take revenge on two men who'd humiliated me and who'd prevented me from earning a nice little wedge on the side."

"What are you talking about?"

"The men you shot at... they attracted silly young girls like flames attract moths, and I'm permanently on the hunt for those sorts of teenagers. I can easily talk many of them into selling their charms and Stevie pays me commission on their earnings. I only had to drop a word in Stevie's ear that the two men had been asking questions about him and he soon sanctioned their killings."

"You bitch!"

"And I must say you made us laugh with the way you went about each execution. You're priceless!"

"I believed I was disposing of some low-life."

"Whatever... but I wasn't the one who came up with the idea of torturing Godfrey with letters and body parts, now was I? I left mother's old love-letters where I knew you'd find them, but your actions exceeded all my expectations. Well done, brother."

"I was trying to make Godfrey think about me... about us... about how we used to be a family and about our good times together. A part of me wanted to hurt him, I can't deny that, but not because of what happened with our dad. I wanted to hurt him for leaving us, yes, but more than that I wanted him back in my life. I wanted to feel I belonged, and was a part of a family once more. Why can't you understand that?"

"Why can't you, Beetle, accept that we lost our real dad because of Godfrey Jones? I was his special little girl. I remember him whispering to me every night as he tucked me into my bed."

"And I was his special little boy, but all I remember is pain and humiliation. Trust me; he would have begun abusing you sooner or later."

"You can't know that." She dismissed the idea with a flourish of her hand. "Anyway, back to my story – don't you want to know how I planned the rest of your downfall?"

*

"ETA two minutes," Forbes spoke into the radio. Unlike the majority of his officers, he hated driving at speed but occasionally it was necessary. "Can anyone see what's happening inside the shop?"

"No visual, sir, they're standing in an internal room, presumably talking with each other. Do you want us to try to make contact via the landline?"

"Wait till I get there. I want armed response officers in place before we attempt anything. Are you absolutely certain no one else is in the building?"

"Affirmative, sir, and we've closed the road and evacuated all neighbouring properties."

*

Sophie raised her tattooed eyebrows. "No answer, big brother? Well I'll tell you anyway, because I'm really quite proud of my achievements. I know my looks are starting to fade, and I know my Stevie sometimes goes for some firmer, younger flesh, for some little bimbo who's so desperate for money that she'll allow him to exercise his violent streak on her. As long as it's nothing serious, and as long as he comes back to me after he's worked off his itch, I don't mind too much. The money I have access to, and the power I have through being associated with him more than compensates for my hurt feelings. But that simpering little, slab-arsed chav of a nurse, Naomi Proctor," she was spitting out the words, "was getting her flat little feet too firmly planted underneath my Stevie's table."

"You knew about Stevie and Naomi? But their relationship was over." He was clutching at straws now. "You had no reason to harm her. You've just said you didn't mind his other women."

"She was seeing him through rose-tinted spectacles and I had to put a stop to that. I left incriminating documents lying around – documents to leave her in no doubt about the number and diversity of illegal and downright cruel businesses that Stevie ran. She challenged him, as I knew she would, but she only received a beating for her efforts. Isn't it funny how some women think they can change a man simply by using the power of what they have between their legs? They never can, of course, but I accept Stevie for what he is and I have never tried to change him. I even help him wherever and whenever I can."

"Did you set me up to kidnap Naomi and the policeman?"

"Oh, your face," she laughed. "It's priceless. I love it. Of course I did, although the police officer was a bonus. When Stevie saw him in the car park, talking with Naomi, he recognised him as someone who'd once arrested members of his family. He was only too pleased to kill two birds with one stone, as it were. Jealousy and bitterness are such consuming passions, don't you think? But of course you wouldn't know about the jealousy – what woman would ever look twice at you?" She looked him up and down.

"I've been living a different life these last few months."

"Don't make me laugh. You're a nobody – a nobody who's going down for multiple murders. Ripper shot Ryan, of course, but you were the one who handed him the gun – a gun that you'd already used. You tied yourself to Ryan's killing, but you were a bit slow getting him into the freezer."

"You've been to the cottage… while I was at work? You took her… you took Naomi… where is she?"

"You mean you haven't found her? Oh dear. I made her walk to the side of the freezer and then I pulled back her dirty hair and slit her throat with the knife you so conveniently left hanging by the door. Thank you for keeping it so sharp. If it's any comfort to you she didn't see it coming. She thought I was there to rescue her. Anyway, then I washed the blade off with bottled water from my car and left it where I knew you'd find it. I know how attached you are to those things and I expect the police will find enough evidence to confirm it as the murder weapon."

"Where is she?"

"Why she's at the bottom of one of your freezers, of course – I had to move so many packages around, before I could fit her in, that I ruined my nails and almost gave myself frostbite. You owe me the price of a decent manicure."

His dreams of building a family around him were dead. He could see that now. He'd handled things badly, to say the least. His head felt heavy with regrets. Wherever his future lay now he would have to move forward knowing his sister would never feature in it. "But, why kill Gary Jones and not Martin?"

"What makes you think I haven't set up years of suffering for Martin Jones?" She flashed that superior grin again. Her arrogance knew no bounds.

"What have you done?"

"I've arranged for the deaths of those closest to him. In fact," she made an exaggerated show of looking at her wristwatch, "his home should be well ablaze by now, with the bodies of his wife and son inside it." She snorted. "The only downside is that with all those police outside those are two deaths you won't be getting the blame for. That was the little job I mentioned earlier, by the way, that I sent Adrian to do. He's killed women and children but he's never torched a house before. He was quite looking forward to it."

She began to laugh. Her screeches grew louder and his eyes narrowed. He watched as she crossed her arms over her midriff and rocked forward with laughter.

The curls on the top of her head were bouncing around. The closer he looked, the more they became those of the strawberry-blonde jogger he'd imagined killing. So many times he'd imagined blasting that smiling woman's features away and turning those curls from the colour of an orange sunset to a dark red, liquid mess.

He took a step back, then another, closer to the doorway, closer to the coat rack. Still she was laughing.

A loaded gun nestled in his coat pocket – ready and waiting.

He pulled it clear of the fabric and the laughing stopped.

Thanks to that jogger, he could kill a woman in cold blood... any woman... even his sister.

Especially his sister!

But before he squeezed the trigger there was one thing he wanted her to know. "Seeing as how we're exchanging all our dirty little secrets," he had her in the palm of his hand now, "Stevie's quite fond of his nephew, Ripper, isn't he? Tell me, do you know where that lad is right now?"

"He's in Romania." Her eyes flashed defiance.

"Wrong... I'm sorry to be the bearer of such bad news, really I am, but he's in my log shed. He was eliminated by one of those guns you so kindly arranged for me to have. It was an accident, but one I guess I'm responsible for. Your precious Stevie believes you found him a killer, but I wonder how fondly he'll remember you when he learns you found him the killer who ended the life of his favourite nephew."

"No, not that... not Ripper..."

"How does it feel to be on the receiving end for once, sis?"

She opened her arms in resignation, as if inviting him to shoot her, but tears were streaming down her cheeks.

He was reading her thoughts – she actually thought he was incapable of killing her. It became his turn to smile as he aimed at her middle.

"He isn't... wasn't... Stevie's nephew..." She gasped the words out as if each one caused excruciating pain. "He was Stevie's son... my son... you've killed my baby boy... your own flesh and blood."

"You're lying."

"In my final year at school, I wanted to be a model, do you remember?" She'd composed herself slightly.

"I remember, and you did some photo-shoots."

"That's where I met Stevie. He was in his early twenties and all the girls wanted him. He chose me and I was flattered."

"Why didn't I know?"

"Why should you – it was sod-all to do with you. You were told I'd moved out to live with friends. Stevie's sister adopted my... our son. I named him Liam, and she kept that."

"Did he know? Did Liam know I was his uncle?"

"Yes, he's known from the beginning. He looked up to you and wanted to tell you, but was waiting for permission from his father… from Stevie." She sobbed out the words. "He was planning to bring you into the businesses properly, so you didn't have to keep on working in that crummy shop."

"If only I'd known…?"

"He was allowed to tell you when he returned from Romania. How ironic is that?"

"I don't know what to say…"

"Sorry would be a start," she was shouting now, and walking towards him with her fists clenched. "You've killed my son and Stevie will never forgive either of us. We're both as good as dead."

"It was an accident. I didn't kill him; I promise you it was an accident. I wasn't even in the room with him when the gun went off."

"You killed him – you and your bloody make-believe father, and your make-believe dreams, and I'm going to make sure you pay for it. I'm going to make sure you both suffer for the rest of your miserable lives." Her legs crumpled and she fell to the floor at his feet. "And the only way you're going to prevent that is to shoot me dead right now."

She was right. Suddenly it was clear. No one would blame him. He'd say he was defending himself against a crazed killer, who just happened to be his sister. Godfrey would still stand by him.

He stared down at the wobbling, blonde curls. "For the deaths I've caused accidentally, and for the murder I'm about to commit now, may the world forgive me." He squeezed the trigger.

Barely a metre from her, he stood and watched her blood draining onto the tiled floor. Unlike in his fantasy, her blonde hair didn't change colour and she took several, long, rasping breaths before she fell quiet.

A head shot would have been kinder but, as he'd found to his cost, he wasn't a particularly good shot, not even at close range. The blood on the tiled wall, where she'd fallen back before sinking down, and the blood on the floor, could stay where it was. The weasel-faced Adrian could clean it up before he was arrested for killing Martin's wife and son. Serve him right.

Back to his own predicament – he'd done it. He finally was a card-carrying, real-life killer, so why shouldn't he play out the final part of his fantasy?

He slipped the gun back into his coat pocket and looked up at the rail above his head. Then he selected one of the larger meat hooks and returned to the body. He couldn't hold back the roar of triumph as he grabbed a handful of blonde hair in his left hand and swung at the top of his sister's back with his right. The spike of the meat hook sunk in easily, just above the shoulder blade. The point was sharp enough that her coat didn't baulk it, but then the sharpness of the hooks had always been his responsibility, and something he'd always taken great pride in.

Using the hook as a handle he dragged her into the cold room, hoisted her up alongside half a cow, smiled as he thought how appropriate that was, and then turned and walked back into the warmth.

She'd been wrong in thinking he'd never experienced jealousy. He'd felt it towards Godfrey's children – they'd lived the lives that he and Sophie should have had. If things had been different then he wouldn't be standing alone now, behind a counter, in a butcher's shop, with only days to go before Christmas and waiting for all hell to break loose.

Chapter 28

"Ian Becket, do you understand the charges against you?" Forbes thought the man was trying hard to communicate.

"Sophie deserved it… I didn't kill the others… none of them… Martin's wife… his son… please… tell me… they're all right… yes?"

Martin's house had been nothing short of a fireball when the emergency services arrived. Accelerant had been liberally used – too liberally according to first reports, and a body had been recovered from the ground floor.

Miraculously, one hour after the arrival of the fire service, Martin's wife and son had returned from the shops. With the help of Ian's garbled statements the body pulled from the house was unofficially assumed to be that of the employee who'd disappeared from the butcher's shop when police officers had first spoken to the owner.

Forbes saw no harm in telling Ian that.

"I'll co-operate… I'll co-operate fully, but I want to speak to Godfrey. When can I see Godfrey?"

"Godfrey's not well. Tell us again where he fits into all of this?"

"Hasn't Martin told you the history of our two families? Ask him… please… ask him."

"We know about your real father's death, Ian, and about the part Godfrey played in it. Is that what all these deaths have been about? Has revenge been your sole motive? Is that why you've killed so many people?"

"You're not hearing me. I only killed Sophie, and that was because she was too evil to be allowed to live. She would have blamed everything on me. Now she's gone you'll have to listen to me – and to Godfrey. He knows I'm a good person. He'll stand up for me… he'll back me up… he promised."

"We've been to your home, Ian. We've found large sums of money and we've seen what you have in your freezers and in your shed."

"I didn't kill any of those people. I cut them up, I'll admit to that, but I didn't kill them. Sophie set me up – Sophie and Stevie Hall. The money was all from Stevie. You have to believe me."

"That's going to be difficult, Ian, with so much evidence against you. You've admitted to taking shots at James Goodall in Matlock, and at Darren Reed in Bakewell, which in both cases resulted in their deaths. And we've found two more hand guns at your home, which along with the one recovered from the shop, made you a very dangerous person to be around."

"It was just business. I needed money, and I needed changes in my life."

"I've no doubt we'll be able to tie those guns to all seven gun-related deaths, and prove that Naomi was killed with your knife."

"I've already told you she was, but not by me."

"You have motives for all the deaths – all except Liam Hall."

"I told you, that was a tragic accident. I didn't know who he really was or I would never have sent him upstairs to pick up a loaded gun."

"So you say. We think that when you found your mothers old love letters you and Sophie decided to take revenge on Godfrey and his family. Then I think that maybe Sophie coerced you into killing two men who'd hurt her feelings, and then into killing Stevie Hall's new love interest. Was Ryan trying to protect her when you killed him?"

"It wasn't like that. Why don't you believe me? Where would someone like me get guns from?"

"Your sister would have had no problems there – not with her contacts. And you've admitted to the abduction and assault on Martin Jones, the removal and dissection of bodies, and to the sending of letters to Godfrey and burial of body parts on Stanton Moor. You can't really expect us to believe that you're, at worst, an accidental killer?"

"I didn't kill anyone except Sophie. After what she'd told me I wasn't in my right mind. I should only be charged with manslaughter, and Godfrey's going to help with my defence. He promised."

"You've been watching too many TV cop shows," Adam said.

"I can become an informer. Everything I've done has been at Stevie Hall's bidding. He's the one who should be sitting here. I'll testify to that."

"We've only got your word, Ian. Even if we believed you, without any evidence to support what you're saying Hall's solicitors would rip your testaments to shreds once they got you into a courtroom. I'm afraid you're looking at a long prison sentence."

"I can cope with that, as long as I know Godfrey still views me as one of his family. He told me he'd never stopped loving me, and I believed him. Nothing matters as much as his love and his belief in me. He knows I need him back in my life, as a father figure. He knows I've never stopped loving him – I told him that last night, and again this morning. Godfrey and Martin are as good as family, they're all I've got left. When you see him, when he's feeling better, you will remind him that I never meant to hurt him with those letters, won't you? You won't need to tell him to come to see me – he'll come anyway. I know that. I'm sure of it."

The door to the interview room opened. "Sir, there's something I think you need to know," DC Bell sounded downbeat.

"Interview terminated at eighteen-thirty. Have a drink and try to relax, Ian. I'm sure Godfrey will speak up for you as soon as he's well enough." Forbes and Adam left the room and closed the door behind them.

"Its bad news, I'm afraid…" DC Bell hesitated. "We've just had a call from Martin at the hospital. Godfrey Jones passed away an hour ago."

Forbes searched for something appropriate to say, but nothing came.

"It seems he'd been infected with the chickenpox virus, and that the illness had gone undiagnosed. At Godfrey's age complications were far more likely. Pneumonia had set in before the paramedics got to him, and because he already had a heart problem, it triggered a massive, and fatal, heart attack. Apparently, there was nothing they could do. I'm sorry, sir."

"Do they know how he became infected?" Forbes asked the question he already knew the answer to. No one answered.

He was acutely aware that there would be no opportunity for him to go back in time. He couldn't un-visit Godfrey. The man was dead because he'd called in on him to make sure he was eating properly and taking care of himself. He'd carried that virus into his old friend's house and they'd come close to falling out, and now there was nothing he could ever do to set either of those things right.

Adam broke the silence. "Shall we tell Ian now, or would you rather leave it until the morning?"

"We'll do it now. Whatever he's done, it's obvious he loved Godfrey. He deserves to be told straight away. We'll do it together."

"OK, sir, but it's going to break him."

"That can't be helped, Adam."

"No, sir; I guess it's just not Ian Becket's lucky day, is it?

Chapter 29
One Month Later

Sophie Becket's funeral was the saddest affair the vicar of the small church on the outskirts of Preston could ever remember conducting. It had been raining heavily all morning and the absence of live bodies in the church meant that the air inside the unlined stone building was as cold as that outside. The funeral director had told him that his bill was being paid by someone living in the town, and the service itself was being carried out as per the instructions enclosed in an email. There were no mourners, no flowers, one hymn was played which only the vicar hummed along to, and one prayer was said which no one was there to bow a head to, after which the coffin was whisked away to the crematorium and the vicar tried to put the whole sorry incident to the back of his mind.

On the same day, at the same time, the rain clouds were finally showing signs of clearing and the All Saints Church in the centre of Leaburn was preparing for the funeral of a senior police officer. Godfrey Jones was to be given a guard of honour on his final journey and an hour before the service was due to begin the church was already packed. In the corner of the car park, a group of three police officers stood talking. After a few minutes, one of them broke away from the huddle and took his phone from his coat pocket.

In an office in Preston, Stevie Hall heard the ping of an incoming text message. He clicked it open:
Coast clear – Ian Becket off to psychiatric hospital today – unfit to plead. Evidence compromised and investigations into you being wound down. Will expect usual payment for services rendered. Your loyal workforce. Be lucky.
    He smiled, deleted the text, and returned his phone to standby.

*

It had been a good many years since there'd been a dog in the Forbes household and on the evening of Beetle's arrest Michael had taken a bit of a gamble on the reception he would get from his father.

On the day of the funerals, in a warm kitchen in a substantial family house on the edge of Leaburn, Angus was enjoying being towel-dried, after his second walk of the day, by a man whose eyes glowed with love and who was a trifle slower in everything than his last master had been.

ENDS

AUTHOR'S NOTES

If you enjoyed reading this novel please consider leaving a review on Amazon. Just a few words mean a lot to me and can help fellow readers.
You can like and follow me for news of my books on Facebook at: fb.me/sylviamarsdenbooks
Or send me a message at m.me/sylviamarsdenbooks
Or you can follow me on twitter @MarsdenSylvia
Feel free to email me at sylviajanemarsden@outlook.com

As with all books in this series, many of the locations are real and can be visited in and around the Peak District.

The market town of Leaburn, however, exists only in my imagination. You won't find it on any map. I see it as being centrally placed between the towns of Bakewell, Matlock, Ashbourne and Buxton with its imaginary team of detectives assisting those in the neighbouring towns when called upon to do so. All the characters and present day events are fictitious, and are not based on any real people or stories, though I do sometimes make references to true or mythical, historical events.

A big thank you goes to those of you who take the time to get in touch and offer their thoughts and encouragement. It means an awful lot to me.

Made in the USA
Middletown, DE
11 March 2019